Scarlet
and
the Keepers of Light

To Chloe

Scarlet
and
the Keepers of Light

Brandon Charles West

Manor Minor Press

Manor Minor Press
© 2012 by Brandon Charles West
All rights reserved.
Revised edition published 2014.

No part of this publication may be reproduced in whole or part, or stored in a retrieval system, or transmitted in any form or by any means, electronic, mechanical, photocopying, recording, or otherwise, without written permission of the publisher.

Interior design by Krister Swartz
Set in Mountains of Christmas and Sabon 12 / 18

ISBN: 978-1-942024-03-3

For my beautiful daughters.
May your lives be filled with love and fantastic stories,
your imaginations always wild and overactive.

Contents

Prologue		11
1	A Surprise Gift	17
2	The Curious Dog	25
3	A Bad Dream	33
4	An Infinite Forest	41
5	The Largest Little Village	51
6	The Conquered	63
7	The Prophecy	77
8	The Tempest	91
9	The Feast	105
10	The Inner Light	113
11	The Mortada	127
12	Dakota Returns	131
13	Chosen's Acquaintances	145
14	Caelesta	159
15	Final Lessons	167

16	The Northern Woodlands	185
17	The Lightning Trip	191
18	A Glimpse of Scarlet	205
19	Melody's Song	211
20	The Hospitality of Dwarves	217
21	Magic Seeds	233
22	A Forced Good-bye	245
23	Welcome Home	251
24	New Friends	265
25	Monsters in the Capitol	275
26	Explanations	285
27	Jefferson's Last Stand	295
28	The Sorrowful Return	305
29	Hulpric's Book	317

Satorium

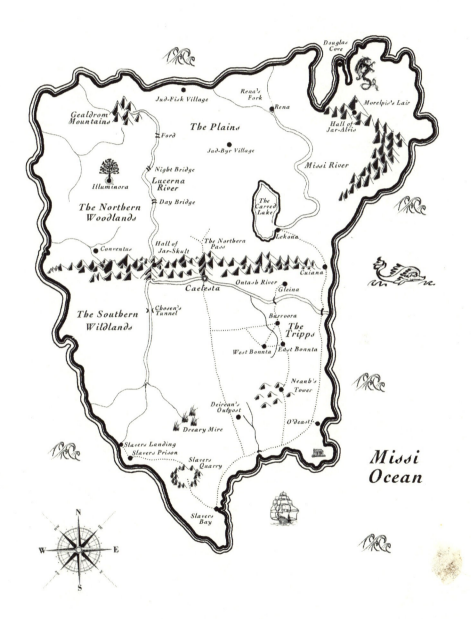

Prologue

Unfolding his glimmering wings, the little man flew cautiously toward the cave, the faint luminescence that clung to his body dimly lighting the dirt and roots around the entrance. It was a dismal place, the moonlight barely penetrating a foot inside. Its inhabitant had to squeeze into it by crouching and crawling, but it seemed immense to the little man, since he measured only six inches from head to foot.

Ten feet in, the den opened into a much larger space. With a wave of his hand the man projected a powerful beam in front of him and then played it over the stone walls of the cavern, which glistened as if damp but were dry to the touch.

Two deep blue orbs glowed from a dark recess. The little man turned the light toward them, finally illuminating the creature he'd come to see.

"It's been a long time." The little man's voice was surprisingly resonant, given his size, and rich with the timbre of wisdom.

"Yes, it has," the creature answered in a deep rumble.

The little man alit near the creature and sat down on a stone, stretching out his wings the way an old man might stretch a stiff leg or back, taking his time. "Would you mind a little more light? It's difficult for me to think in this darkness."

The creature nodded.

The man held his hands in front of him, palms facing, and moved them in horizontal opposing circles as if he were rolling clay into a ball. A tiny point of light formed between them, steadily growing to the size of an apple. With a flick of his wrist, he sent the ball of light floating up toward the roof of the cavern, filling the space with a warm, comfortable glow.

"Now, that's much better." He took his first proper look at his host. "You're showing your age."

"As are you, Xavier. And you take a great risk, leaving the protection of your forest."

"I doubt I'll find an enemy who'd follow me into the home of the Lord of Wolves, Udd Lyall."

The creature reflexively snarled at the mention of this

name and title, which had not been spoken for some time. The little man smiled and reached into his pocket, drawing out what looked like an emerald in the shape of a child's top.

"I had hoped that the signs were only my imagination," said Udd Lyall.

"No, old friend. I'm afraid not."

Xavier held the top tightly in his palm, head bowed, searching for the right words.

"Are you absolutely sure?" Udd Lyall asked, before Xavier could begin.

"Yes, I'm sure." Xavier's voice was distant.

"I'd come to think that it would not take place in my lifetime."

"That it did is one of the few things that gives me any real hope."

After a long silence, Xavier opened his palm, and the top began to spin, sending flecks of intense green light whirling out across the cavern. Slowly the flecks converged on the farthest wall, and an image came into focus: a child, sleeping in a woman's arms.

"She's human?"

"Yes, and more vulnerable than I ever imagined." Xavier closed his hand over the glowing top, and the image vanished. "She must be protected until she can begin her training."

"How long do we have before he is powerful enough to challenge us?"

"Not long enough."

"You have a plan?"

"I do." Xavier smiled sadly. "Someone must watch over her until we can bring her to Illuminora."

"Many have tried to cross over through the years, and failed. How do you plan to get someone to her?"

"It's . . . complicated. It will require all my knowledge—and a very powerful friend. One as dedicated as I am, and willing to sacrifice much."

Udd Lyall looked down at Xavier, studying his good friend for a long time. He trusted Xavier absolutely, though the winged man's ways might be mysterious. "I know enough of the human world to know I would not fit in. There I'm the stuff of nightmares, not dreams."

"That," Xavier said solemnly, "is a crucial part of the plan."

"Who is it? . . . The dark one."

Xavier looked pained. "The prince of the Dorans."

"The boy? Thanerbos? Surely not . . ." Udd Lyall trailed off, distressed. "He can't be more than two years old."

"I'm afraid so. His father, the king, has already banished him, much as it tore at his heart to do so."

A long, quiet moment passed. "I saw the boy once, at the celebration of his birth," Udd Lyall said finally.

"As did I."

An unspoken grief passed between them, both for a life lost and for the trials to come. There was little else to be said.

Xavier stood, and began making his way back to the opening.

"When do I leave?" Udd Lyall called out.
Xavier looked back with a somber smile.
"Soon, my friend. Soon."

1
A Surprise Gift

Though Charles Hopewell had first taken to the woods as energetically as the two-year-old black Lab bounding ahead of him, that didn't last long. About two miles in, feeling a little out of shape—at least, for a firefighter and former soldier—and very old, he was regretting his decision to take the family dog out for a jog instead of kicking back with a soda and John Wayne. To make matters worse, it looked like the storm the local news channel had been talking about for days was coming in a little ahead of schedule.

He was trying so hard not to think about his burning muscles that he didn't notice Cricket's leash going slack until a sudden backward jerk pulled his feet out from under him, and his behind hit the mud. He glared at the dog, who'd stopped to snuffle at a bush by the trail, then smiled ruefully. At least no one had witnessed his ignominious fall.

Climbing gingerly to his feet, Mr. Hopewell hobbled back to Cricket and patted her on the rump.

"Whatcha got there, girl?"

Cricket looked up at him with anxious brown eyes. He pulled her away and tried to look under the bush, but it was too dark to see much. He paused. No sound. Nothing moved. Just as he'd begun to straighten up, writing it off to a squirrel, he heard an unmistakable whine. Barking wildly, Cricket started pawing at the bush.

"Easy, girl." Charles kneeled by the bush and reached in, touching soft fur. A damp tongue licked his hand. Carefully he pulled the little creature out of the bush: a skinny, dirty puppy with startling blue eyes, which Cricket immediately began to nuzzle.

Taking off his sweatshirt, Charles wrapped it snugly around the pup. He shook his head. Who'd be cruel enough to dump a puppy out here? If he hadn't found it before the storm . . .

Cricket looked up at him, tail beating hard, clearly pleased with herself. "You're a hero," he told her, rubbing her fondly behind the ears.

Back at the house, Melody ran out to greet her father. "What's that, Daddy?" she asked, tugging at his pant leg.

Charles smiled at his five-year-old daughter. "I'll show you when we get inside." He glanced anxiously at the darkening sky.

In the living room, he unwrapped his sweatshirt to reveal the pup as the whole family looked on. Both girls were enchanted. Within minutes Scarlet, their elder daughter, had uttered the inevitable magic words—"Can we keep him, Daddy? Can we?"

She held the little creature close to her chest, pressing her cheek to his. Charles glanced uneasily at his wife, who didn't look quite as thrilled. Allie was a petite woman, with short blond hair and one of the most wonderful smiles Charles had ever seen. But she wasn't smiling now.

"Charles, I don't want to be the bad guy on this one." Allie leaned back against the arm of the sofa and gazed at her husband, trying to look stern.

Finally it was quiet in the house, and the lamps glowed softly in the living room. By the time they'd settled the puppy into a makeshift bed, convinced the girls that he needed a little peace, and gone out to get some puppy food, it had been dinnertime, followed by the girls' usual night routine. Scarlet had begged that she be allowed to keep the puppy in her room, and Allie finally gave in, making her promise to let him rest.

"You know we already have a dog." Allie sighed. "And we know nothing about this puppy—where it came from, who might own it, why it's here."

"I know, honey, but I think it'd been lying under that bush awhile. I'm sure it's been abandoned. I couldn't just leave it out in the storm."

"Still, we need to make sure no one's looking for it." Allie knew what a soft spot Charles had for his daughters, not to mention for helpless pups. It was part of what she liked about him, but with his easygoing attitude, the house might fall into chaos if she weren't there to keep things grounded. "We don't want Scarlet to get too attached before we know for sure."

"You're right. Strange, though, how quickly they seemed to hit it off. It just seems meant to be. Even Melody didn't try to take him away."

Allie's face softened. "I know. But let's make sure he doesn't belong to someone else." She glanced over at the framed family pictures on the mantel. "Cricket's the family dog. Maybe Scarlet can have her own—learn a little about responsibility."

"That might be going a little far. Scarlet is just a little girl."

Allie smiled inwardly. Some part of her husband wanted that to be true, she knew. "She's not our little baby anymore, Charles. Look at those pictures—she's grown so much. She'll be a young woman soon."

"You're right," he said reluctantly, gazing up at the mantel. "I just can't believe she'll be fourteen next week."

"And with age comes responsibility. . . . Charles, let's give it a week to make sure the puppy doesn't belong to someone else, and teach Scarlet how to take care of him. If all goes well, he'll be her birthday present."

Scarlet woke to the soft, wet nose of the puppy against her neck. She giggled as he licked her face.

"You're going to need a name," she said softly. "That is, if you get to stay."

A week had gone by, and still no one had called the number on the notices her parents put up. No one had lost a puppy. Her parents had explained that she would have to prove she could take care of a dog on her own. It had been hard at first—she'd never realized how much work it was. She had to remember to feed him twice a day, make sure dog food was on the shopping list when necessary, take him out, and teach him to behave. That last part wouldn't be hard, though—he already seemed to know how to act. Sometimes it even felt as if he was taking care of her, helping her prove that she could handle things. She'd made mistakes, but she thought she'd come a long way. Hopefully her parents felt the same way.

Setting the puppy down gently, she headed downstairs with a hopeful skip in her walk.

On the kitchen TV the weatherman was droning on about another storm. *Again?* The weather had been crazy lately.

Scarlet slid the glass patio door open to let the puppy out. Pulling her red hair absentmindedly into a ponytail, she watched the two dogs frolic in the yard. If she didn't know better, she could have sworn the puppy was playing fetch. He'd grab the tennis ball and, using his tiny neck muscles, hurl it with surprising strength out into the yard, where Cricket would chase it down and bring it back.

Finally Scarlet turned and sat down at the breakfast table. Neither of her parents looked up. Her father was reading the paper, her mother filling out today's sudoku.

"Good morning." Scarlet grinned. Her parents loved this little act, year after year.

"Oh, I didn't see you there." Her father glanced up briefly. "Good morning."

Her mother kept her eyes on her puzzle. "I was thinking we might run a few errands today, dear," she said to her husband.

He grunted. "I could use a trip to the hardware store."

Scarlet shook her head, but she didn't mind her parents' game. It was kind of a family tradition. To be honest, she'd miss it if they stopped.

This time, she thought, she'd play along. "I'll go with, if you don't mind. I need some school supplies."

Both of her parents looked up simultaneously, surprised. Then, unable to keep straight faces any longer, they laughed and got up to hug their daughter.

"Happy birthday!" they exclaimed.

At Scarlet's party that afternoon, the puppy played dutifully with her small cousins, never protesting at the occasional pulled ear. He never got underfoot while the guests milled around, playing party games and eating cake and ice cream.

He sat, lay down, rolled over, let out his tiny bark, even shook hands, all at Scarlet's father's command.

Finally he sat dutifully beside her, watching with quiet interest as she unwrapped each gift—clothes, board games, and most of all, books. When all had been opened, her mother snuck out and returned with a small rectangular box.

"I know you already got your presents from us," she said, handing Scarlet the box, "but we just couldn't help ourselves. Here's another one."

Scarlet opened the box. Then she leaped from her chair and threw her arms around her mother's neck. "Thank you, thank you, thank you, Mom!"

"You're welcome," her mother answered, her eyes misty. "Happy birthday."

"And you too, Dad." Scarlet hugged him and then picked up the puppy, who nuzzled her cheek.

Still clutched in her hand was a small red collar.

"Don't worry, little one," Scarlet whispered to the pup in her room that evening. "You're home now." He nestled himself into the crook of her arm, almost immediately falling asleep.

It was funny, though.

Just before he closed his eyes, she could almost swear he winked.

24 Brandon Charles West

2

The Curious Dog

Scarlet woke to rain driving against her window.

"Scarlet! Up you get," her mother called. "Dress warm. They say this new storm is gonna be a cold one."

Cricket was still sleeping by Scarlet's bed, but Dakota—as she'd named the puppy—had already left the room. In the few weeks that had passed since her birthday, he'd tripled in size. His paws were comically large, nearly twice the size they should have been, and the rest of him was sleek and powerfully muscled for such a young animal. Though he looked like a German shepherd, with his black mask and saddle over a rich reddish tan coat, he had the most unnaturally blue eyes—not the pale blue of a husky or Australian shepherd, but a deep cobalt blue that almost seemed to glow.

She showered and dressed, grabbed the backpack she'd put her schoolbooks in the night before, and headed downstairs. At the bottom of the stairs she lingered a few seconds, her hand resting on the ball ornament at the end of the banister, looking into the living room.

Dakota was sitting in front of the TV, staring raptly at the screen as the weatherman pointed at his map, which showed another storm front coming in. The weather had been getting stranger and more frightening. Power outages were ravaging the East Coast as high winds blew trees onto power lines, and flooding was widespread.

"Morning, Dakota."

Dakota barked once without looking away from the TV.

"Dakota just said good morning to me," she said as she sat down at the breakfast table.

"He *talks*?" Her father sounded startled.

"Oh, I just meant he barked back when I said good morning."

"You had me for a minute there! I gotta say, that dog seems so smart, I'd almost believe he spoke English."

Scarlet laughed. "I know what you mean."

Once she'd finished breakfast, Scarlet stood up and looked around, a little puzzled. Her backpack wasn't where she usually hung it, on the kitchen door. Maybe she'd left it at the bottom of the stairs.

When she walked into the hall, though, there were Dakota and Cricket, sitting at attention by the front door, Dakota holding Scarlet's backpack, Cricket holding Melody's.

"Cricket, too! Good doggie!" Melody patted the black Lab on the head.

"Well, thank you, Dakota," Scarlet said in mock formality. "How kind of you."

Their mother laughed as the two girls put on their sweaters and raincoats and took their bags from Dakota and Cricket, though she'd seemed a little disconcerted when she first saw the dogs holding the backpacks. "You pay attention to your teacher, Melody," she said, opening the door. "And Scarlet, good luck at the assembly."

A couple weeks into each new school year, the principal welcomed the students with an assembly in the auditorium. This year was special, though. Before school let out, Scarlet's English teacher, Ms. Thandiwe, had asked each of her students to write a short story for a contest over summer and bring it to her on the first day of school, so she could announce the winner at the assembly.

Scarlet had jumped at the chance. For several years she'd been dreaming about a magical world, and writing stories based on those dreams; she had a whole folder at home. She'd chosen one and worked on it most of the summer to get it perfect, and her hopes were high.

In homeroom she fidgeted, so excited she could hardly sit still. Finally everyone filed into the auditorium. A few metal and plastic chairs were lined up on one side of a podium, and on each side of the stage hung flags—the American and state flags on one side, the county flag and one displaying the school's mascot, a ferocious-looking wolf, on the other.

Scarlet was so preoccupied with the results of the contest that she hardly heard the principal's welcome speech. Finally he called Ms. Thandiwe's name, and the young teacher stood and walked gracefully to the podium from one of the chairs on the stage. Her long black hair was pulled tightly into a bun and she wore an austere gray suit, but the gaudy pink reading glasses hanging from a chain around her neck added a lighthearted touch.

"I'd like to thank all those students who submitted stories." Ms. Thandiwe's voice was soft and lilting, with a hint of an African accent, and the crowd hushed to hear her. "I felt honored to read so many wonderful submissions."

She announced the third- and second-place winners, and still Scarlet's name hadn't been called. Scarlet sat on the edge of her seat, almost unable to breathe.

"Now, when I announce this year's contest winner, I would like to ask the student to come onstage and read their story, for all of the students and teachers to enjoy."

Scarlet's heart plummeted. Read her story in front of the whole school? Suddenly she wasn't so certain she wanted to win.

"And the winner is—Ms. Scarlet Hopewell," Ms. Thandiwe announced. "For her story 'The Lightning Fairies.' "

Scarlet was frozen in her seat, unable to speak.

"Ms. Hopewell?"

How long could Ms. Thandiwe possibly wait before moving on with the assembly? Scarlet sank deep into her chair.

"I guess Ms. Hopewell isn't here today," Ms. Thandiwe said finally. "That's a shame. You're all missing a real treat." She turned to the principal and thanked him before taking her seat.

A wave of guilt washed over Scarlet. She thought about the talks she'd had with her parents about Dakota and responsibilities, and she knew she'd made a mistake. She couldn't just hide from whatever made her uncomfortable. Ms. Thandiwe had chosen her story, and Scarlet had not even acknowledged her choice. Then another thought struck her. Surely the powers that be were making sure Scarlet learned her lesson. Ms. Thandiwe's class was Scarlet's last of the day.

When the bell rang for the last period, Scarlet marched off to Ms. Thandiwe's classroom, resigned to her fate. Flooded with dread, she hardly heard a word in class, even though she usually loved listening to Ms. Thandiwe, who was a wonderful teacher, bringing her subject alive. Books transport you into another world, she'd tell the class. When she described the first time she'd read Shakespeare's play *The Tempest,* the class was caught up completely in her spell.

Finally the bell rang. Scarlet waited until the last student had left, gathered her courage, and walked up to Ms. Thandiwe's desk.

"Yes, Scarlet?"

"I'm . . . um . . . not absent."

"Yes—I noticed that when I called roll." Ms. Thandiwe's warm brown eyes gleamed with gentle humor, but then she looked graver. "I'm sorry about this morning, Scarlet."

Scarlet's jaw dropped. *Ms. Thandiwe* was sorry?

"You see, Principal Edwards explained to me that you might have been embarrassed, put on the spot like that. I'm new to teaching in the United States. In South Africa, where I come from, public speaking is emphasized quite early."

"Oh," was all Scarlet could manage.

"All the same, young lady, you shouldn't have been embarrassed to share your work. You're a very talented writer."

"You think so?"

"I do, and I think that the next time someone asks you to share your work, you should jump at the chance. You don't want to let too many opportunities pass you by—you never know when they might come around again." Ms. Thandiwe got up from her desk and placed her hands on Scarlet's shoulders, gave her a little wink, and walked her to the door.

"There's nothing for you to be embarrassed about. Now scurry along. I'll see you tomorrow."

In a joyful mood nothing could shake, Scarlet hurried out of school just in time to see her bus pulling away. She didn't live far away, but the weather was awful. Clouds blanketed the sky, so dark and thick that it felt as if dusk was already descending. So far there'd only been rain, but another storm was definitely on the way.

Scarlet steeled herself for the walk, lowering her head against the wind. But then her eyes went wide. There was Dakota, seated patiently at her feet.

"What are you doing here?" she exclaimed, both pleased and shocked.

Dakota let out a short bark, then walked around Scarlet and stood at attention by her left side.

"Did you come to walk me home?"

Dakota spun in a circle, let out another short bark, and wagged his tail furiously.

Scarlet bent down and ruffled Dakota's fur. "Well, thank you," she said, and they began the walk home together.

They got home before the storm, but the temperature was dropping fast. Over this last week, they'd been warning of a terrific storm on the news, a strange new kind of storm unheard of in this region, though the weatherman said it sometimes happened on the shores of the Great Lakes—thundersnow, he was calling it.

When Scarlet opened the front door, Cricket was on her way down the stairs. Dakota trotted up to meet her halfway, and they touched noses in a doggy greeting. Cricket turned and trotted back upstairs, while Dakota headed for the living room, where the television was broadcasting an urgent weather update.

Upstairs in her room, Scarlet slid her story back into the thick pink folder where she kept all the rest. There must be at least a hundred, she figured, running her finger over the top edges of the pages. She put the folder back in the drawer and looked out the window at the storm clouds on the horizon. For a second it felt as if they were coming directly at her. Coming *for* her. She shivered, then shrugged the feeling off and headed down to dinner.

3
A Bad Dream

Cricket snored tranquilly beside Scarlet's bed, the only sound disturbing the night-before-Christmas quiet. Dakota was sitting at the window in a silent vigil, ears pricked; something about the coming storm seemed to worry him. In five months he'd grown nearly twice as tall as your average German shepherd, and now he weighed 180 pounds. Somehow his vigilance was comforting.

Scarlet had just woken from the dream world she visited so often in her sleep. There she'd wandered in a deep forest, surrounded by fairies that danced around her, tickling her face and landing softly in her hair, through a radiant landscape of emerald and silver. This world had seemed as familiar to her as her own home.

In the dream, she always found herself in an enchanting village, alive with light, sheltered under the wide-stretched limbs of a great tree. At the foot of this tree Scarlet's family and friends, among them many animals of the forest, would be gathered to greet her, as if she'd been long awaited. It was always a grand homecoming. Both dogs would be there, speaking English as if it were the most natural thing imaginable. She and her sister would play in the woods all day with their animal friends, under a canopy of glittering leaves, and in the evening they'd sit outside and watch the fairies put on shows of astounding magic, with wondrous displays of light and color. When the dream's evening came to a close, Scarlet would lie down, tired but happy, on a bed woven of springy twigs, cushioned by leaves longer than her body yet soft as fine suede.

Tonight, however, something dark had begun to stir in the dream, some unnamed fear. She'd woken suddenly, this ominous darkness hanging over her like a shroud. Outside the window, through the cracks in her blinds, the night sky was an abyss. The moon was hidden behind thick clouds and the snow fell in dead silence, so thickly that she couldn't see the house across the street.

She rolled over, punched her pillow, and tried to go back to sleep. She'd nearly drifted off again when a thud—much too loud to be a knock at the door— shattered the silence, followed by a cracking, splintering sound, like a tree limb being wrenched away.

She bolted upright, looking for Dakota, but he was missing. Her door was ajar, and she was alone. She jumped out of bed and made a beeline for the comfort of her parents' room, as she'd done so often as a little girl.

"Charles, there's no dial tone," her mother was saying as she fumbled desperately with the phone, the tremble in her voice betraying her own fear though it was obvious that, seeing Scarlet, she was doing her best to look calm.

Her father grabbed a heavy wooden ax handle from the closet and rushed to the stairs. "Get Melody."

"Stay here, baby." Her mom had run to Melody's room and back before Scarlet had a chance to think. She gathered both her daughters up and sat them on the bed, taking a stand by the door like a soldier guarding his post. Scarlet couldn't remember ever having seen her so scared.

BOOM! CRACK!

The sounds were even louder this time. Scarlet's stomach clenched. The air seemed to grow darker though the lights were still on, a strange thickness filling the room. It was how Scarlet imagined a smoking house might look when her father went in to fight a fire, but she knew it wasn't smoke. Smoke was real, and this—well, she could see the darkness, but she knew it wasn't really there. Somehow that didn't make it any less frightening.

BOOM! CRACK!

"Come here!" Her father appeared suddenly in the doorway, making them all scream. Her mother gathered herself and grabbed Scarlet and Melody's hands, pulling them toward her husband.

"We'll go to the basement," he said, lifting Melody into his arms. "Cell phones aren't working either. We'll run out the back and get to the neighbor's—use their phone."

They'd rounded the bend in the stairs, the basement door only feet away, when a final CRACK rang out, and the wood of the doorframe gave way.

Standing in the doorway were three tall, slim figures dressed in black. They were beautiful, their pale skin luminous against the darkness all around them, their golden hair long and flowing. Shadows danced across their fine-boned faces and gathered in the bottomless black pools of their eyes. They stepped forward gracefully, their smiles warm, almost friendly, as if they were invited guests. But the air seemed to grow even thicker and darker before them as they entered.

Scarlet's father put Melody down and swept his wife and daughters behind him. He looked fierce and brave now, and somehow younger.

"*The girl,*" all three figures said in unison, their voices like every awful sound he'd ever heard. It was babies screaming and dogs whelping, nails across a chalkboard, a mother wailing and bones breaking.

"Get out of my house," Scarlet's father said, teeth clenched, his knuckles white where he grasped the ax handle.

"*Not until we have the girl,*" the dark ones lilted, this time in a mystical song, compelling and all-consuming. Their voices seemed rooted in Scarlet's brain, festering.

For a fleeting moment, unbelievably, it looked as if her father was considering obeying. He turned to look back at Scarlet, and she felt her stomach lurch at the blankness in his eyes. But a moment later the light came back into them. He swung back toward his tormentors. "Over my dead body!" he shouted, lifting the ax handle.

The figures stepped toward him again.

"*And over mine.*" The voice from behind the girls was deep, and seemed to roll over each word like a growl.

Scarlet whipped her head around, expecting a new enemy. What she saw was even more shocking. Moving up to join them, teeth bared, hackles raised, unearthly blue eyes trained on the intruders, was Dakota. Scarlet shook her head to clear it. There was no way the dog could—

"*Follow me,*" said a new voice, similar but somehow softer and more feminine. "*Dakota hold them off.*"

This time there was no doubt. Cricket, the black Labrador, had spoken.

For a moment Scarlet was frozen to the spot. She looked from the figures to Dakota and back again. Any youthful playfulness had vanished from the scrawny pup her father had rescued only five months ago. What she saw now was something so impossible, so fierce, it defied imagination.

"Now," Dakota growled, and Scarlet's father caught her hand and tugged her out of her trance, pulling her after Allie,

Melody, and Cricket down the stairs. It felt as if the darkness were chasing them, and above she could hear terrible snarls, thuds, and the sound of snapping teeth.

"*Hurry,*" Cricket called from behind them, running to the back door. "*We must make woods.*"

Suddenly the basement door flew open, snow rushing in with a howl of wind. The family halted. It's over, Scarlet thought. We're surrounded.

But it wasn't more of the dark figures—though to Scarlet it seemed worse. Her father pulled her and Melody tightly to his chest, reaching out for Allie.

Five massive wolves, each easily twice the size of Dakota, were slinking into the basement.

Scarlet wasn't afraid of the wolves. After all, she had seen them before. This very night, in fact, she'd been running with them in her dreams.

"*You make it!*" cried Cricket. "*Dakota say you come.*"

"*It's a long journey,*" the biggest wolf growled. "*Where is . . . er . . . Dakota?*" But the commotion upstairs told him before anyone could answer. "*Hurry, into the woods!*" he barked, before rushing up the stairs.

In a flash Scarlet was running, her mother gripping her hand. They staggered through the backyard after Cricket, trying to keep up with the leaping dog as they floundered through the deep snow. It was like one of those nightmares where every step is a struggle. She could hear her father's heavy footsteps right behind her as he ran with Melody in his arms.

Any second they would break through the trees and be in Mrs. Anderson's backyard. They would use her phone to call the police, and this would all be over. After all, the little stretch of woods behind their house was only five or ten trees deep. First their yard, sixty feet of grass, a playground with a swing. Then the tree house their dad had built for the girls, in the large maple at the edge of the woods. Maybe eight trees beyond that, some brush, and then . . . this should be Mrs. Anderson's yard.

Yet every time Scarlet thought this must be the end—now they must be emerging into the beginning of Mrs. Anderson's backyard—the woods only seemed to multiply, growing both in density and scope.

And something else strange was happening. The snow kept falling more lightly, until it had faded completely away. That might not have been so strange, but the air seemed milder too, and suddenly Scarlet realized that everything around her was green. Green, lush forest unfolded endlessly before them, velvety clumps of moss underfoot, like the plushest carpet, beneath the emerald canopy. The world was spinning—it was beyond comprehension—and yet there it was, for them all to see and hear and feel. The trees became larger as the group moved along underneath them, towering taller and wilder. The leaves thickened until the world was a sea of green.

Cricket ran effortlessly just ahead in the expanding forest. She seemed overjoyed at this phenomenon that was making Scarlet's senses reel. "*It here!*" she called back excitedly, frolicking like a pup. "*It happening, just like Dakota say!*"

Scarlet wanted to ask what she meant, but she could barely catch her breath. She was an active girl, but she'd never run so far in her life. Her amazement at the ever-expanding forest that had once been only a skip or two in her backyard was gone. Now she just accepted it, almost her entire mind consumed by the burn in her failing muscles, fear driving her on as she dodged the massive trunks of trees and ducked under low-hanging branches.

Once she glanced behind her at her father, doing his best to shield Melody from the branches and leaves that whipped at them as he ran. It was a comfort to have him at her back.

What was happening? How was any of this possible? She tried to shake off what must be a nightmare. Surely she must be back in her dream.

A low branch struck her in the face, a sharp pain radiating back from her nose. You can't feel pain in a dream, she thought. Not actual pain.

It had to be real. This was all really happening. There would be no waking up. Something incredible, unbelievable, was happening, and it was happening to her.

4
An Infinite Forest

Dakota was furious with himself. There was no reason to be; he could have done nothing more. It was all a part of the magic that had brought him to this world as Scarlet's guardian. He'd known it would take time to reach his full strength, and that even when he had recovered, he could never again be what he once had been. Never again would he resume the body that had once been his, the body that had been born the Lord of Wolves. That had been part of the sacrifice—a fruitless sacrifice, if Scarlet didn't escape from the hunters in time. Nothing was more relentless, more evil, than the Mortada. Theirs was the darkest magic, and in his new form he was no match for them. As it was, he'd barely held his own against the three of them, and if the Stidolph hadn't come when they had—well, no matter now. They had. He hoped they'd bought the Hopewells enough time.

His mind churned with questions. How had the Mortada found them? How had they crossed over? Had they been wandering, lost between worlds, as he had?

It had taken him fourteen years to find Scarlet. In that time, he'd had no contact with anyone or anything. Everything could have changed. The world he thought he was leading Scarlet toward, a world where she would be safe, where she could be trained to fulfill her destiny, might offer no safety at all. But there was no alternative. Not with the Mortada on their heels. Even if the prince had overrun Satorium, their only hope was to get Scarlet to Xavier.

Still, Xavier's plan had worked. Somehow he'd held open the crossing for Dakota and, when the time came, for the Stidolph as well. Maybe that was how the Mortada had crossed. He hated to think what that might mean for Xavier. Luckily something about the crossing had weakened the Mortada. No doubt Mr. Hopewell's great love for his children had helped him to resist, but even that wouldn't have prevailed against a Mortada at the height of its powers. For his part, Dakota had made it through the fight with only a bloody scrape on his right shoulder, but it throbbed deep in his muscles as he ran. *Please, Cricket. Get them to safety. Let there be safety still through the barrier.*

He knew in his heart, though, that she would succeed, and that safety was still to be had on the other side. He had prepared Cricket well, and although she wasn't originally from his home, she had a bigger heart than any warrior he'd ever known. Besides, her loyalty to the Hopewells was beyond mere dedication. She loved them, and Dakota had learned over his long life that love could make up for many weaknesses.

For a dog who until meeting Dakota had been content to live each day as a mere pet—not that, after living with the Hopewells for five months, Dakota held any contempt for that role—Cricket was a quick study. Every night they had gone over the route through the woods and across the barrier to Satorium. Every night she repeated the plan perfectly, asking few questions. Her devotion was all that mattered to her.

The rhythmic thumping of the pack's paws drove Dakota onward despite the pain in his leg. Any second now they would catch up with Scarlet and the family.

"Cricket," Mr. Hopewell called, a note of doubt in his voice, as if he wasn't sure whether he was still in charge. Cricket looked back, slackening her pace. "We have to rest," he said, his breath labored. "The girls need a break."

Cricket stopped, her nose automatically searching the air for the scent of danger. "*Dakota told me not stop until we reach Tounder,*" she barked, worry in her voice.

"I'm sorry, but I don't know what any of that means. For a minute, though, we have to stop—I can't carry Melody much longer without a break. Let's catch our breath," Mr. Hopewell pleaded. He leaned against a tree, chest heaving, still cradling the sleeping Melody in his arms.

Cricket nodded reluctantly, taking up a guard position between the family and the house. *Don't stop. Don't rest or believe you're safe.* Dakota's words were hammering in her brain as she strained to process all the new information she was responsible for now. She was just a dog, after all—a regular family dog. What did she know of magic and the Mortada and protecting her family against these things? Before Dakota came, the most important decisions she had to make in any given day had been who to bring the ball back to, and which of her family looked the most willing to give her a belly rub. This was all too much—but there was no alternative. Dakota . . . her family . . . they were all depending on her.

But just as panic was beginning to rise in her, she felt a familiar hand scratch her behind her ear, just where she liked it best. "I can't believe you can talk," Scarlet said, smiling down at her. Her face was flushed from running, almost hiding the freckles on her nose. "Could you talk this whole time?"

Cricket tried to smile, though that didn't work so well on a dog, since it looked more like baring teeth. "*No, not until Dakota show me how.*" She knew her pride at having mastered the language, a feat that seemed impossible for a dog, shone in her eyes.

"How did Dakota learn?" Scarlet asked.

"*I don't know.*" Cricket was starting to get nervous again, her eyes darting from shadow to shadow. She could just catch the scent of something in the distance, but could not quite make out what it was. She was quivering with fear. *Please let it be Dakota*, she pleaded silently.

Whatever it was, it had to be close now. It was something powerful, she knew that much. *The Mortada*. Had Dakota failed? There was no way to know until it was too late. If it was *them* she was smelling, she didn't know what she could do. They had so much power, she could feel it, and she was just an ordinary dog.

"Who were those men?" Scarlet asked. "And what was the dark . . . smoke stuff? Was it magic?"

"*That is best for Dakota to answer. We have to move. We not safe until we reach land where Tounder live,*" Cricket implored. She felt as if time itself were an enemy, hunting them down as surely as the Mortada.

"What are the Tounder?" Scarlet asked, sounding much more curious than scared. "The name seems familiar, but I can't think why."

Cricket wasn't sure how to answer. She certainly had never seen these beings, and the description Dakota had given of them made little sense to her. "*Not sure. Just know Dakota said we safe once we reach their land.*" Her hackles had begun to rise involuntarily, and she shifted uneasily. *"To me, sound like little bird people in books you talk to Melody."*

Scarlet frowned. "Little bird people? What in the world?" Then she smiled. "Fairies. You mean fairies. Like the Tinker Bell books."

"Yes, those. Tinker Bells."

Scarlet wanted to laugh at the absurdity of this surreal night. Fairies? As if talking dogs, evil men, and mystical forests weren't ridiculous enough, now fairies? But now, with Cricket trembling under her fingers, her warmth and the texture of her fur much too real to belong to a dream, humor was giving way to fear.

"Mr. Hopewell!" Cricket's bark had the ring of panic. *"We have to move. We not safe here."*

Scarlet looked over at her parents. Her dad was sitting with his back against a tree trunk, still cradling the sleeping Melody in his arms. Her mom had been sitting next to him, resting her head against his chest, but now she straightened up, looked at Scarlet and Cricket, and spoke for the first time since they'd run out of the house. "Where are we going, Cricket? What is all this?" She sounded puzzled, and a little annoyed.

She still thinks it's a dream.

Cricket whimpered a little in frustration. *"I not best to ask. Dakota or Tounder will answer questions. We have to move."* The longer they waited, the more panicky Cricket looked, and now she was shifting her feet, barely able to keep still, as if she were waiting to run after a ball.

Scarlet's father began to climb to his feet, but her mom stopped him, placing a hand firmly on his chest.

"Cricket," she said firmly, "I don't know if you can understand how crazy this all is to us. We can't just go chasing after a talking dog in the middle of the night. Someone broke into our home. We have to call the police."

But Cricket wasn't listening. She sniffed the air frantically, turning one way and the next, as if searching for a scent. *"Please. We need to go."*

"We're not running into the middle of nowhere like this anymore. We need to reach the police." Scarlet's mother had crossed her arms. She looked as unmovable as a boulder.

"Maybe we should just go with it," Scarlet's father suggested. "Whatever those things were, I'm not even sure the police could help."

Scarlet's mom shot him a be-quiet-and-let-me-speak look. "What *are* those things?" she demanded. It was plain she wouldn't be budged.

Cricket whined. It was too late. Whatever she'd heard rustling in the brush was close. No, it was here. They wouldn't be able to escape. She had failed.

"We have to try and hide. Hurry!"

But now there was a great rustling in the trees from the direction of the house. There wouldn't be time to hide. Cricket planted herself firmly between the danger and her family, steeling herself against whatever might burst through the trees. She would give it the fight of her life. However little good it might do, she would die protecting them.

The undergrowth parted, and Dakota emerged from the thick green shadows, panting heavily and bleeding from his shoulder. He slid to a sudden halt in front of Cricket, looking at her and the family with desperate eyes. The pack came to a more graceful stop behind him.

"*Why did you stop?*" Dakota barked. "*I told you not to stop until you'd reached the Tounder.*" He was holding back his anger, but it showed in his flashing blue eyes.

Cricket lowered her head and nuzzled Dakota's neck. "*I sorry,*" she whined.

"It's my fault," Mr. Hopewell called out, walking to stand next to Cricket. "I told her to stop."

Dakota looked from Cricket to Mr. Hopewell, and his eyes softened. It was completely understandable that she had listened to her master, Cricket read in them; he couldn't fault her for it. "*We're not safe until we reach the Tounder,*" he barked. "*We can't afford to stop.*"

"Scarlet is tired. She can't handle this running much longer," Mr. Hopewell said. Cricket suspected that he spoke for himself as much as Scarlet. After all, he was carrying Melody.

Dakota lifted his head and barked. It sounded curiously as if he was laughing—perhaps he'd had the same thought.

"That's a problem easily fixed," he said. "Ulrich, Fael!"

Two of the largest wolves—no, Stidolph, Cricket corrected herself—came forward, silently communicating with Dakota. Then the one Dakota called Ulrich approached Scarlet.

"Climb on my back, my lady," he said, his voice low and gruff, as if he rarely used it and wasn't quite sure it worked.

Scarlet smiled and, without hesitation, jumped onto Ulrich's back. Fael went to Mrs. Hopewell and motioned for her to do the same. After a great deal of hesitation, she did, and Mr. Hopewell handed her Melody.

Dakota looked at Mr. Hopewell. *"How are your legs?"*

"I'll be fine," he answered, a little doubtfully.

"Then let's be off." Dakota took the lead, darting off into the forest ahead of them.

Limbs and leaves flashed by in a dizzying blur, almost faster than Scarlet could see them. Despite the tremendous speed at which Ulrich ran, she had no fear of falling off. She wrapped her arms around the Stidolph's mighty neck and reveled in the wind rushing through her hair. Stealing a glance at her mother, she was surprised to see much the same expression on her face, even if it was a bit more reserved. With the Stidolph carrying them, now, everything seemed like it would be okay. She looked back and saw her father and Cricket running side by side. Never had she seen her dad run so fast.

After several miles, a familiar sensation washed over her. Her heart seemed to be dancing. Inside she was filled with a warmth that staved off the cold. It felt as if nothing in the world could ever be sad again. Even in the dark, the forest around her glowed so alive and green, shimmering like emeralds carved into the shapes of leaves and ferns. There was a strange tickling in her hair, a tickling she knew she'd felt before. Just above her, in the canopy of the trees, she could swear she saw dancing lights of every imaginable color.

The trees parted to reveal a circular clearing, a massive oak standing majestically at its center. Scarlet gasped. Clothed with iridescent gold and silver leaves, the oak's limbs spread wide to form a glittering canopy against the night sky. All along its branches, up and down its mighty trunk, glistening lights danced in every hue.

At the base of the tree, much smaller than she remembered it in her dreams, was the entrance to the village.

5
The Largest Little Village

Dakota stopped at the base of the massive oak, bowed his head low to the ground, and then lifted his muzzle to the heavens and let out a mighty howl. Cricket and the wolves did the same, the canine chorus rising to a crescendo, echoing out into the night.

The myriad points of lights that had been dancing around the tree began to swirl together, forming a cyclone of vibrant colors that encompassed the Hopewells and the canines. Scarlet felt a tingling all over her body, radiating in circles just beneath the surface of her skin. Through the lights that swirled around her, she could just make out the foliage, and as the speed of the luminescent cyclone grew, so did the size of the tree above her. Within moments the ferns that had been underfoot now seemed as tall as trees, and the great oak, which had already been a mighty specimen, was now incomprehensibly vast. After a few moments the tornado of light slowed, and Scarlet could see that each light was actually a person, dressed in shimmering cloth, floating gracefully to the ground on wings that seemed made of the same iridescent material. This, Scarlet correctly guessed, must be the Tounder.

One of the Tounder landed in front of the family. "I am Xavier," the winged figure said. "Elder of the Tounder and Keeper of Light." He bowed elegantly and then waved his arm to introduce the many winged figures behind him.

The little man looked very old, with a long beard and hair that matched the glistening white of his wings. He was smaller than the other winged figures, and quite thin. The eyes that lit up with his warm smile were clear amber and shone with a radiance of their own.

"Ch—er—Charles. Charles Hopewell," Mr. Hopewell mumbled. "I'm with the talking dogs."

Xavier laughed. It was the most beautiful sound Scarlet had ever heard. "But of course you are. Come with me—you must be exhausted." He beckoned them toward the massive archway at the base of the oak.

Confusion washed over Scarlet in waves. Nothing from the moment she had woken made any sense. It was as if she had never left her dream, and when she thought about it, that really was the most likely explanation for what was happening to them. A desperate need to wake warred within her with an insatiable curiosity, a sense of wonderment she could not shake. Perhaps if she focused on one unbelievable thing at a time? Work backward, if she must, to a final explanation. She took a moment to study the world around her, focusing not on the whole of the evening but simply on what was before her now.

Finally it came to her. It wasn't the forest that had grown. They had shrunk.

Xavier looked at the bewildered family and frowned. "Have you told them nothing?" he asked Dakota.

"There was no time," Dakota answered faintly. "I barely had time to reach some degree of maturity. The Mortada came earlier than expected. I lost a lot of blood and strength in the fight."

Xavier nodded. "We couldn't know how long it would take to get you over. That's my failing. . . . You must be more than a little confused," he said apologetically to the family. "Come into my home. You can rest while I do my best to explain what I can."

He turned to Scarlet and smiled, bending down so they were eye to eye. "Yes, my dear." He chuckled. "We shrank you."

I didn't say that out loud, did I? Scarlet thought. As if in direct reply, Xavier winked at her.

Mr. Hopewell was an easygoing sort of man, but still, he liked to consider himself a rational person. It wasn't that he lacked imagination or didn't enjoy the occasional fantasy movie or book, but when it came to the world of nonfiction, what you see is generally what you get. He tried to wrap his mind around what he saw in front of him. Rational really wasn't going to cut it. There was no rational way of explaining the circumstances of following a winged man, who called himself what amounted basically to "the old fairy," through a hole in a tree that moments ago he wouldn't have been able to fit his hand into. Not to mention that the tree was now twice the size of the tallest skyscraper Mr. Hopewell had ever seen.

He reached out and took Mrs. Hopewell's hand, giving it a reassuring squeeze. To her credit, she just smiled and shrugged, having obviously given up her earlier confrontational attitude as futile. Perhaps she was right. There was no point in trying to rationalize away any of this, for the moment at least.

Hand in hand, they walked beneath the arch and into the tree trunk.

Mr. Hopewell had been expecting the space they entered to look like, well, the inside of a tree. Instead, beyond the entranceway stretched a great hall lined with glorious stone columns, carved in the shape of winged figures. The hall was alive with light, though there were no lamps or candles anywhere to be seen. A glow seemed to come from nowhere, and yet everywhere.

"There is a column for each of the elders past," Xavier said, walking beside Mr. Hopewell. "All fathers of my fathers, going back to the beginning of recorded time."

There must have been nearly a hundred columns, Mr. Hopewell realized.

They followed the Tounder down a wide stone staircase that wound for what seemed like miles below the earth. Finally they emerged onto the cobblestone street of a medieval village.

Scarlet couldn't believe her eyes. It was a place familiar from her dreams, but those dreams had done nothing to prepare her for the grandeur of the reality. It was as if they weren't underground at all. Light was everywhere, filling the space with a glowing warmth so much like the light of a summer's day that her mind was reeling. Hadn't she just climbed down an impossibly long staircase? Surely in her dreams she hadn't imagined entering a hollow tree and walking beneath its roots.

Everywhere she looked were unbelievable sights—magnificent gardens, full of fairy-tale flowers, columbines and larkspur and Canterbury bells, around velvety lawns punctuated by dancing fountains; shops selling everything from strange fruits in jewel tones to golden loaves of bread to shimmering fabrics. The main street was lined with statues of fabulous creatures that seemed to be carved out of light. At the center of the town square stood a massive windmill, its long blades turning in languid circles, powered by what looked to be solar panels mounted on them.

Next to this glorious reality, the world of her dreams had been only a faint echo. Now, in the Tounder village, all of her fears and exhaustion melted away. Everywhere busy Tounder were milling around, working, shopping, gossiping, going about their lives as if this were the most normal place in the world.

Scarlet had been shuffling along behind her parents and the old Tounder, but as they passed an open pavilion, she stopped, drawn as if by a magnet to the scene she saw there. Seated on the floor underneath the awning, a group of young Tounder were watching what must have been their teacher working with his hands to form an orb of light. The young Tounder watched him, some taking notes on rough parchment, while others carried on their own quiet conversations, much as Scarlet and her friends did in math class. The teacher circled his hands over the orb, making it grow and shrink and then causing its light to brighten and flicker.

"It must seem quite astounding to you, dear," Xavier said from right behind her. She started and turned to face him, her face flushed with excitement. "I imagine all this must be." He paused, smiling at her, and then leaned in close, continuing in a voice just above a whisper. "I can assure you, though, it's just the beginning of the wonders yet to come."

Reluctantly, Scarlet pulled herself away from the class to follow Xavier down the street again. As they rounded a bend, what she had seen as only the hint of spires in the distance came fully into view, a gleaming white structure, something between a cathedral and a castle—a palace, maybe, Scarlet thought. It soared above the buildings around it, a spire rising from each of its four corners and generous windows of crystal, carved in the shapes of creatures both familiar and exotic, set into its walls. Two colossal roots descended from the oak tree behind the palace, flanking the spires at the back, running along the ground on each side of the building, and finally meeting to intertwine in an elaborate pattern at the front, where doors would normally be, guarding the main entrance to the palace. At Xavier's approach the roots slowly unlaced themselves and curled back to allow the group to enter.

Xavier guided them through the grand foyer and into a warm sitting room with couches of wood, upholstered luxuriously with soft leaves filled with dandelion-seed down. Xavier motioned for them to sit on the sofa near the fireplace that dominated the far end of the room. Exhausted, the four humans sat, feeling the fatigue lift from their muscles, a feeling of security and warmth enveloping them.

Dakota seemed to be arguing with one of the Tounder, while Xavier took his seat in a large chair across from the family. He motioned to Dakota, who was reluctantly leaving the room through a doorway hidden in the wall. "He is loyal to a fault, I think. He doesn't even want to leave you to get his leg fixed."

"Um," Mr. Hopewell fumbled. He seemed to be struggling valiantly against an intense desire to close his eyes and go to sleep. "Yeah, he's a great dog."

"Yes." Xavier laughed. "That he is. I guess some answers are in order."

"That would be nice," Mrs. Hopewell said wearily.

"Mommy, I'm hungry," Melody whispered. Somehow she'd managed to sleep through almost the whole ordeal.

"Oh, how rude of me!" Xavier waved to a group of Tounder waiting by the doorway. "Perhaps the ladies might like to retire for food and rest. I'll explain what I can to you, Mr. Hopewell."

Mrs. Hopewell was reluctant, but, looking at the exhausted children, she agreed to follow the Tounder out of the sitting room with Scarlet and Melody. Cricket followed, not wanting to let the girls out of her sight.

Once they had left, Xavier turned back to Charles, handing him a glass of cool liquid that a Tounder had brought in on a platter. Charles drank it down quickly, feeling his thirst instantly quenched.

He looked quizzically at the glass. "What was that?"

"We call it water." Xavier smiled. "I guess you might call it fairy water." He let out a bellowing laugh, apparently finding this a grand joke.

Charles smiled back uncomfortably, too tired to enjoy the humor. "Of course. What else would it be?" Looking down at the glass, he realized that it was full again. He was too weary to be shocked, so he just gratefully took another sip.

He'd fully intended to listen keenly. Now, he hoped, he could get some answers, make sense of what was happening to him and his family. He had so many questions, so many fears. Yet somehow just now they didn't seem as urgent as they had just moments before. A profound feeling of peace enveloped him. Surely it wouldn't hurt if he laid his head back to rest, just for a moment . . .

Within seconds he was fast asleep.

Xavier had expected this. After all, what Mr. Hopewell and his family had been through was exhausting in every possible way. He motioned for another group of Tounder to come and take Mr. Hopewell to his family, then sat down again, relief washing over him.

For the first time in fourteen years, for a moment at least, he could be at peace.

It had been a long time to wait for the greatest gamble of his life to pay off. Although he'd had full faith in Udd Lyall, he could not help but worry whether he'd played his own part well enough. But now that Scarlet was safely under his protection, Xavier could fully concentrate on the next phase of the plan.

Prince Thanerbos was growing stronger with each passing moment. Xavier had no way to tell how long they had left before he reached the full height of his powers. There was no time to waste.

Although he knew that Udd Lyall would only shrug off any expressions of gratitude, Xavier decided that he would try to offer thanks anyway. Even if he hadn't known where the castle Tounder had taken him, it would not have been difficult to find Udd Lyall. Xavier could hear his disgruntled growls of protest the second he left the sitting room.

He found Udd Lyall lying in the castle's infirmary, a well-lit room that, small as it was, sufficed for the needs of the entire village. A larger space was not needed; Tounder rarely experienced injuries or got ill, and when they did, it was usually something simple and easily treated.

The Tounder treating Udd Lyall seemed to be quite energized at the chance to handle such a nasty wound. This would be the worst injury most of them would ever witness, and they found it a real treat to hone their skills on something so significant. Udd Lyall, on the other hand, did not appear to be amused in the slightest.

"Watch it," Udd Lyall growled as one of the Tounder poured a cleaning solution on his shoulder.

Xavier approached the table where Udd Lyall lay, giving his friend the warmest of smiles. Udd Lyall looked up at him with a flash of anger. "Thank you," Xavier said to the Tounder healers. "You may go."

Reluctantly the Tounder left, leaving Xavier and Udd Lyall alone. Xavier placed one of his hands over the wound and began singing in a voice so quiet that even Udd Lyall, with his superior canine ears, had difficulty hearing him. It was a soft, lilting song, and as Xavier sang, his hand began to glow with a warm yellow light. The wound on Udd Lyall's shoulder closed, healing in a manner of minutes.

Xavier fell silent for a moment, looking down at his old friend. "Thank you, dear friend. You have saved us all." There was so much admiration and gratitude in his voice that it seemed on the verge of breaking.

Udd Lyall shrugged off the thank-you, as Xavier had known he would. "How long do I have?" he asked, his voice resigned.

"I don't know for sure." Xavier sounded sad. "I have not found much in my library about the life span of dogs. Mr. Hopewell might actually know better than I—"

"No," Udd Lyall interrupted. "It doesn't matter anyway. We don't intend to take our time."

"You're right, we do not," Xavier responded. As Udd Lyall began to pad out of the infirmary, he added, "Are you going?"

"You don't need me for this part. It's you she needs now. I have some explaining to do to the pack." And with those words, Udd Lyall trotted out of sight.

6

The Conquered

Brennan was scared. There was no point in denying it or trying to act otherwise. There was no one left to act tough for except himself, and he knew better. After all, he couldn't fool himself. It just didn't work. He was not, however, afraid of the jail cell he found himself in, or the overwhelming cold that sank deep into his bones. He wasn't even afraid of the jailers who had kidnapped him, thrown him into this dismal place, and beat him so unmercifully. No, he was afraid of the loneliness and the sorrow. His mother was gone, and now he was the last of his people. The last of the Conquered.

It was hard to believe that it had come to this. For all his mother's sheltering, her constant vigil, her obsessive looking over her shoulder, she was gone, and he was right where she had always feared. He looked over his body, lean and fit, his skin brown with the sun. Until this morning there had not been so much as a scratch on him, and now, after only half a day as a slave, his skin was marked forever. There were sharp, angry whip marks across his back, and an especially deep one ran the length of his chest, slicing a symbolic partition through his heart. This was his fate, as it had been that of all his people. Despite his mother's attempt—which had only led to her death—there was no avoiding destiny.

His mother had not believed in fate and had fought it most of her adult life, but there was no denying simple fact. Every man and woman of Brennan's race had been hunted down and sold into slavery—the women for their unparalleled beauty, the men for a natural strength and hardiness that made them invaluable as laborers for the mines and quarries in the southwest. Brennan had often wondered how, considering his peoples' physical strength, they had become slaves to a weaker people. Not in all the libraries of the world could he have found an answer. There was no history of the Conquered, as his people were called. No record of a time before servitude. All that a young Conquered needed to know was that he had been born, he labored, and he would die. Even this brief history was no longer of any value. With the passing of his mother, Brennan had become the last of his kind.

That, of course, made him the most valuable Conquered ever to walk this land. He might be of little value to the mines now, but the dark and twisted souls of Satorium would pay a high price to own the last Conquered on earth. He would be kept like an endangered species at a zoo, in a cage for all to gawk at. Perhaps they might even put him in an arena. The last Conquered to have that honor had been a champion for fifty years before his master poisoned him to make for a more exciting contest. Unfortunately the Conquered gladiator had dropped dead before the match even began.

Brennan stirred and shuffled farther into the dark corner of his cell. Footsteps were echoing against the stone walls of the corridor outside, and that could only mean one of two things. They were coming to beat him again, or to move him to another, equally dismal place. Either way, fate or not, Brennan had decided he would not go quietly this time. When they first came for him, his shock over the loss of his mother had been too fresh, too numbing, for him to care for anything else. Now the pain was as sharp as a razor's edge, honed to a deadly point of pure anger.

Perhaps in response to the violence around them, or as an attempt to better endure the life they faced, Brennan's people had always been peaceful. The Conquered gladiator was such an anomaly that in a thousand years he had been the only one. Well, Brennan had no elder to speak calm words to him, to tell him to quell the anger inside. No mother to help him calm his mind against the flood of emotion that rattled him. His anger was all he had for guidance, and he saw no reason to deny it.

Deep in his core he felt the familiar heat rising, though he knew it was in vain. The Tempest, his people called it—a force latent within all Conquered males that could give them an incredible surge of strength. With this force, legend had it, the Conquered had built the Great Wonders in the Northern Mountains, the Dorans' capital city, Caelesta, and the tower prison of Leona, where it was said that the dark one was being held. The construction of these ancient works would have been a feat even in modern times, and yet they'd been built by hand centuries ago by the Conquered. As an act of rebellion, the Conquered elders—acknowledging that the Tempest had become merely something for their enslavers to exploit, rather than a force that could throw off their bonds—had refused to teach the youth the ability to harness this power, and the knowledge had slipped away with the elders' deaths. Now all that was left of the Tempest was a gentle suggestion of the bridled power within.

Brennan could now hear voices along with the footsteps, and he readied himself. The voices were familiar; they belonged to his jailers. Brennan tried in vain to unearth the Tempest, but it was like trying to find treasure that might be buried anywhere across an entire continent. Without a map, it was hopeless.

Though for a moment, when he had found his mother's body and heard the laughter of her murderers, he'd almost thought—

It made no difference now. It was buried too deep.

"Can't believe this is the last one."

Brennan could make out the voices clearly now.

"We can retire on the money we make with him."

Brennan could see the faces of the two men, who were indeed his jailers. The head jailer reminded Brennan of a rotten tree—large, cumbersome, giving a menacing appearance from a distance. Up close, however, the weakness and decay were evident. His assistant, much younger and smaller, had yet to show the ravages of a lifetime spent in prison; instead, he wore filthy rags in a feeble attempt to ape his mentor's style.

"Whaddaya mean, retire?" The head jailer snorted, hacked up some phlegm, and spat on the wall.

"I mean, if he's the last, we're gonna get rich selling him. Make a lot more than we do with these normal creatures." The younger man gestured toward the other cells. "Hasn't been one of the Conquered up on the market in ages."

The head jailer stopped and looked at his assistant, who obviously had the lion's share of what little brains the two possessed. His head tilted, and he frowned, trying to figure out what the younger man was getting at.

The assistant threw the head jailer a worried look. Brennan had watched the two often enough to guess why—the big man would be none too pleased if his assistant figured something out he himself hadn't or couldn't. In any other circumstances, the scene would have amused Brennan.

"We get ten percent of what they sell for at the market, yeah?" the assistant said apprehensively, having decided to press on. Reasonable enough, thought Brennan, forgetting for a moment that it was his fate they were talking about.

Surely the big man would be pleased he'd be getting rich, whoever he heard it from.

"Oy," said the big man.

"Usually it's the same. We sell a beast for a hundred, we get ten. We sell a rare beast for two hundred, we get twenty. Well . . . seeing as that big fella is the last Conquered anyone seen in ages, he's gonna go for a lot more."

"Oy."

"Okay . . . So ten percent of a lot more is . . . a lot," the younger jailer announced, quite proud of himself.

There was lengthy silence while this all sank in. Finally the head jailer cracked his assistant on the head with the handle of his whip. "You think I didn't know that, boy?" he snarled and, without another word, started toward Brennan's cell.

Brennan knew it was useless to fight the two men. It wasn't that they could possibly be a match for him, but there was nowhere to go. The jail was four stories belowground, and surrounded by guards. Perhaps he should just take the way of his people and be at peace with his fate.

No, he couldn't do that. He wouldn't do that. He thought of his poor mother, who had died trying to keep him safe. He thought of their life together, running from place to place, never at peace, never at home. What honor would it do her memory to just accept being a slave, when she'd given up so much to keep him from becoming one? No, this Conquered was going to put up a fight. At least that way she would not have died for nothing.

Brennan had backed up against the slimy wall farthest from the cell door, steeling himself for the fight ahead, when he was hit with a sudden realization. At sixteen, he'd never fought before. Would that matter? He hoped not. He was strong—very strong. At nearly seven feet tall, he was broad-shouldered and thickly muscled. Once, traveling with his mother through deep woods, he'd lifted a tree trunk easily out of their path. Never, though, had he used his strength in anger or violence.

The jailers reached his cell, and the older one guffawed.

"Lookie there. He's hiding in the corner."

The younger jailer didn't share his senior's sense of humor, but he faked a laugh anyway. He didn't see Brennan as a cowering child. To him, Brennan looked more like a cornered wolf—dangerously so.

"You gonna cry, slave," the head jailer taunted in a high-pitched, scratchy voice. When Brennan remained silent, he scowled. "Open the door!" he yelled at his assistant.

"I wouldn't do that if I were you," came a voice from behind the jailers. It was so unexpected, the younger jailer yelped.

They turned to see a tall hooded figure standing calmly only a few feet away, almost hidden in shadow. The head jailer recovered from his initial shock first, and his face flushed with anger.

"Who are you?" the jailer snapped. "Get outta my jail!"

The figure emerged into the light, moving with a slow, easy confidence. He stopped inches from the head jailer and removed his hood, revealing himself as a man of astounding beauty, his long hair woven into golden braids, his skin porcelain smooth and radiant. If it wasn't for the man's shoulders and his size, he could easily have been mistaken for a woman.

The sight of the man without his hood brought a sudden sense of dread upon the jailers. They backed against the bars of the cell and began to cower, averting their gaze from the man's cold gray eyes.

"I—I—I'm sorry," the head jailer quivered. He looked as if he had seen death itself.

The man stood motionless for a long moment, then said simply, "Open the door and leave."

The older jailer obeyed at once, fumbling with the keys and dropping them several times before finally finding the right one and turning the lock with a metallic *click*. Once the jailers had scurried off down the corridor, the mysterious stranger entered the doorway to Brennan's cell.

"I do apologize." The man's voice had an almost musical lilt. "But these heathens have not even bothered to discover your name." He smiled. "I have no idea how I should address you."

For a long moment, Brennan simply stared at the man, unsure whether to speak to him or attack. Surely this was some sort of trap. But something about the exchange between the figure and the jailers, the fear the newcomer provoked in them, had piqued his curiosity. It wasn't as if he had much of a choice, anyway.

"I'm Brennan. Why would that matter to a jailer?" Brennan responded, watching the man closely.

The stranger laughed in a warm and friendly manner. "I'm no jailer," he said. "I am called—well, I guess, Chosen would be the best translation. Not exactly right, but it will do. May I?" he asked, gesturing to the inside of the cell, as if he were making a simple house call and the barren stone chamber were a cottage in the country.

Brennan nodded, and Chosen strode gracefully to the center of the cell, effortlessly avoiding the puddles of blood on the floor. He stopped a few feet from Brennan and looked around in dismay.

"There doesn't appear to be anywhere adequate for two gentlemen to sit for a conversation. If you will permit me?" Chosen motioned through the cell door, and the jailers reemerged from the darkness of the hall, each carrying a wooden chair, their faces fixed in a look of fear, verging on horror.

Brennan found that he was thoroughly enjoying the way the jailers, who just this morning had been acting so tough, cringed in abject terror. For the moment at least, he banished the idea of attacking Chosen from his mind.

The jailers scuttled into the cell cautiously, eyes darting about. They placed the chairs facing each other, as close as they dared to Chosen, and scurried back out, nearly tripping over one another as they fought to get through the narrow door.

"There, that's better," Chosen said, motioning to a chair. "Please."

Seeing no harm in sitting down, Brennan sat. Chosen sat shortly after, acting the role of a grand host so well that

Brennan could almost imagine the dismal surroundings transformed into an elegant drawing room.

"So, you are to be a slave," Chosen said after a pause, crossing his legs and leaning back in his chair.

"That's what they tell me," Brennan replied, a little curt; he didn't appreciate hearing this fact spoken of in such a flippant tone.

"That's a shame. You are much too young to be looking at such a fate," Chosen said, more gravely.

"Why are you here speaking to me?"

"Why indeed? When word reached me of the last of the Satorians, I had to—"

"The what?" Brennan interrupted.

Chosen chuckled. "I always find it a shame when history passes out of common knowledge, especially out of the knowledge of the people it directly involves. I suppose I could say Conquered, but that's a name given by kidnappers and murderers. The real name of your people is Satorian, the first people of Satorium. It is an ancient language from another land, but it is yours."

"My mother never mentioned it, and she knew a lot about our history." This was only partially a lie. His mother knew more than almost anyone about her people, even if in reality that was still very little. But then here was a stranger with effortless confidence giving his people a name that his mother had never used.

"No one knows a lot of Satorian history, my friend. Still, it is as I say, and you *are* the last. It would in my opinion be a great shame to see you dead, here in this cell, or worked to death in a mine. I have always thought the mines were a poor use for people of such considerable gifts. Much like using an ax to peel a grape. But then again, nobody ever asked my opinion on the subject."

Brennan was taken aback by the manner in which the man spoke and carried himself. Brennan would have been apprehensive only visiting this dark place, but Chosen looked as comfortable as if he were lying in a meadow on a breezy summer's day.

Brennan did not have the benefit of age or experience; for one of a race that lived exceptionally long lives, his sixteen years were no more than a scratch on the surface of adolescence. But now he was being forced to face adulthood much sooner than was his mother's plan. And though it had taken him a while to figure it out, he realized that this strange man might be his only way out of the cell—if he wanted to get out alive and unchained, at least.

The only way forward was to push the issue, he decided. "What do you want?"

"Straight to the point. I like that. I want to free you, and give your life some meaning." Chosen reached into his cloak and removed a root that Brennan did not recognize. Biting off a small piece of the root, he began chewing on it methodically. Brennan was expecting a further explanation, but Chosen didn't offer one.

"What meaning? You're going to free me to do what? What's in it for you?" Brennan asked suspiciously.

"I'm looking for someone."

"How could I possibly help you find anyone? I don't know anybody or anything about the world out there." Brennan's frustration was mounting. "My mother is dead. She was the only other person I knew. Just tell me what you want!"

"Not one of my stronger points, being direct." Chosen leaned forward, his eyes locked on Brennan's. "Perhaps the traits that I admire in others, I should make better use of myself. But then nobody's perfect."

And now, in those eyes, Brennan saw what he had not before, what he imagined most, enchanted by the man's beauty and lilting voice, did not see. Something about the man put Brennan at ease—until he met his eyes. A darkness lurked behind those clear gray irises. It consumed Brennan, bore down upon him like a great weight, heavy with sadness and despair. He felt himself sinking into that gloom, almost lost in it.

With an effort he shook the feeling off, lifted his shoulders and rolled them backward, as if physically shedding the despair. Slowly he stood, looming over the man called Chosen.

"I'm not in the mood for games. I asked you a simple question, and I'd like it answered." Brennan wasn't sure he meant a word of what he had just said, but it sounded good to him. Firm, strong, threatening. Besides, he had to do or say something to stop Chosen's gaze from pulling him under. He could still feel the draw of that darkness. "You keep jerking me around, and I don't care if I never get free, I'll knock you out," he added, instantly regretting it. His voice had failed him at the last few words, and he felt his confidence falter.

"Please, young Satorian. Don't posture. I've offered you a chance at life, and I'm short on time. Not that I haven't enjoyed our conversation." Chosen stood, but still had to look up at Brennan. "Your choices are few and simple. Die with them, or live by leaving with me. My reasons, explanations, any further talk—none of it's necessary. I want you to come with me, but I assure you, you are in no way indispensable. If I leave without you, I'll have lost nothing. I'll just have to change my plans, that's all."

Brennan allowed himself a moment to look into Chosen's eyes. If it hadn't been for the evil he saw there, this would have been such an easy decision. After all, this man was giving him a chance at life. Whatever kind of life that might be, at least it would be considerably longer than it had been only minutes ago. For all his sixteen years, his mother had sheltered him and hid him from the outside world, sacrificing her own way of life to give him a chance. A chance to survive. She had paid with her life, and mingled with the rage and sadness was a heavy guilt that joined to crush Brennan—guilt over not having been there at the crucial moment to save her. Guilt over the life she had been forced to live for his sake. And guilt that he had allowed himself to be taken prisoner, her efforts and sacrifice all in vain.

He tried to think what she might have wanted for him in this moment. What choice would have made her proud? How would he best respect her beliefs and her hopes for his future? This Chosen was not what he seemed on the surface, and even that surface was confusing and difficult to read. *The eyes are where men hold their deepest desires and true motives*, his mother had always warned him. *A man can learn to lie with words, and even hide his intentions with veils of cunning, but if you look hard enough, the eyes will always reveal the truth.* The truth was that Chosen was a dark and mysterious man at best. He was not to be trusted. But Brennan couldn't overlook his current circumstances. If he didn't at least pretend to go along with whatever plan Chosen had for him, he would die.

"I'll go with you," he said finally.

"Fantastic," Chosen responded, gleefully moving his chair aside. "I take it you'll be packing light." Gesturing to Brennan, the man strode out of the cell.

7
The Prophecy

Scarlet woke in a room at the top of one of the rear spires, the view from her window partially obscured by one of the giant roots. The bed she found herself in was beyond comfortable, the mattress filled, like the couches they'd sat on earlier with dandelion fluff. She imagined it in a sunny field, white and wispy, ready for a wish or a breeze to carry it away.

The room was beautiful. The walls were inlaid with living branches from which sprouted bright green leaves of exotic shapes and flowers with large maroon petals that reminded Scarlet of dark poinsettias. In fact, the whole room had a festive look that made her think of Christmas. The furniture even looked frosted and snowy, and ornate carved crystals hung from the ceiling, sending the morning light dancing across the ceiling as if through a prism.

She stretched and reluctantly got out of bed. Her legs were a little sore from running the day before, but all in all, she felt delightful. Ever since she'd arrived in the Tounder village, a warmth and comfort had enveloped her, never leaving her, regardless of what troubling thoughts crossed her mind. Her dreams in the land of the Tounder, ironically, had been of home.

The Tounder ladies who had helped Scarlet and Harmony to their rooms had given them soft nightgowns to wear. Looking down at her plain white gown, she realized that she had nothing to change into. The Tounder had taken away her old clothes, to be washed, she assumed.

But before she could worry about that, she caught sight of a beautiful dress in the corner of the room, hanging from a stand shaped remarkably like herself. As she walked toward it, light shimmered across the strange fabric, causing it to shift from deep forest green to light seafoam and back again. She ran the fabric through her fingers. It was incredibly light, soft, and expertly sewn. Actually, Scarlet wasn't sure it had actually been sewn at all. She couldn't find a single stitch anywhere.

There was a knock at the door. Still transfixed with the dress, Scarlet mouthed, "Come in."

A pretty young Tounder with long golden hair and a tiny button nose came into the room. She smiled at Scarlet.

"I'm quite sure it will fit you," the Tounder said. "Xavier asked the best dressmakers in the village to work all night on them for you, your mother, and your sister."

"It's very beautiful," Scarlet said.

"Well, they are the best," the Tounder responded, just a little too sweetly. "I'm Lindi. I was sent to collect you and bring you downstairs."

Scarlet crossed the room and extended her hand. Lindi just stared, making Scarlet feel awkward and silly. She dropped her hand back down to her side, not sure what to say or do next.

"Maybe you should go ahead and get dressed," Lindi said. "I'll be just outside."

When the door closed, Scarlet went back over to the dress, took it down, and slipped it on. Lindi was right. The dress could not possibly have fit any better. Scarlet had never had anything tailor-made for her, but she imagined that this must be what it was like, even though she doubted that any normal tailor could have made something so perfect.

Once dressed, she went to the door to ask Lindi where Melody and her parents were. She had so many questions. What were those horrible things that had come after them? Why had they wanted to take "the girl"? Which one of them did they want, Scarlet or her sister? How could Cricket and Dakota talk? How did Dakota seem to know so much? How had they gotten here?

She opened the door and found Lindi standing impatiently; obviously she felt that Scarlet had taken longer than was necessary to get dressed. "Ready then, are we?" she snipped.

Scarlet had thought she was imagining the Tounder girl's standoffishness—perhaps the custom of shaking hands wasn't known to the Tounder—but now she was sure the girl was being deliberately rude. For some reason the young Tounder did not like her. It was all over her pretty face and the sneer of her forced smile. Scarlet couldn't imagine what she could have done to upset the girl. She'd only been here for a night, and she hadn't met anyone but Xavier.

"Can you take me to my parents?" she asked timidly.

Lindi shook her head and rolled her eyes, but waved at Scarlet to follow her and began moving down the spiral stairs that led to the main section of the castle. Scarlet had to hurry to keep up; Lindi chose to float down many of the steps, which proved to be much faster than walking.

Her awkward feeling vanished when she got to the bottom of the steps and saw her parents. Rushing past Lindi, she jumped into her father's arms.

"Daddy!" she squealed, more delighted to see him than she had ever remembered.

Her dad lifted her off the ground, holding her for a long moment. Finally he set her down and turned his attention back to the efficient-looking Tounder he had been speaking with.

"I understand your concerns, Mr. Hopewell, but Xavier was called away to tend to, ah, Dakota, and the Stidolph—the, um, wolves. Some of their injuries were—well, they required special care." The Tounder looked frustrated, as if this was information he had just recently been given.

"I understand that Xavier was called away. I wouldn't want to interrupt him if he's helping Dakota or the wolves—they saved my family's life." Scarlet's father looked as exasperated as the Tounder. "What I don't understand is why you can't answer my questions. You obviously know a lot more than we do, seeing as we don't know anything."

"Mr. Hopewell, please—"

"That's okay, Raden," interrupted Xavier, who'd somehow appeared without anyone having noticed him. "I'm here now, and I'll be happy to answer any questions the family may have."

"Xavier, sir, I wasn't sure what I should say, so I—well—"

"It's quite all right, Raden. Go and attend to the rest of the castle. I'm pretty sure I saw two young ones sneaking into the old armory. The one hiding behind a tapestry as I passed was Delfi." Xavier said this last as if it was a rich source of amusement; the Tounder called Raden flew off at once, obviously not sharing Xavier's sense of humor.

Xavier began walking back into the sitting room they'd been in the night before, burbling away as he did so, his merriment infectious.

"Young Tounder are always trying to sneak into the old armory. They tell wonderful stories about what's inside, and get themselves so worked up that eventually curiosity gets the best of them. What's really funny is that the last young Tounder to actually make it into the armory itself was Raden."

He sank down into the large cushioned chair, gesturing for the rest to join him. The four Hopewells fit easily on the couch across from Xavier. They all leaned forward with identical looks of feverish anticipation.

"Questions, questions," Xavier said cheerfully. "You must have so many."

Several Tounder brought in trays with a teapot, cups, and an assortment of what looked like pastries. Xavier genteelly began to pour the tea into cups and handed them around. Scarlet took a sip just to be polite, but found that she rather liked it. Melody seemed to agree, and soon they were both munching on pastries as if aware for the first time how hungry they were. Even their father took a moment to eat, though he was obviously dying to get to the questions.

"Now, that's better. A bit of something in the stomach does wonders for the brain. Who's to be first, then?" Xavier looked expectantly at the family.

Melody was the first to speak, uninhibited as she was for a five-year-old and unencumbered by a need to figure it all out. "Does everyone get wings?"

Clearly frustrated that his little girl had asked an irrelevant question when so much needed answering, Scarlet's father was about to interject when Xavier put up a hand to stop him. "All questions are important to those who ask them." He turned to Melody. "The answer to your question, my sweet little girl, depends on who 'everybody' is. If you mean, do all of my people, the Tounder, get wings, well then, the answer is yes. They are a gift from the great oak that stands above us, and all Tounder are born with wings. If you mean, do you and your family get them now that you have come here, sadly, no. I know that is disappointing to you."

Melody nodded.

"Would it cheer you up to know that in the land of Satorium—that is, the land you now find yourselves in—wings aren't the only way a person can fly?"

Melody nodded again, this time with great enthusiasm.

"What is going on?" her father cut in before Melody could ask something else.

"My, that is quite a question. I don't think we'll have time for anyone else if we try to answer that all at once," Xavier said cheerfully.

Just when Charles was starting to get angry, the worried look on Xavier's face made him stop and think. He remembered the way the little man had slyly sent Scarlet and Melody off to bed the night before, so that he and Charles could be alone. Perhaps there were things about what was happening that would be too much for young children to hear.

Charles decided to ask a question he thought he already knew the answer to. Perhaps that way, he might show Xavier that he understood why he might be reluctant to speak openly in front of the children.

"Are we safe here?"

Xavier gave him a knowing smile. "Quite safe. I am proud to say that there is no place in the two worlds safer than here at my home. For now, you have nothing to fear."

For now. Charles didn't like the sound of that last statement, but at least he and Xavier understood one another.

"How can our dogs talk all of a sudden?" Scarlet asked. Charles was pleased; this was definitely something he too wanted to know.

"As for your lovely dog Cricket, I expect that the dog you call Dakota taught her. Not an easy task, considering that dogs don't really have the right equipment, physically that is, to speak. But then again, Dakota has abilities that have more than surprised me before, so I can't say I'm surprised at this."

"And Dakota?" Charles added.

"He has always been able to talk," Xavier said matter-of-factly. "Well, ever since he was old enough, that is."

"He wasn't very talkative when I found him in the woods, or any of the five months we had him as a pet," Charles said.

"Ah, of course. I had forgotten that you might still be under the impression that he was only five months old. Dakota is not, I'm afraid, exactly what he seems, and I'm not sure how much he would want me to tell you. I will say that he is from Satorium, and your finding him in the woods that day was not an accident. He was sent to protect Scarlet and your family, and had we not made the decision to send him . . . well, some things are better left unsaid."

The girls continued to ask questions, while Charles waited as patiently as he could to speak to Xavier alone. Yes, they had been shrunk with magic from the great oak, Xavier told them. The Tounder lived exclusively in Illuminora, the village beneath the tree, and they were also called the Keepers of Light, although explaining that title properly would take more than an afternoon. The Hopewells had been in danger at home, Xavier conveyed delicately, and he and Dakota had brought them here to keep them safe.

After about half an hour of questions, Xavier suggested that they take a break.

"I would think that two young girls such as yourselves," he said to Scarlet and Melody, "would love to explore such a strange and wonderful place as this must seem to you."

"Oh, yes!" they both answered.

"If you will permit, Mr. Hopewell, I can assure you, they will be quite safe," Xavier said.

Charles was reluctant, looking to Allie, who'd been silent this whole time, for guidance, but eventually he agreed; he needed real answers from the old Tounder, and he wouldn't get them with his daughters present.

"You watch after your sister," Allie said sternly to Scarlet.

"Will do," she promised, taking Melody's hand and heading for the entrance hall.

The two girls were giggling and running toward the entrance hall, their heads swimming with ideas of what to try and see first, when they caught sight of Dakota speaking to the group of wolves who had helped them escape. Melody was about to call out to Dakota, but Scarlet put a hand to her mouth.

"Shhhh. Wait a minute," Scarlet whispered, pulling Melody behind a pillar just inside the entrance hall. Dakota and the wolves were standing in the entrance to the castle, and Scarlet could just make out what they were saying, although she had to strain hard to hear.

"*I don't understand,*" Ulrich was saying. "*You mean the change is permanent.*"

"*Yes,*" Dakota answered. "*There was no other way.*"

"*But a dog, Udd Lyall!*" Ulrich moaned.

"The dog who came here with us is a braver and more noble creature than many Stidolph I've met in my day," Dakota snapped back. Stidolph was clearly the name for the magnificent wolves, Scarlet realized.

"*I've nothing against dogs. That's not what I meant,*" Ulrich said defensively. "*It's just that, well, dogs— They don't—*"

"*I know, old friend. But it's a small price to pay for saving her life. A small price to pay if it means winning the war that's to come.*" Dakota lowered his head solemnly.

"*Well, at least you're a big dog,*" Fael added cheerfully, though Dakota didn't look that big next to the two Stidolph.

Just then Scarlet felt something rub against her leg, and she jumped, making Melody squeal. Looking down, she saw Cricket standing next to her. When she looked up again, the Stidolph had gone. Dakota nodded to the girls but didn't come over, leaving instead through another passage out of the hall.

What was all that about? Scarlet wondered. What had Dakota sacrificed? Had he once been a Stidolph like the other two, and why did they call him Udd Lyall? He had obviously changed into a dog so that he could come to live with her family, but if he had changed into a dog, why couldn't he change back? And what was it that dogs don't? It had certainly made Ulrich look sad enough. Her list of questions seemed to be growing exponentially with each passing hour. She would have to find out later, though; today she was going to explore the land of her dreams—only this time she'd be awake.

"You want to come exploring with us?" she asked Cricket, feeling a little funny talking to the family dog.

"*Can I?*" Cricket asked excitedly.

"Of course," Scarlet responded, and the three of them set off out of the castle and into the village.

Unlike Lindi, every Tounder they saw seemed overjoyed to meet Scarlet as they walked down the main street. Everyone waved and pointed. To Scarlet, it felt a little like being a movie star rather than a guest. It was hard to decide where to go first, it all was so weird and wonderful.

Melody was drawn to a shop with carts sitting out front bearing strange but succulent-looking fruit. She stared wide-eyed at the multicolored assortment, finally focusing on what looked like silver grapes.

"What are those?" she asked boldly, when the shop owner approached her.

"Those are guildagrapes," the shopkeeper answered pleasantly. She removed a bunch from the stand and handed them to Melody, who wasted no time plopping one into her mouth, her eyes lighting up with pleasure. "Try one, Scarlet. They're so good!"

Scarlet took a couple from the bunch and ate them slowly, savoring each one. It was difficult to describe the taste—like the sweetest grapes Scarlet had ever eaten, but with a hint of something else that she had never tasted before.

"Thank you," she said.

"It is my pleasure," responded the shopkeeper. "It is such a happy day that sees you here and safe with us." The shopkeeper bowed slightly and went back into her store.

The store across the street drew their attention next. It was filled with glowing objects of every imaginable shape and size. As they entered the store they were bathed in the soft illumination of hundreds of these objects. It was difficult to figure out exactly what they were, but if Scarlet had to guess, she would have said that they were decorations or trinkets.

"They are toys," the shop's owner said, appearing from a back room carrying a small orange ball pulsing with light. "You have that look of curiosity that I welcome in my store. We haven't had any visitors to Illuminora in quite a while," he explained.

"They're beautiful!" exclaimed Scarlet. "What are they made of?"

The toymaker turned his head quizzically. "My, you are from far off, aren't you? They are made of light, sweetie."

"*Made* of light?" Scarlet asked, puzzled. "How can that be?"

"When you know the secrets of light, it is no more difficult than building something out of wood or stone, which of course is to say that it's quite difficult if you're trying to create something truly art-worthy. But not impossible." The toymaker laughed. "Would you like one?"

"Oh, thank you, but we don't have any way of paying you," Scarlet answered bashfully.

"Paying me?" the toymaker rebuked. "I could never accept payment from the For Tol Don."

"What's a fortoldon?" she asked, confused.

A look of worry crossed the toymaker's face. "You mean to say you don't know?" he said in a hushed whisper.

"I've never heard those words before," Scarlet admitted.

The toymaker looked around his shop, his eyes shifting guiltily. He came very close to Scarlet, lowering his voice to an even softer whisper. "You are the hero of a great prophecy that we Tounder have known all our lives. And now you're finally here. Just in time, if you ask me—not that anyone is, mind you. Only a matter of time before the dark prince will be ready to challenge us . . . well, you. It is a glorious day, but please—I should not be the one telling you this. I would appreciate you not telling anyone I told you."

"I won't," Scarlet promised reluctantly. She wanted desperately to ask the Tounder what he had meant, but the worry in his eyes told her to leave it alone. A dark prince? A prophecy? It all sounded surreal, and at the same time so ominous. "Besides, I don't even understand what you did tell me," she added.

The toymaker backed up and laughed, his expression lightening. "You will," he said. He took a small cube of light, about the size of a board game die, and placed it in Scarlet's hand. "Until the day you create your own light," he added cryptically and then hurried back to the room from whence he'd come.

The rest of the day passed quickly, with one wonder-filled moment after the next. It was difficult to take in all the glorious sights of Illuminora, as each and every thing the girls saw was new and exciting. When finally they decided to call an end to their explorations, they headed back to the castle, feeling hungry and sleepy. Scarlet's first thought was to find her mother and father and ask them what they had learned from Xavier.

Her questions, however, would have to wait. A large group of young female Tounder met in the entrance hall, and informed them that they had to hurry and dress for the feast. A grand celebration had been prepared for Scarlet and her family.

Forget feeling like a movie star. Now Scarlet felt more like royalty.

8
The Tempest

Brennan was cold, hungry, and exhausted. He and Chosen had been walking all day and well into the night. His ordeal in the jail cell had left him weakened, and the pace Chosen kept was unrelenting. Making matters worse, they had now entered the Southern Wildlands, which, aside from being extremely difficult terrain physically, was also some of the most dangerous territory in all of Satorium.

Brennan's mother had told him many stories of the dark creatures that inhabited these lands. Once when their travels had taken them near the edges of the Wildlands, she had become visibly nervous, a trait his mother never displayed without good reason. Chosen, on the other hand, plodded straight through this sinister landscape with no more concern than a man on a Sunday stroll through the park. When Brennan mentioned that he'd thought it dangerous, Chosen's only reply had been that it would take ages to walk around.

The Wildlands' dense forest and swampland were bisected by a fast-moving river whose treacherous currents rendered it nearly impossible to cross. Upon entering the Wildlands at the delta, a traveler was forced by the impassable marshland to the river's east to instead negotiate the formidable forest along the west bank. Eventually, however, the terrain would flip, and the traveler would have to cross the river again at the southern border of Leona, the kingdom of the Dorans—an impossible task for anyone without an intimate knowledge of the river and the surrounding terrain. Brennan wasn't sure how well any man could know the Southern Wildlands, but Chosen certainly seemed familiar with it as he moved effortlessly over the rough terrain.

Brennan tried his best not to think about how tired he was, instead concentrating on what would be waiting for him on the other side of the Wildlands. The Dorans ruled over the greater portion of Satorium beyond the Wildlands, and at the heart of Leona was Caelesta, their capital city. Brennan's mother had told him about the city, which she had once seen as a little girl. In her stories it was a place of such beauty that all other sights paled in comparison. Brennan was smart enough to realize that part of her description was more than likely based on a child's wonderment, from a time when his mother was happy and innocent, and therefore to be taken with a grain of salt. This realization didn't dampen his desire to see it himself, though, if only to have something that he could share, even posthumously, with his mother.

But despite his best efforts, fatigue eventually got the better of him, and he began to fall behind. Soon Chosen had gotten so far ahead that Brennan lost sight of him in the thickness of the trees. As troublesome as this was, Brennan had to stop; he just couldn't continue without rest, even if just for a moment. Slumping against the trunk of a large willow tree, he tried to catch his breath.

He paid little attention to the rustling in the brush at first, figuring that Chosen had realized he was no longer right behind him and doubled back. His eyes closed, and as he took in deep, desperately needed breaths, Brennan felt that if he wanted to, he could fall asleep right there beneath the willow tree. After all, what was the worst that could happen? Chosen would scold him. Tell him he needed to wake up. A small price to pay for some long-overdue rest.

But then a dreadful thought occurred to Brennan, making his skin crawl as if a thousand spiders had began creeping under his clothes. Chosen was ahead of him; the rustling sound was from behind.

In a flash Brennan was on his feet, searching the trees for any sign of movement. The problem was that everything moved. The slender, drooping branches of the willows caught even the slightest of breezes. Looking out into the forest, Brennan saw a constantly shifting landscape of dappled greens and darker shadows. Panic struck, in a dizzying onslaught.

"Chosen!" he called out, not bothering to hide the fear in his voice. There was no answer.

Brennan started to run over the uneven ground in the direction he thought Chosen had gone. The ground was matted with a tangle of underbrush and roots, and each step Brennan took threatened to fail beneath him, sending him sprawling headfirst onto the forest floor. The sound was growing louder as whatever was in the trees behind him also picked up its pace. Throwing all caution to the wind, he plunged headlong through the trees, running as fast as he could, dodging tree trunks and limbs, leaping over roots and brush.

He barely had time to notice the bramble sprawled across his path before he'd tripped over it and went flying, sprawling on his hands and knees into a small clearing, his clothes torn and his skin bleeding from numerous cuts and scratches. He rolled out of the way just in time, as a massive creature leaped over the brambles behind him and landed feet first right on the spot where Brennan had been.

On his back, deeply shaken, Brennan looked up at the enormous figure, only a few feet away. Easily twice the size of a normal man, the creature was covered with thick orange and fawn fur. Although its arms and legs resembled those of a man, thickly muscled and bulging, its most striking features were its long, sharp claws and catlike face. As Brennan watched helplessly, paralyzed by fear, the fangs that already protruded over its bottom lip lengthened until they reached past his chin.

"Long way from home, aren't you, boy?" the creature growled.

Horrifying as the creature looked, that it could speak was even more shocking to Brennan. Should he talk to it? Reason with it? It was so difficult to reconcile the savage appearance of the creature with the notion that it could speak, that it was even . . . intelligent?

"I'm just passing through," Brennan fumbled, searching the area around him for something he could use as a weapon.

"No," the creature said, taking a step forward. "You *were* passing through." It crouched, ready to spring.

Suddenly it froze and then righted itself again. Chosen had emerged into the clearing from the far side and was now standing, as relaxed as ever, against one of the trees on the clearing's edge.

"Just like an animal, waiting until your prey was separated from its pack before you could get up the nerve to attack," Chosen chided. If the size and viciousness of the creature worried him at all, he didn't show it.

He'd obviously struck a nerve. The creature's eyes narrowed. "I just don't bother with tainted meat," it seethed, snarling at Chosen.

"Ah, so that's why you waited until the boy had fallen back and was alone. I figured it was just that you were a coward," Chosen responded, removing the dark root from his tunic and biting off a piece.

The creature let out a deafening roar, its muscles flexing as it raised its massive arms to the sky. "Others might tremble at the sight of you, dark one, but not me," it raged.

"You're probably right, although you sound like you're trying to convince yourself, not me. Besides, it's not me you should concern yourself with."

The tension in the creature's muscles eased as it looked at Brennan and laughed. "Is there a third with you? A scentless figure." The creature made a dramatic pantomime of sniffing the air. "No, I don't think so. Just a dark twisted soul and a sizable fresh boy. Fresh . . . meat."

Without any further warning, the creature pounced, landing on top of Brennan with a crushing force. Brennan just had time to seize the creature's wrists, its claws inches from his face. It bared its snarling teeth as it bore down with its full weight and strength. The force was tremendous, and Brennan could already feel his own strength failing him. The claws edged closer to Brennan with every second.

Then Brennan felt it, that warm tingling sensation all over his body, from his core to the tips of his fingers. It was the same feeling he had felt when he'd found his mother murdered. Brennan knew what it was, and it gave him little comfort. The Tempest was buried too deep to actually help him, and this hint of its presence was more torment than grace, taunting him with the knowledge that had he only known how to harness what was inside, he could save himself . . . could have saved his mother.

Visions of his mother filled his mind, and the creature faded away. Now she was all he could see. She was smiling at him, trying to act happy and brave, but he knew better. She was lonely. It was her people's way to accept fate and make peace with it, but she couldn't accept such a life for her son. She had taken him and run, and in rebelling against her people's beliefs, she'd lost the man she loved. Risked everything—and for what? So he could die, eaten by some horrible creature in the middle of the Southern Wildlands?

No. Brennan wouldn't allow it. That was not how her sacrifice—her love and devotion—would be repaid. If he was to die, so be it, but it would be for something. For someone. His mother's face faded from his mind's eye, replaced by the snarling creature, smiling like the Cheshire Cat down on what he thought was his next meal.

What had only been a warm tingling sensation now burned through Brennan's body like wildfire. He felt a deep and primal stirring from within, and then slowly, almost imperceptibly at first, the claws were receding. Unbelievably, he was pushing the creature back. He lifted his chest off the ground, then got his legs underneath him.

Straining under the weight of the creature, Brennan began to rise to his feet, still pushing the creature back. His legs wobbled beneath him, but they did not fail. For a long moment they faced each other, neither giving any ground, but the vicious sneer on the creature's face was now a grimace of shock and fear. With a second surge the Tempest raged through Brennan, and with a swift, effortless movement, he released the massive beast's wrists, seized it by its shoulders, and flung it into the trunk of a tree, where it fell motionless at Chosen's feet.

For a moment Brennan couldn't comprehend what he had just done. He couldn't take his eyes off the crumpled figure lying motionless on the ground. Then the Tempest began to fade, and he felt his weakness and exhaustion flooding back in. The trees and shadows began to shift again.

"Take deep breaths," Brennan heard Chosen say. He looked up from the dead creature and locked eyes with the man, who was smiling broadly.

Brennan sank to his knees, unable to hold himself up any longer. He was filled with rage and confusion. Chosen had just stood there, not raising one finger to help. Not that Brennan was under any illusion that they were friends, but he couldn't have just watched while another person was killed and eaten right in front of him. Suddenly he wanted to walk over to Chosen and knock him out, hit the man so hard that he would feel as weak and frail as Brennan did now. But it was no use. All he could do was lie down on the earth, his consciousness fading.

Chosen walked slowly to Brennan and crouched beside him. "We'll camp here," he said mockingly, as Brennan's world went dark.

When Brennan woke, the sun was filtering through the trees, warming his skin. He could smell a fire burning and the savory aroma of food. He rose onto an elbow and looked around the clearing. Chosen sat by a small campfire, dropping vegetables into a pot suspended over the flames.

"Good afternoon," Chosen said, his voice welcoming and cheerful. He leaned over the pot and inhaled deeply, clearly pleased with his cooking. "Not much to work with, but I think I've managed to make something of it."

Slowly Brennan rose to his feet, walked over to the fire, and sat down across from Chosen. He wasn't sure what to say to the man; he still felt confused, and more than a little betrayed. The rage that had consumed him before he passed out had abated somewhat, but an undercurrent of anger remained.

Chosen ladled the soup into two bowls and passed one to Brennan, who took it and immediately began to drink the broth. The taste was earthy but good, and Brennan realized that he was starving.

"I've added something to help with your fatigue and put a little weight back on you. I underestimated how much your time under the jailers' care had taken out of you." Chosen paused to drink some of the broth. "I should have been making this all along, but I wanted to put as much distance between us and the jail as possible."

Brennan concentrated on the soup. He could feel his weariness fading with each sip. Only after he'd drained the entire contents of the bowl did he finally speak to Chosen.

"I could have died," Brennan said, as levelly as he could.

"But you didn't," Chosen said casually.

"You just stood there," Brennan objected, trying not to sound as betrayed as he felt.

Chosen ladled more soup into Brennan's bowl. "And what would you have had me do?"

"Help me!" Brennan cried in exasperation.

"You are obviously very naive when it comes to the world around you. This was no doubt your first encounter with a tiranthrope. They are one of the few creatures that are quite immune to any gift I possess, and you can attest firsthand to how vicious they are. I would have only been a hindrance to what, I have to say, was an amazing display of strength and perseverance." Chosen motioned for Brennan to drink more of the broth. "You should be thanking me."

"*Thanking you?* For watching me nearly get eaten alive?"

"For helping you find it." Chosen smiled knowingly.

Brennan decided to ignore the comment and the smirk. "What are we doing here?" Frustration and a multitude of other emotions still grated in his voice, sharp as broken glass.

"I told you, it is the shortest route through—"

"I don't mean in the forest," Brennan snapped. "I mean what are we doing? Who are you looking for? Why do you need to find that person? Why do you need my help? Why me?"

"I should think that the 'why you' would be obvious after your little display," Chosen teased.

"Stop playing games. I have a right to know."

Chosen stood, his handsome features turning suddenly cold and expressionless, though his gray eyes flashed with anger. "You insolent, ungrateful boy. How dare you question me?"

Brennan rose to his feet as well and faced Chosen, his face stony. The broth had done wonders; he now felt a great deal like his normal healthy self. He didn't want to hurt Chosen—after all, he'd rescued Brennan from a life of slavery—but when he saw the man standing passively by, watching as he was attacked, he'd felt a great deal of the debt he owed him slipping away. He needed answers, and if he didn't get them now, he didn't think he ever would.

The stalemate lasted for several minutes, neither Chosen nor Brennan moving or speaking. Finally Chosen laughed and sat back down, and Brennan reluctantly followed suit.

"There is a very special girl that I need to find," Chosen said, "and when I do, I have something I'll need you to do."

The look Brennan gave him told Chosen that such a meager explanation would not nearly be enough.

"We all have a destiny, Brennan. Mine lies with this girl. I have to find her."

"I don't believe in destiny."

"That's because you're a fool, and you think yours was to be a slave."

"No, it's because I think I have a choice," Brennan snapped back.

"That's fine, believe what you will." Chosen looked intently into Brennan's eyes. "I have a destiny, and in this I have no choice."

"Fine, so you have to find this girl. What do you need me for?"

Chosen didn't answer at once; he seemed to be struggling with his pride. "I need you to protect her until I can finish what needs to be done."

Brennan shook his head. Even when Chosen did give information, it was still vague and shifty. "I'm just a sixteen-year-old Conquered. How am I supposed to protect anyone?"

"No, Brennan. You're a sixteen-year-old Satorian who is the first person in recent history to survive a battle with a tiranthrope."

Could that possibly be true? There was no way for Brennan to know, and he had little faith in anything Chosen might say. The man obviously had an agenda, and he struck Brennan as someone who would say or do anything to get what he wanted. What sense did it make to choose a sheltered sixteen-year-old Conquered as a protector? Brennan had no idea how to protect anyone. He wasn't even sure he could look after himself. All he knew of the outside world that came from stories told to him by his mother. Until this encounter, he had never even known tiranthropes existed.

Brennan looked over at the motionless beast. The Tempest. He had actually tapped into it, used it. Fought with its power raging through him. Why now, though? Why couldn't he have harnessed it when his mother needed him? Was he really so self-absorbed that only a threat on his own life had allowed him to channel it? What kind of bodyguard was that? Not a very good one, Brennan supposed. Yet Chosen seemed to act as if what had happened with the tiranthrope was a positive sign. He certainly seemed impressed by it.

But he'd get no answers just now—that was clear enough. He'd table the subject for the time being, but he wasn't going to let it go. If Chosen wanted Brennan to stay with him, he'd have to come up with some decent answers soon.

9

The Feast

The dining hall ran the entire length of the castle, and from what Scarlet could tell, it was spacious enough to fit all of the inhabitants of Illuminora. Scarlet and her family were seated at the head of the longest table, with Xavier and a group of Tounder he called his council. The remaining tables, all long and elegantly carved, were arranged parallel to this central table on either side, forming a stair-stepped diamond pattern. The walls and ceiling of the dining hall glowed with a pleasant radiance, neither too bright nor too dim. Even though they lit the whole room uniformly, Scarlet found that she could look directly at them without hurting her eyes.

Before the food was brought in, it was customary for Xavier to speak to the crowd, offering a prayer of sorts to bless the meal and those about to eat it. The little man looked smaller than ever standing at the center of the dining hall, but his voice had no trouble filling the space.

"My friends," he began. "What a glorious day!"

A loud and hearty cheer erupted from the Tounder, and Xavier waited for it to subside before continuing.

"As you know, we have very special guests with us in our humble home. Though many of you may have already met them, it is my pleasure to formally introduce all of you to Miss Scarlet Hopewell and her family, Charles, Allie, and Melody." Xavier motioned for them to stand, which they did to another rising cheer from the Tounder. "They have traveled far to be with us today and have already had their fair share of toils, so I will ask you to extend to them your warmest welcome and to help to make them feel that this is as much their home as it is ours."

Xavier paused for a moment, allowing the warmth of the introductions to pass before continuing.

"The path ahead lies dark and treacherous. And while we will all do our part, it is for those select few that destiny calls upon to carry the light into the darkness. We, the Keepers of Light, shall give them the means to face what is to come. Together we will light the way."

Xavier lowered his head, and the Tounder followed suit.

As one chorus they began to sing, their voices more beautiful than any choir Scarlet had ever heard. The sound filled the hall, washing over Scarlet and her family. To Scarlet's astonishment, every scrape or scratch on her body began to heal, right before her eyes. All negative feelings, no matter how buried in the recesses of her brain, faded away, leaving only a joyous sensation of hope and enlightenment. At that moment, among the soft lilting voices of the Tounder, she felt that there was nothing she could not accomplish, no dream she couldn't make come true.

The chorus faded, and Xavier raised his head, his benevolent smile full again on his aged face, and clapped his hands.

"Let the feast begin!"

A large crew of Tounder flew in at once from the kitchen, carrying tray upon tray of food, setting before Scarlet and her family an assortment of exotic fruits and vegetables, magnificent pastries and breads, and soups and stews. Then they filled crystal goblets to the brim with a sweet milk, made from the acorns of the great oak that hid the entrance to Illuminora.

The food was not only strange but wonderful, and Scarlet found her appetite stronger even than her curiosity over Xavier's mysterious speech. Some things tasted as familiar as her mother's cooking, while others were tastes she had never experienced before. The biggest surprise was the acorn milk. When she was younger, Scarlet had tasted an acorn after watching a Disney Chip and Dale cartoon. She remembered it being extremely bitter and giving her a stomachache. Either being shrunken changed her taste buds, or this was from a very different sort of acorn. The milk was sweet, refreshing and made her stomach feel pleasant and warm.

The feast turned out to be the grandest of celebrations. The Tounder ate and laughed with such abandon that any ominous or foreboding thoughts seemed impossibly distant. Once Scarlet had taken the edge off her hunger, she couldn't help but share in the Tounder's merriment. But occasionally she would steal a glance at her dad, and then she felt a shadow pass over the room. Despite the music and revelry, he looked preoccupied; he didn't seem to be enjoying the feast. Plenty of time to worry about that after the feast, she told herself, shaking the feeling off; for the moment, she would just enjoy the magic and spectacle of this wondrous celebration.

Her father, however, wasn't the only thing that threatened to dampen Scarlet's mood. Near the end of the feast Lindi appeared—for the first time during the celebration, or at least Scarlet hadn't noticed her before—behind her with a pitcher of acorn milk. This time the young Tounder was making no effort to hide her contempt. Her face was set in a look of disdain as she refilled Scarlet's goblet, sloshing the milk onto the table and muttering "Oops" in a snide, overly bright tone.

For a moment, Scarlet thought about coming right out and asking Lindi what her problem was, but then she decided that this wasn't the best time to risk causing a scene. The girl's attitude rankled, though. The next time she was alone with Lindi, she would find out what was going on. It just didn't make any sense.

For now, she made a point of thanking Lindi in the sweetest voice she could muster.

After a long, mostly glorious evening, the feast began to break up, and slowly the dining hall emptied. Xavier asked Scarlet and her dad to stay, along with the Tounder council. Her mom agreed to take Melody up to bed, but said she would be back down to talk to Scarlet and tuck her in as well.

With the hall now empty of everyone except those Xavier had asked to stay, the mood shifted. It was as if the darkness hinted at in Xavier's speech, held off by the merriment of all the revelers, had at last descended on them like a cloud. Xavier turned to Scarlet's dad, his face still calm and cheerful; behind the clear amber of his eyes, however, she could see a degree of anxiety.

"Would you like me to explain things, Mr. Hopewell, or would you rather give it a try?" he asked, his voice full of genuine concern.

Her dad placed his hand over Scarlet's and gave her a worried look. "I'm still trying to figure it out, myself. It might be better if you . . ."

"I understand completely," said Xavier. "Miss Scarlet, my dear, as you've probably already realized, you are a very special person to us. Not just the Tounder, but all of us. I've known about you since before you were even born."

"How can that be?" Scarlet asked.

"Try not to interrupt, darling," her dad said, squeezing her hand. "Let him finish, and hopefully it'll be clearer."

Xavier smiled warmly, giving Scarlet and her dad a moment before continuing. "The Dorans are a race of men and women who live in our land, Satorium. They are much like you and your family and all the other men and woman you know, with one important exception. Much as we are keepers and users of light, they too have the ability to perform what to you might seem like extraordinary things." Xavier paused, lost in thought for a moment. "They are magical. They can use magic." He paused again, longer this time. "We have a prophecy. Do you know what that is, dear?"

"Sure," said Scarlet, trying her best to take it all in; she could feel that something big and dangerous was coming, but she couldn't figure out what it was. She couldn't help feeling a strong sense of foreboding. "It's like a prediction of the future."

"Very good," Xavier said, sounding so wise and grandfatherly that it made Scarlet smile, despite her apprehension. "That is exactly what it is. Although I'm afraid that when it comes to prophecies, it's not always so simple. Many things can affect how a prophecy comes to be, and it is always difficult to try and figure them out. Most times we don't even bother. There have been many prophecies spoken over the course of even my long life, and usually they are ignored. After all, there's not much anyone can do about something that is supposed to happen anyway.

"The prophecy I want to tell you about is quite different, though. Unlike most, this one tells of two possible futures.

One is full of hope—the other, of despair. You see, the prophecy says that from the Dorans will rise a great and evil force that will threaten all goodness in the two worlds. It says that this force will enslave those without the gift of magic, and rule over the rest of us with tyranny and hate.

"That force has been identified. He is the prince of the Dorans, and his name is Thanerbos. He will have powers beyond what any living being possesses. He has an unlimited capacity for evil and a mastery over dark magic that I can barely match with light. The only reason he hasn't made his move to take over, Scarlet, is because his father, the king, knowing what he was, had him locked in a prison, where he is guarded by all the magical power the king possesses. But the king grows weak as the prince grows strong. The attack on your family is proof of that. He can't yet leave the prison, but he commands the Mortada, and he is able to use part of his power from the confines of his tower. No one knows exactly how long we have before he is free, and when that day comes, a mighty war will begin. This war, those of us who wish for peace and good in the two worlds will have no hope of winning."

Scarlet's head was spinning. A large part of her brain wanted not to believe a word of it. And yet here she was, in a village hidden beneath a tree, where no one was over seven inches tall and they made toys out of light.

"So what can you do to stop him? I don't understand," she said, strain in her voice.

"That is only one of the possible outcomes. You remember, I said there were two," Xavier's smile returned. "The prophecy also speaks of a hero. A great sorceress who will wield her magic from within, and will match his power. The For Tol Don. A woman from the nonmagical world. This sorceress will stand against the dark one and save us."

Xavier let these words hang in the air as if they needed time to breathe and grow. His smile didn't fail as he looked tenderly into Scarlet's eyes.

"That woman, my dear, is you."

10

The Inner Light

Scarlet had decided not to ask any questions of Xavier the night of the feast; she had too many to even decide where to begin. Exhausted from a day and evening filled with sights and sounds that tested her concept of reality, she had gone to bed with a cramped brain and a heavy heart. Xavier had thrust a tremendous weight upon her shoulders, and she didn't even really understand what it was, or whether she had a choice in carrying it out.

Several days passed in relative calm, resting and regaining some sense of equilibrium. She played with Melody and Cricket and explored areas of the castle and village that they had missed on their first outing. The castle in particular was much more expansive than it had first appeared, full of hidden rooms and winding passageways. Scarlet found particularly fascinating a suite of rooms with one dedicated to each season. The winter room was bitterly cold, its floor dusted with snow, the resinous tang of fir needles in the air; the summer room, blazing hot, with a floor of sand; the fall room, sparkling and cool, carpeted with richly colored leaves that rustled underfoot and smelling of distant woodsmoke; and, her favorite by far, the spring chamber, mild and fragrant with the scent of cut grass, violets and wild narcissus scattered across the floor. Scarlet learned all she could about the Tounder and Illuminora, asking anyone who seemed willing to talk about them, as well as about the two worlds, the Dorans, and the places outside Illuminora. She didn't find out much, but what she did learn—for one thing, that the oak tree above Illuminora, with its sheltering roots, gave the castle many magical properties that were not inherent to the Tounder—was fascinating.

For reasons she didn't herself understand, however, she avoided asking the one person who might be able to answer all of her questions. Perhaps it was a fear of the real answers, or perhaps she wanted to be better prepared before those answers came. Xavier, for his part, didn't attempt to force the issue, and Scarlet assumed that he sensed she wasn't ready. At least for the moment, he seemed patient to wait her out, and let her come to him.

Three days after the feast, Scarlet found herself wandering through the castle, enjoying for the moment not having her sister, her parents, Cricket, or a throng of well-wishers tailing around. It was a relief just to be alone and think.

Climbing up a spiral staircase through one of the castle's front towers, she reached a terrace at the top of the castle that looked out over all of Illuminora. From this height, it almost looked like an ordinary village. The translucent wings of the Tounder below were barely visible; she couldn't distinguish between those who flew just above the ground and those who simply walked. It could have been any small village in Europe, the inhabitants going about their ordinary routines of shopping and working.

"It's nice up here," a voice remarked quietly, just behind her. Startled, she turned around. A Tounder about her age, with curly chestnut hair and mischievous elven features, was regarding her through cheerful baby-blue eyes. "I'm sorry—I didn't mean to scare you. I'm Delfi."

Scarlet smiled and extended her hand, and Delfi took it awkwardly, obviously having no idea what the gesture meant. For some reason she felt as if she had heard his name before. "I didn't know anyone else was here," she said. "I'm—"

"Scarlet. Scarlet Hope."

"Hopewell, actually," Scarlet corrected. "It's nice to meet you, Delfi."

"I come up here a lot. It's a peaceful spot." Delfi looked embarrassed. "I should go. You probably wanted to be alone, what with your training starting tomorrow."

"No— I mean— Stay, please. I haven't really met anyone except Xavier. Certainly no one my age— Well, Lindi, but she—"

"Is a pain and a bully," Delfi said, giving a mischievous smile. "Don't worry about Lindi, I don't think she really likes anybody." Scarlet was giving Delfi a suspicious look. "Sorry. It's a horrible habit of mine, but I tend to notice things about people, and I overhear a lot. I saw the way she treated you at the feast. Best to just ignore her—we all do."

Scarlet suddenly remembered why Delfi's name sounded so familiar. "Aren't you one of the Tounder Xavier said was trying to get into the armory?" she said abruptly.

Delfi's face turned a bright crimson. "Uh . . . yeah. That was me," he answered.

"Oh," Scarlet said, regretting having asked now. She hadn't wanted to embarrass Delfi. "I didn't mean to bring up a sore—"

"Don't worry about it. I almost got in, and my punishment wasn't so bad. I'll get in next time, though. I've got all the bugs worked out." Delfi's voice held more than a trace of excitement.

"What do you want to get in there for, if it's not allowed?" Scarlet asked.

"I don't know. Maybe *because* it's not allowed." Delfi chuckled. "I have a knack for finding those sort of things. Keeps life exciting. At least until you're restricted to the castle. I'm not allowed into the village for a week," Delfi complained.

"That's terrible," Scarlet sympathized.

"No, I got off easy, to tell you the truth."

"Why do you want to get in the armory so badly—really?"

"It's supposed to be incredible." Delfi said this in such a matter-of-fact tone that Scarlet giggled. She'd been expecting a much more complicated answer. What she hadn't expected was for Delfi to talk like any regular boy.

"*Incredible*, huh," she said.

"Well . . . that's what they say, at least. I've never actually been in there. Funny thing is, Raden's been in there, when he was young. And now he acts like it's the worst thing in the world that others try. Kinda full of himself, now that he's in charge of the castle grounds." Delfi tried to sound stern, even angry, when he spoke of Raden, but his eyes held a mischievous twinkle. "He also happens to be my big brother."

Scarlet laughed again. Delfi was instantly likable, and she found herself drawn to him. It didn't hurt that he was very cute. Suddenly she remembered something from earlier in the conversation. "You said I was going to begin training tomorrow—what did you mean?"

"I overheard my brother and Xavier talking. Xavier told Raden to keep everyone away from the library so that you and he could have your first lesson without a bunch of curious Tounder milling about. You're the most exciting thing to happen around here in a long time," said Delfi, moving to the stone seats at the center of the terrace. He sat down and took a piece of what resembled chocolate from his pocket, broke it in two, and offered half to Scarlet.

Scarlet sat down beside him, took the candy, and tentatively took a bite. Expecting some unusual flavor, she was quite surprised to find that although it was very good, it tasted . . . well, like chocolate.

"Thanks," she said.

"You're welcome." Delfi paused, obviously weighing his next words. "Don't tell Xavier that I told you. I wasn't supposed to be where I was when I overheard them, strictly speaking." Scarlet nodded vigorously, her mouth full of chocolate. "You're lucky, you know?"

"How's that?" Scarlet asked, holding her hand delicately over her mouth while she chewed.

"Xavier hasn't taught anyone in a very long time. It's quite an honor, even for the For Tol Don, I expect." Rather than appear misty-eyed or reverent when he said the Tounder's name for her, Delfi acted as if he had merely called her by any regular name.

"I don't really even know what that means, truly. I know to the Tounder it makes sense, but to me it sounds like a fanciful story."

"I can understand that," Delfi admitted. "I'm sure there are a lot of things about where you're from that would seem the same way to me. You're going to learn our magic—how to keep and manipulate the light. The first non-Tounder to ever do it, as far as I know. And Xavier is going to teach you. He can do things that many of us have never dreamed of, and he's been around for longer, as well."

"How long?"

"I don't know. There aren't any Tounder around who were alive before he was born. Once heard him talk about meeting a dragon. Haven't been dragons in Satorium in . . . well, I don't know how long, to tell the truth. A long time."

Scarlet couldn't believe her ears. Dragons? Every time she thought that she couldn't be surprised anymore, there was something new. "Were there really dragons?"

"Of course there were. Loads of 'em from what I understand. I think there is even supposed to be one left up in the Northern Mountains, but that's probably just flickering light, if you know what I mean. Can't imagine something that big staying out of sight for this long." Delfi plopped his last piece of chocolate into his mouth.

"How big are—were they?" Scarlet asked.

"Don't know. My brother used to tell me that they were as big as a house. Xavier would be the only one who'd actually know for sure, though."

Delfi looked out over the village. "It's getting late. I better go. Raden'll be all over me if I'm not in my room when he comes to check on me. Worse than our parents, that one is." Delfi stood up and put his hand out, awkwardly imitating Scarlet's gesture when they first met. Scarlet stood and took his hand. "I'd get some sleep, if I were you," he added. "The first lesson can take a lot out of you."

Scarlet woke up feeling fresh and eager; she'd taken Delfi's advice and gone to bed early, sleeping as deeply as she did every night in her room at the top of the spire. At breakfast, her dad told her that they'd be going to see Xavier to begin learning magic. She could tell by his face that he felt as silly saying the words as she did hearing them.

The library where Scarlet would be taking her lessons encompassed the entire second floor of the east wing of the castle. Unlike almost every other building and room in the castle and the village of Illuminora, the library didn't glow with light playing in and on every surface. Here the light was subdued, background to the splendid, ornate woodwork.

The library was nearly a full three stories high, with shelves lining the walls from floor to ceiling. Halfway up, a dark wood balcony ran around the room, giving access to the higher shelves. Glittering mosaics were set into the domed ceiling, illustrating—as Xavier explained—the saga of Hulpric the Great and the eventual dividing of the two worlds. Their rich, deep colors made the cavernous space feel smaller, more intimate. At the far end was a stone fireplace easily large enough to hold Scarlet's whole family; inside, flames danced gently, warm and inviting.

Xavier, who was sitting in a high-backed chair underneath the dome, motioned for Scarlet and her dad to join him. As they did, he opened a large leather-bound book and set it on the table between them.

"How are you, dear?" he began, his voice calm. "I'm sorry it took so long for me to talk to you again. There were many things that needed to be worked out."

"That's okay," Scarlet said without hesitation. She too had needed the time.

"If you remember, I told you that we don't know how long it will be before Prince Thanerbos will be free and his strength at its fullest. We must act as though time is short, in case it is. You need to begin learning to deal with him."

Xavier glanced down at the book. Scarlet could see the pages, full of hand-painted illustrations and what looked like handwritten text. It was a beautiful object, and just the look of it piqued her curiosity.

"Aha!" Xavier exclaimed suddenly. "These pages are always changing. Never the same place twice. I've found it, though."

Scarlet looked again at the book. Although Xavier had not turned any of the pages, she saw that the text and illustrations were different. She looked up at Xavier, thoroughly confused.

"In my younger days," Xavier said wistfully, "I would chase what I was looking for all through the book. Old age has given me the patience to just open and wait. The right page always comes. . . . Look here." Xavier turned the book so that Scarlet and her dad could see properly. The illustration was of two indistinct figures, one little more than a shadow, the other a white shape that might be a woman, varicolored beams, flashes, and sparks colliding between them. On the ground a tangle of roots encircled the two figures, while over their heads a wave of water collided with a ball of fire. "You, obviously, are the woman in white."

Scarlet stared at the picture. She knew that she had never seen the illustration before, but something about it felt ominously familiar, like a name on the tip of her tongue she couldn't quite remember, a name linked to something bad.

"I'm sorry if this scares you, Scarlet. I wish it didn't have to be while you are still so young," Xavier said. "You can see from the picture that the woman of the prophesy appeared to be full grown, although I must admit that the vagueness of the drawing leaves a great deal to the imagination. At least we got the woman part right."

"I'm not scared," Scarlet responded immediately. "I'm just confused—by all of it. How can I be this person?" She started to point at the illustration, but found that somehow a new one—what looked distinctly like a dragon—had taken its place.

"You will have to trust me. I have waited and searched for you my whole life."

Suddenly her father, looking as if he couldn't sit still and listen another minute, grabbed her hand and leaned forward. "I can never thank you enough for saving my family, but this has got to stop. It's all too ridiculous. I can't let my little girl go off to fight some evil magician." His voice quavered with his frustration and fear for his family. "It's— I just can't."

Xavier leaned in and placed a comforting hand on both of theirs. "I understand. I do. I wish there was some other way than to involve your family, and most especially your children. But Thanerbos is coming, and the only way you can protect Scarlet now is to let me help prepare her. Whether you agree to let me teach her or not, I assure you that it will make no difference to Thanerbos. Killing her will be one of the first things on his mind after he's freed."

Scarlet's dad frowned, visibly struggling with what Xavier had told him. "I'm sorry . . . I just can't accept that," he said finally, but his voice was heavy with resignation.

"Let me show you," Xavier said, sitting back and giving him his most reassuring smile. "Would that be okay with you, Scarlet? Just give it a try." Scarlet nodded. "Thank you—you're a brave girl.

"This doesn't have to be all doom and gloom." Xavier leaned in even closer to Scarlet. "Not yet. Right now is the time for something quite extraordinary. With one exception, never has someone outside the Tounder learned our magic. I have taught many over the years, but I have to say that I'm a little excited about teaching you."

"What do I do?" Scarlet asked.

"Well, at the beginning, it's not so much *do* as it is *feel*. The light begins inside you. If you can imagine a place where your soul resides, that is where the light must begin. Close your eyes." Xavier's voice dropped nearly to a whisper, as calm and quiet as if he were a hypnotist. Scarlet obeyed, closing her eyes and feeling a sense of relaxation come over her. "What do you see?"

"Nothing," Scarlet answered.

"Oh, I don't believe that. Let your imagination roam. Turn your mind inward." Xavier waited patiently, watching Scarlet's face. When her face changed, betraying the slightest of smiles at the corners of her mouth, he asked, "Now what do you see?"

Scarlet flushed and, feeling slightly embarrassed, answered, "Um . . . a friend."

"Good. You can open your eyes. That was the first step, simple but quite important."

Scarlet looked at him with confusion. "Picturing a friend is the first step of magic?" Her disappointment was evident.

"Well, it's all in how you manipulate it—so, yes, it's the first step. There was darkness, and, using your imagination, you pushed it away. Let's go to the next step."

Scarlet pursed her lips, feeling very silly, but she nodded, ready to move on. Again Xavier told her to close her eyes.

"This time I want you to imagine something in particular. I want you to picture a perfect round sphere made of light, like those trinkets at the village toy shop—you've seen those, right? Can you picture that?"

"Yes."

"Good—is it radiating light?" Scarlet nodded. "Excellent. I want you to picture bringing that light back into the ball, so that it no longer lights up anything but itself."

Scarlet nodded again. She could see the ball clearly, and, concentrating, she was able to do as Xavier asked. She felt a warm sensation radiating through her as she pulled the light back into the sphere. It was as if she had drunk a cup of hot chocolate after having come in from the cold.

"Now, bring that light farther into the ball, until all that remains is a pinpoint of light in the center. Hold it there."

Scarlet sat motionless, concentrating as hard as she could. The warmth inside her was now hot, almost uncomfortable. Her picture of the ball with its pinpoint of light seemed so real that she could reach out and touch it. In a tiny corner of her consciousness, she could see her dad staring worriedly at her.

"Scarlet," Xavier said, his voice almost imperceptibly soft. "When I give you the next picture, I want you to imagine it quickly. Don't think it through, just make it happen, all right?"

Scarlet nodded.

"Let the light out, Scarlet. Let it fill the room."

Scarlet trembled for a moment, and then began to glow, herself. Without another warning, a blinding flash of light expanded from her, moving in a wave out to the perimeter of the library. Her dad and Xavier threw up their hands to shield their eyes.

"Did you see that, Daddy? Did you see that?"

But her dad couldn't speak. He looked bewildered, and she felt a pang for him, grappling again with the impossible.

Xavier put his hand on her dad's shoulder. "There is no doubt." He sounded on the verge of cheering. He turned to Scarlet. "That is beyond what any young Tounder has ever accomplished on her first day, my dear. And you aren't even Tounder. You have just accomplished the impossible. I hope that you can appreciate how amazing that is. Of all the Tounder I have taught, not one has been able to produce such a light on her first try."

Scarlet could feel that she was still glowing.

This time, though, it was with inner pride.

11

The Mortada

If evil could be given form, given life, a body, breath, and thought, it would be the soul of a Mortada. Merciless, they served only that which brought the world closer to chaos. Thriving on the pain and misery of others, they were relentless, supremely powerful—and beautiful. It was a cruel joke that few beings in either of the two worlds could match the splendor of these malicious creatures, with their flawless skin and long golden hair.

Three of the Mortada stood motionless just outside the forest of Illuminora. They had searched the entire land of Satorium on the small chance that the obvious was not true. It was. Their prey was under the protection of the Tounder, where not even the Mortada could get to her. They would wait for her as their lord commanded. He had assured them that eventually she would emerge. She had no choice, if she was to fulfill her destiny.

What great pleasure it would be to kill her—not for the reward that awaited them when they delivered her to their lord, but just for the joy of killing someone so young and full of life. So full of untapped power.

"How long will we have to wait, Letum?" one asked, his voice a lilting song.

"As long as it takes, Gelu," Letum answered, staring into the distance.

They watched for a long moment in silence. As the wind moved through the trees, rustling the leaves, it parted around the Mortada, moving past them without so much as stirring a strand of their hair.

"Did you hear what became of our brothers who crossed over to find her?" Gelu asked.

"They failed," Letum answered, his gaze still focused away.

"Obviously," Gelu sneered.

"He disposed of them. They failed," Letum answered, his tone so nonchalant that he might have been discussing which local baker made the best pastries.

Gelu smiled, seeming to enjoy the news of his fellow

Mortada's death. "I would like to kill that tree," he said, looking at Illuminora's great oak, rising high above the other trees in the forest.

"Why?" Letum asked, his voice showing no sign of actual interest.

Gelu didn't answer, but his smile was a wicked thing to behold.

12
Dakota Returns

Scarlet sat by the fountain that had become one of her favorite spots in the village. It was a dazzling sight, a pink marble sculpture of wolves that reminded Scarlet of Dakota, who she hadn't seen since her second day in Illuminora. The wolves were posed playfully, chasing each other through the water as light spilled around and above them. It reminded her of a day at the lake near their home, when everything had been simple and safe, and she and Melody watched as Cricket and Dakota swam, chasing sticks and each other. It was one of those perfect days that would stay with her always.

Ever since her session in the library with Xavier, Scarlet had found that if she concentrated hard enough, she could direct the light from the fountain, once even so well that she was able to make two spheres of light chase one another. What amazed her most about her new ability was how natural it felt, as if she had been doing it all her life. Although her power was limited by experience, her imagination had been running rampant with all the possibilities.

A little distance from the fountain, Dakota stood, watching Scarlet. Her red hair was gleaming in the light from the fountain, sending rays of gold all around her. She was smiling as she made the light dance around the fountain, looking so innocent, so childlike. She seemed unaware of the danger gathering around her, although Dakota knew better. Scarlet was a smart girl, and he had little doubt that she had figured much out on her own.

Dakota closed the distance between them, and spoke. "Your abilities are quite extraordinary already."

Scarlet turned and, catching sight of the large dog, leaped from the side of the fountain to throw her arms around his great neck. But then she stopped short, and Dakota could see uncertainty flooding over her. He knew what she was thinking: Dakota was no longer the dog she had known, not really the puppy who'd snuggled beside her all those nights, even though he looked just the same. Scarlet was confused, Dakota knew, caught between betrayal and longing.

"Thank you," was all she managed to say.

"I'm sorry it took so long for me to speak to you, Scarlet. That wasn't fair. I know that," said Dakota, genuine remorse in his voice. "There was much for me to do . . . but that's not really an acceptable excuse."

"I have been kind of confused. Especially by you. Strange or not, at least everybody else is who they are. But you aren't, are you?" Scarlet asked, her voice quivering a little.

"It's complicated—"

"*Everything's* complicated," Scarlet snapped back, perhaps a little too forcefully.

"It's not that I'm someone different, Scarlet. Just . . . well . . . older, for one thing."

"How old?" asked Scarlet, walking back to the fountain and sitting down on its edge.

"About a hundred and three," Dakota admitted.

"Wow." Scarlet sighed. "*People* don't even live that long."

"You'll find that in Satorium, things tend to live a lot longer than you're used to."

Scarlet let her hand fall so that her fingers brushed the cool water of the fountain.

"How old is your father?" she asked tentatively, then looked down and flushed. Dakota knew what she was trying to ask. He did his best to disguise the look of anguish that flashed in his eyes as the thought of his father stirred up painful memories.

"When my father died," Dakota answered, the slightest tremble in his voice, "he was five hundred and thirty-three. That was many years ago."

Scarlet's jaw dropped. "Five hundred and thirty-three years. That's unbelievable!"

Making a determined effort to keep his voice level, Dakota added, "Would have been much longer, if it hadn't been for the Mortada." He would keep no secrets from Scarlet, not anymore. He had promised himself that.

"The Mortada . . . they killed your father?" Scarlet asked, meekly.

"They killed my parents, my brother, and my sisters." Dakota looked away for a moment. "The oldest Stidolph I've ever heard of lived to be one thousand years old. Died on the anniversary of his birth. That might better answer your real question."

"So do you start over then, since you were a puppy again?"

Dakota laughed, a pleasant sound despite the harsh growl in his voice. "No, I don't start over. That would be something, if I did."

"So when you were a puppy, it was like a spell or something—a trick?" Scarlet couldn't keep the disappointment out of her voice.

"No trick. I had to be born again into innocence and youth to make the journey. There was no other way at the time. Once I finally crossed over, Xavier was able to use my . . . essence, I guess you'd call it, to send the Stidolph pack to us."

Scarlet stared at Dakota, bewildered. "Should I try and understand what that means?"

"You should try and understand everything. Sometimes acceptance is important, but never without an attempt to understand—" Dakota stopped, realizing that he was preaching. He didn't want to talk like that to her. Not after the time they'd spent together before the Mortada came. It would be too confusing, even hurtful, to a young girl who had essentially lost her pet . . . her friend. "Everything around you now, everything you're learning, it's not beyond your understanding. It's strange and confusing, but not beyond you. Remember that."

"Okay. I'll try."

"Good. That's going to be important in the times to come," Dakota padded over to the fountain and sat down beside Scarlet. Though Scarlet was seated off the ground on the fountain's edge, Dakota's head was level with hers. "Even with Xavier's magic and mine together, the barrier between Satorium and your world was too great to pass as we did when we came back to Satorium. We had to find another way, and there was only one. I left my body behind and wandered, searching for a way to find you. By the time I finally did, fourteen years had passed. I had to choose a form from your world. Something that would not be out of place. Something your family would allow to get near you. I chose a dog. The rest you know."

Scarlet waited a while before responding. "It makes sense. It's unbelievable, but it makes sense. Where did you go? After we got here, you left us."

"I had to work the soreness out of my shoulder, and I had some explaining to do to the Stidolph. They were notably curious as to why I was no longer . . . myself . . . and a little upset when I told them I never would be again. They had a hard time with . . . well . . . they had a hard time accepting it."

"Why did you come back?" Scarlet asked, her face hopeful.

Dakota could see that she'd missed him, and that she wanted very much for him to stay, even though she was confused. "I am your guardian and your mentor," he reassured here. "I will be with you as long as I'm able. Hopefully to the end. You have a great task ahead of you. You are more than capable, but it won't be easy. I will help see you through the best I can," Dakota responded, trying to keep a hint of sadness out of his voice.

They sat quietly, Scarlet letting things sink in, Dakota giving her time, watching with admiration as the lights of the fountain danced with her varying emotions, although she was unaware of what she was doing.

Suddenly the lights flickered and went out before returning, even more intense, colored a deep scarlet.

"What are you thinking right now?" Dakota asked.

"I was thinking about . . . the darkness," Scarlet admitted apprehensively.

"Interesting . . . " Dakota's voice trailed off.

"What is?" Scarlet asked.

"Look at the fountain," Dakota said, tilting his head toward the water.

Scarlet's eyes went wide as she saw the crimson light. "Did I do that?"

"Yes, and I think you will probably be able to skip your next lesson. All colors are within white light, as I understand, but it takes a good deal of experience to single out a particular color. You are having a powerful reaction to Thanerbos already."

"How could I possibly be expected to beat a sorcerer who's known magic his whole life?"

"That is an excellent question, one I'm glad you asked. Xavier might be upset at me for jumping ahead, but I've always been a fan of knowledge. I will never lie to you again, Scarlet. You have my word, and what I know, you will know." Dakota took a minute to let his words sink in. "Magic exists in nature, in the wind, fire, water, in the minds of others, in the forces of gravity and the passage of time. There is also the magic of light and dark. All who reside in Satorium have the gift of magic in some form or another. What is common among all those who know magic is that they can only practice the form of magic they are born with." Dakota paused for a moment, trying to think of the best way to explain. "Think of it like your hair or your eyes. Your mother and father both have something inside them that they passed on to you when you were made that together gave you your green eyes and your red hair."

"You mean, like DNA or something?" Scarlet asked.

"I don't know what DNA is," Dakota admitted.

"I don't completely know either, but it has something to do with the genes that you get from your mother and father, and that's what makes you have certain color eyes and skin and stuff."

"Then yes. Like DNA. The peoples of Satorium inherit their magic from their mothers and fathers. There are many forms and many ways in which magic is used. Some use staves they imbue with magical properties. Some speak to nature using ancient words of great power. Some can control flame with the power of the minds. What is similar among all these practices is that they involve using magic to manipulate what is already there. They are born with magic, but they can only control things outside themselves. The magic of light and dark is different. All the powers of light and dark come from within. The Tounder alone possess the power of light, and the Mortada . . . the darkness." Dakota paused and then added, "Are you following?"

Scarlet tilted her head playfully. "Again, the whole understanding-but-trouble-believing thing."

"Magic requires a great deal of knowledge, strength, and stamina. It takes a great deal of energy to manipulate the world around you. Everything has its own will, even things that you might not think of as alive. To get those things to act against their will requires skill, knowledge, and strength. The more powerful and dramatic the magic, the greater the toll it takes on the magician.

"The pirates of the North Sea, for instance, are born with magic that enables them to manipulate water. They can make the sea answer to their commands, but the greater the magic they perform, the weaker they will be, and the longer they will need to recover.

"The Tounder and the Mortada are different. Their magic does not come solely from knowledge of how to manipulate the light and dark around them. It comes from their own inner source of power. It is much easier to control your own will than the will of something else. The Tounder are born with the light inside them. They can not only manipulate light but create it. They are keepers. Now what if a sorcerer were born with this inner magic, but instead of being like the Tounder and Mortada, who keep only the light or the dark, this sorcerer was the keeper of all magic. They would be able to use magic—"

"Without limitations," Scarlet interrupted.

"Yes and no. Even the Tounder and the Mortada tire with the use of magic. But their power is greater than that of other users of magic. Now imagine if you were born with every color hair, and you could change that color whenever you wanted. You and Thanerbos have this ability. You were born with all the magic inside you. You can create what isn't there, not simply manipulate what is. And in all of history there has only been one other, so you can see why you are so important—so special." Dakota stood and arched his back, stretching his powerful muscles.

"That still doesn't explain how I, even if I were to learn all this magic, could beat someone who has known magic all his life."

"Ah. . . . Well, there is a catch. You may be born with the ability to perform any magic that exists, but without someone to teach you how— It would be like knowing the secret to life but having no way to communicate it. The Tounder will never teach Thanerbos how to find the power of the light, Scarlet. You alone will have that. He may possess the ability inside him, but without someone to help him awaken it, it does him no good."

"But he'll have the dark."

"If all goes as planned, you'll have the dark as well," said Dakota, without a trace of doubt.

"Why would I want the power of dark? Isn't it evil?" Scarlet asked, her face twisting in alarm.

"The Mortada are evil, Scarlet. Darkness is a force—easily abused, surely, but as natural and vital as any part of the magical world."

Scarlet gazed absently at the fountain, putting the pieces together in her mind, trying to process it all. It was as fantastic as everything she had seen so far, even more so. It wasn't that she didn't trust Dakota. It was just . . .

How could she be the greatest sorceress in the world? She was just a girl.

"Give it time. You will understand all in time. Train well," Dakota said. "Pay attention and concentrate. I promise I'll be close."

She watched him pad off. She'd give it time.

What else could she do?

Later that day Scarlet was summoned to the library again, this time meeting Xavier there without her dad. Reluctant as he was to have his daughter put in harm's way, he had agreed that training her would only make her safer, at least until he could find another way to stop those who were after her.

They would be learning to focus the light now, Xavier explained. By focusing the light, she would be able to create a powerful offensive force when she was forced into battle. Listening to Xavier's description, Scarlet at first pictured a large laser beam—but the actual focused light was much more fantastic, she found.

With a little practice, she was able to move the inner light—the same light that in her previous lesson she had expanded into a great, blinding sphere—into the palms of her hands. At a thought from her, a beam of crimson light shot out from her hands into the fireplace, boring a hole into the wood, which quickly caught fire.

Xavier seemed as pleased as he could be, telling her that the best pupil he'd ever taught before her had learned focus after a month, and the next closest had taken nearly an entire year to get the concept.

The next day, her lesson was on illuminating other objects, turning them into permanent or temporary sources of light. Scarlet illuminated books in the library, Xavier's chair, a goblet, and finally the entire mosaic ceiling, making the tesserae glow like radiant gemstones.

Sent off to practice, she happily took to delighting Melody with her newfound gift. The next lesson, Scarlet decided, must be a particularly complicated one, because Xavier said that he wouldn't teach her again until she had shown great progress with what she'd learned so far.

The week passed quickly. At one point, Scarlet had to ask Xavier to come and help her de-illuminate her room; she had turned every object into a lantern, and it was so bright that she found it impossible to sleep.

Late in the week, Scarlet saw Lindi for the first time since the feast. Scarlet was hovering a softly glowing ball ahead of her as she walked down a corridor that was, unusually for the castle, dimly lit.

"*That's* supposed to save us from the prince?" an all too familiar voice called out from behind her.

Scarlet's orb instantly dissipated as she turned to face the girl. "What do you want, Lindi?"

"Oh, nothing. I've just been watching you. Can't say that I'm impressed."

"I don't remember asking for your approval," Scarlet snapped back. She didn't know what the young Tounder's problem was, but she'd had enough of being nice.

"You have no idea what you're doing, do you? Getting everyone to believe that you're some kind of hero. As if a human could possibly—" Lindi seethed with rage. Whatever hatred she was harboring, she obviously couldn't contain it any longer.

"I'm not *getting* anyone to do anything," Scarlet answered, backing up a couple steps. Lindi had begun to glow with an eerie purple light.

Scarlet racked her brain. This was no good at all. Even with all her practicing, she wasn't ready for a fight, especially not a fight using magic. A moment ago she had felt ready to face anything; now she was overcome by feelings of inadequacy. She felt small and helpless.

"Everyone else might think you're some mythical hero, some great hope, but you don't fool me one bit." Lindi's glow grew brighter.

"What is the matter with you?" Scarlet pleaded. "I barely even know you. I haven't done—"

Without warning, Lindi sent out a beam of purple light that struck Scarlet square in the chest like an anvil. It didn't seem possible that light could have such mass, such force, but as she fought desperately to regain the breath that had been driven from her chest, Scarlet didn't need any more convincing.

Lindi strutted over to Scarlet, who was still too shocked to move. The Tounder's glow was now painfully bright.

"Let's see what everyone'll say after this," she shrieked, focusing another beam into her hands.

Then suddenly Lindi was flying back away from Scarlet. It had happened so fast, Scarlet hadn't even seen what had hit the girl. She could only watch in astonishment as Lindi landed with a crash against a far wall.

"What are you playing at?" Delfi shouted at Lindi, bending over Scarlet to check on her. "Are you okay?"

"I'm fine," Scarlet croaked.

"I'll be right back," Delfi said, straightening up and walking cautiously over to Lindi, lying in a motionless heap ten yards away.

Lindi was making painful groaning noises, and finally she managed to turn her head and look up at Delfi, whose anger melted away at the sight of Lindi's pitiful expression. He was visibly torn, trying to decide what to do.

"Get out of here," he said finally. "Don't let me find you within shouting distance of Scarlet again, or I swear . . ." His voice trailed off.

Lindi got up slowly and, after taking a few tentative limping steps, flew off out of the corridor as Delfi went back to Scarlet and helped her up.

"Let's get you to your room."

Scarlet nodded. She was still in considerable pain.

"You could've walloped her, you know," he added with a smile.

13

Chosen's Acquaintances

Brennan was still shaken from his battle with the tiranthrope. Physically, he was almost back to his former self; at least he was no longer on the verge of passing out from lack of food and exhaustion. His muscles had become used to Chosen's relentless tempo.

It had taken nearly a week to get out of the Southern Wildlands, and although they had done so without any further run-ins with tiranthropes, their venture had not been without incident. Chosen was one of the few who knew the

Wildlands well, it soon became obvious. As they threaded their way along beside the raging river that seemed to snake endlessly through the trees and rocks, coming ever nearer to the impassable marshlands, Chosen stopped suddenly. The place he'd chosen looked no different than any other—a dense clump of trees, a craggy bank next to an unfordable river. Chosen looked briefly to the left and right, then walked straight toward the riverbank. He seemed to shrink and then was gone.

Brennan ran to the spot he had last seen Chosen, only to have his feet slip suddenly and his stomach heave into his throat as the ground dropped away. Before he could realize what had happened, he was sitting on his bottom, staring down a dark tunnel with small streams of water trickling from the ceiling. Chosen was twenty yards ahead, making his way under the river to the other side. The ground was covered in wet stones, and Brennan had to place each foot carefully to avoid slipping.

He'd been concentrating intently on his feet, trying his best to see through the gloom, when a flicker of light caught his eye. He looked up and saw a flurry of small birds, no bigger than butterflies, their wings glowing above. Chosen was out of sight, having already emerged from the tunnel on the far side. Brennan stopped, transfixed by the beautiful birds and wondering what they were doing in such a confined space beneath a river.

Without warning, the birds scattered, fleeing down the tunnel and out the far side. A strange emotion filled Brennan at seeing the birds fly away. He couldn't explain it, but he felt as if he and a good friend had parted company.

But then the sensation of being watched pushed all other feelings aside. Every nerve on his body tensed.

Turning slowly, Brennan saw five men, dressed exactly like Chosen, standing at the entrance to the tunnel, where he and Chosen had come from. They smiled malevolently, seeming to feed on Brennan's fear. He had a moment to decide: fight or run? There were five of them—but then again, what are five skinny men compared to a tiranthrope? he wondered, allowing himself an uncharacteristic moment of arrogance.

There was something off about these men, though. Something told Brennan that fighting would be the wrong choice. It was the same eerie presence that Brennan had felt when he first met Chosen.

Turning on his heels, Brennan sprinted headlong down the tunnel, slipping and fumbling over the rocks as he hurtled toward the exit. Crashing through brush and thickets, he emerged into the pre-dusk light, nearly running into Chosen, who stood impatiently, leaning against a tree.

"Well, it certainly took you—" Chosen swallowed his words, noticing the panicked look on Brennan's face. "What is it?" he scolded, the answer to his question immediately following his words in the form of the five figures charging from the tunnel.

Brennan had expected Chosen to react as he had, with great alarm, but Chosen merely looked amused. The five figures flashed strikingly beautiful smiles, and Brennan had the impression that if he were asked to tell one from the other, he would not be able, so alike were the flawless features and flowing blond locks of hair.

"*Mortada*," Chosen whispered to Brennan.

"How unusual to find you traveling in these times, Devoveo," one of the figures hissed, making no attempt to mask his contempt, a jarring note that marred the normally musical tone of the Mortada.

Brennan looked curiously at Chosen. Devoveo?

"How unusual to find one who has failed the dark one so miserably walking Satorium alive," Chosen said coolly.

The Mortada who had spoken became visibly angered, his face flushing for a moment and his jaw clenching. He recovered quickly, though, his smile returning.

"You have heard wrong. I was not a part of their failure," he argued, trying very hard to keep his voice level.

"It's possible," Chosen quipped back. "Not that you would have done any better. With your previous failures it's probably best that you *didn't* volunteer to cross after the girl. I'm not sure the dark one would have been as forgiving . . . as just to kill you, that is."

The cloaked Mortada could no longer control his anger. He stepped aggressively toward Chosen, pulling a long, curved knife from beneath his robes. In his anger, he had neglected to pay attention to Brennan, who he was nearly brushing past.

Brennan had only a second to make a decision, although for that moment time seemed suspended, allowing a multitude of thoughts to pass through his mind. He was not particularly fond of Chosen; after all, Chosen had only watched while Brennan had fought against the tiranthrope. Then again, without Chosen, Brennan was completely alone and purposeless, a fate he wasn't sure would really be any better than prison. And it had been Chosen who'd saved him from that prison, regardless of what ulterior motives lay behind his actions.

In the end he reacted on impulse, his fist darting out as the figure passed by him, striking the Mortada solidly in the face. There was a loud thwack as Brennan's fist collided with the Mortada's forehead, sending him tottering backward several paces. What happened next was difficult for Brennan to fully understand.

The Mortada howled, not in pain but as a declaration—a pronouncement that Brennan was about to die. The features that had only moments ago been so beautiful were twisted into such anger and violence that they could easily have belonged to some ferocious cold-blooded animal, perhaps a crocodile. A whirl of smoke gathered around the Mortada's hands, and his eyes began to glow in the failing light.

Then Brennan found himself sprawled on his back as Chosen shoved him out of the way, moving with amazing speed and agility. Chosen was on top of the Mortada before Brennan had fully settled on the ground. The black cloud grew, quickly cloaking the entire group of Mortada. Brennan's hands went to his ears as a deafening crack broke the air; it was like standing inches from a bolt of lightning when the thunderclap follows.

Silence, deeper and more complete than any Brennan had ever known, descended. The sounds of the forest were completely absent. Nothing stirred. Slowly the black cloud began to dissipate, becoming more and more translucent until it finally faded away. Standing alone, five cloaked figures lying motionless at his feet, was Chosen.

He turned suddenly to Brennan. "We have to move. Now."

From that moment on, not a word passed between the two. For a week they traveled at a desperate pace through the treacherous depths of the Wildlands. The tension between Brennan and Chosen was so thick that even the relief of emerging from the Wildlands hardly made a dent in it.

Chosen had offered no explanation for what had happened by the river. Brennan, although he burned to know who the men were, how they knew Chosen, and what had happened to them, hadn't dared to ask. Now, more than ever, he sensed something dark about Chosen, something not to be trusted, not to be trifled with. He needed to figure out how to escape from the man. Whatever Chosen wanted from this girl he searched for, it surely wasn't to protect her—or at least, that wasn't the full story.

Brennan's mother had told him tales about these Mortada, men who had mastered dark and evil magic—cunning, wicked men who'd sold their souls for power and beauty. Until now, Brennan had regarded her stories as just that, fables told to entertain, and to warn of the dangers of the world. In fact, until that day by the river, he had forgotten all about her stories of the dark ones. But ever since, these stories had been echoing in his mind. He couldn't believe that he hadn't thought of them the moment he saw Chosen.

On its north side, the forest gave way to pastureland, a rippling expanse of grass covering gently rolling hills. Occasionally they would pass a farmhouse, but they never saw any signs of people, or any sign of life other than fields that had once been tilled but were now barren. Brennan tried to remember his geography, but since all he knew was what his mother had described to him, and he had never seen a map in his life, it was difficult to place where they were. If he had to guess, he figured that they must be somewhere near the land of the Dorans, somewhere in Leona.

Something was wrong, though, if they were in fact in Leona. His mother had always told Brennan of the prosperity of the Dorans, their fertile farms, their abundant crops. Yet all around them, at each and every farm they passed, they saw only fallow fields and abandoned houses. Many miles along the empty road, they had yet to see a single Doran. Surely this was not the land of enterprise and plenty that Brennan's mother had described.

At nightfall Chosen led them into one of the abandoned farmhouses where, he informed Brennan, they would be spending the night. So tired and so glad to see a warm place with a roof was Brennan that he didn't even think to question who the house might belong to, or whether they might be trespassing.

He would need to find out more before he could leave Chosen, Brennan had decided; he didn't know enough about this world to venture off on his own without at least knowing where he was and who he could trust—if indeed he could trust anyone. It would do no good just to run off into the waiting arms of more slavers. After all, for all he knew, the Dorans could themselves be a part of the slave trade that pervaded the south of Satorium. He debated asking Chosen, but decided that this would only betray his true intention. In the end, he just found a room and lay down on a bed, falling asleep almost instantly.

As he slept, Brennan dreamed of a young girl with red-gold hair and pale skin. She was being chased by something that Brennan could not see, hunted like game through a dense and dark forest. The girl was somehow very powerful, and yet she was afraid. She was lost and had nowhere to go; the hunter was closing in on her.

Brennan had never seen the girl before, but for reasons he couldn't explain, he felt a strong desire to protect her, to keep her safe. He tried first to catch up with her, tell her that he would help, but no matter how fast he ran, he couldn't close the gap between them. If he couldn't reach her, he decided, he would attack whatever was after her, so he turned, plunging headlong through the forest to intercept the hunter. With each step he took, however, the forest grew darker and denser until he could barely move through the brush. The trees began closing in on him, and now it was he who was afraid.

No matter where he turned, no matter how hard he struggled, Brennan couldn't move. He was overwhelmed by panic and dread. He tried calling out to the girl, but he had no voice. Then Brennan realized what he must do, and he reached deep within for the Tempest. He called to it, begged it to come to him. The warmth began to rise . . . and then it faded and was gone.

Brennan woke with a start, covered in cold, clammy sweat. The sun was filtering through the dusty windows of the small farmhouse onto his face. He rose, blinking in the light, and wondering how long Chosen had let him sleep. Normally they were up before dawn; Chosen liked to have been walking miles before the sun rose. He tried to remember the details of the dream, but found that the only thing he could recall with any clarity was the feeling of panic.

Brennan made his way to the farmhouse's parlor and found it empty. He checked the other bedrooms and found them empty as well. Chosen had ventured far ahead of Brennan while they were traveling, but he had never left him alone before. A shudder of fear ran through Brennan. Had the men from the woods followed them? Had they taken Chosen? No, it couldn't be. Those men were dead. Brennan had seen their lifeless eyes.

This could be his chance. Depending where Chosen was, Brennan could be miles away before Chosen even knew he was gone. Where would he go, though? Which direction?

The door opened, ending all of Brennan's thoughts of running. Chosen entered the house, carrying a bag that he promptly dumped on a table. An assortment of vegetables and roots tumbled out.

"Start boiling some water," he commanded. "We'll need full stomachs for the last leg to Caelesta."

Caelesta, Brennan remembered, was the capital city of the Doran Empire. More than any other place in his mother's tales, it was one he had always wanted to see. Its beauty was legendary, and Brennan's people had built the king's castle when the Tempest was still accessible.

"You were thinking of leaving," Chosen said flatly. Taken completely unawares, Brennan was unable to hide the surprise; the look on his face all but confessed that it was true.

"Yes, I was," he responded, deciding that at least being honest would count for something.

"That would be a mistake," said Chosen, sorting the vegetables in groups and then slicing them into bite-size chunks. "There is a war coming, sooner than I had hoped. We have little time left to find the girl, and I promise you that we do not want to be caught on this side of Caelesta when the fighting starts. Besides, I highly doubt that you will be able to make it through Caelesta's mountain pass without me."

Brennan looked away, his mind a tumult of thoughts. "What you did—back in the woods—that was dark magic?"

"Yes, it was. Do you have a problem with that? As I remember, it saved our lives."

"My mother always told me that the users of dark magic were . . ." Brennan's voice trailed away. His nerve was failing.

"Your mother was a sheltering, overprotective woman who had been so abused that she was afraid of her own shadow. I expect that most of what she told you is oversimplified rubbish," Chosen said coldly, turning back to his chopping.

Brennan felt a surge of anger. His mother had not been afraid of her shadow. She was brave and strong. How dare this twisted man speak of her like that? How dare he defile her memory? "Don't ever speak about my mother that way," he snapped.

Chosen stopped his work on the vegetables and looked up at Brennan. A wicked sneer curled his lips. He stared at Brennan for a long, uncomfortable minute.

"Have I struck a nerve, boy?" Chosen said scornfully. Brennan's arms flexed, and his hands bunched into fists. "You are going to need a thicker skin. Tell me, what did I say about your mother that you take issue with? What did I say that wasn't true?"

"My mother was not a coward. And she did not lie to me."

"And you do not listen. A trait that will get you into more trouble than most things. You are also an inexperienced boy who knows nothing of the world."

"You said she was afraid of—"

"Yes, *afraid*. That has nothing to do with being a coward. I said she was afraid of her own shadow because she feared too much, sheltered you too much. Left you unprepared. Her running away with you was an act of courage, nevertheless. She knew it would end in her death, and yet she did it anyway." The words were kind, yet there was no compassion in Chosen's voice, no attempt to soothe Brennan's mourning soul.

"What do you want with the girl?" Brennan asked suddenly.

"I have told you that it is my business. Yours will be to keep her alive. It's my price for your freedom."

"And what if I don't choose to pay that price?" Brennan quipped.

"Then you are without honor and useless to me anyway," Chosen answered dismissively.

With those words, Chosen had him; Brennan could feel resolution descending within him. If there were one thing his mother would have asked of him, it would have been to live an honorable life. When he walked out of that cell with Chosen, he had as good as given his word. Does your word count when it's given to a devil? Brennan didn't know.

The answer came to him as if he had known where it was all along, but never bothered to look for it. Chosen wanted him to protect some girl—for what, Brennan didn't know.

He couldn't possibly imagine what Chosen would want with her, or what dark plans he held in his twisted brain. It didn't matter. Brennan would stay until they found the girl, and then he would do exactly as Chosen had asked. He would protect her from anyone who would do her harm. Including Chosen.

14
Caelesta

By sunset the following day, Brennan and Chosen had reached the outer walls of Caelesta. Massive ramparts encircled the city, with only two breaches allowing passage through the towering walls of stone, the massive metalwork gates at the southern end of the city and, at the northern end, a tunnel, also protected by metal gates, that had been bored under the moat to provide one of the few passages through the mountain range on Leona's northern border. As mesmerizing as the walls of the city were, it was what rose inside those the walls that defied Brennan's wildest imaginings.

White towers loomed over the surrounding land, gathered in a spiral of progressively taller spears, and ending in a final spire that seemed to defy heaven itself.

Brennan stopped, his mouth hanging open and eyes wide. He had seen a few towns and settlements in his short life, and he had tried to imagine what a city would be like from his mother's stories, but nothing in his mind's eye had come close to such grandeur.

"I suppose even I was taken aback the first time I saw her," Chosen admitted in a rare moment of civility. He had walked back to Brennan's side. "It is a shame that the Dorans claim her as their own, when it was your people who built her."

"I can't imagine how anyone could have built such a castle," head tipped back to gaze up at it. "Surely it must have been magic of some kind."

"Of some kind, maybe. That depends on your definition of magic. Cunning, will, and the strength of the Tempest. If that is magic . . ." Chosen took a moment to admire the structure, although his admiration did not come from pleasure in its beauty but from respect for its technical prowess.

Brennan's enchantment with Caelesta did not diminish as they moved closer to the city. With every step the towers seemed to further defy possibility. A small crowd of Dorans joined Brennan and Chosen within a mile of the gates, and Brennan did not have to guess that many of them were the owners of the abandoned houses and fallow farms on the road to the capital. All carried themselves with a look of defeat, their clothing tattered and soiled, their skin sallow, and their bodies weak.

"What's happened here?" Brennan whispered to Chosen, who seemed to have barely noticed the Dorans around them.

"War is coming. They are here to seek shelter within the city." Chosen shook his head with disgust. "This is not good for us. It will be harder for us to get in if we are taken for refugees."

Brennan didn't understand why this would be the case. After all, if they were mistaken for Dorans, surely it would be easier to get into the city. He didn't ask Chosen, however. He didn't feel like being shot down again or made to feel like a child for not understanding.

In any case, when they finally arrived at the gates, it became clear what Chosen had meant.

The crowd thickened, a dense mass of people shoving and shouting, pressing toward the city, trying to move to the front of the pack. Armored guards stood above them on the walls to either side of the massive gate, while others blocked the entrance, checking everyone who wished to come inside.

"What do we do now?" Brennan asked.

"Quiet," Chosen snapped. "I have to find the captain of the guard."

Brennan followed closely behind Chosen as they wove their way through the crowd. A few of the more brazen men shot nasty looks at them, but turned away or even cowered when they looked up at Brennan or caught sight of Chosen and his cloak. When they finally reached the gate, Brennan saw a burly guard arguing with an equally brawny farmer.

"This is our city as much as yours," the farmer was shouting. "We have as much right to its protection as you do."

"You just crawl out from under a rock, peasant," the sergeant barked, his voice as gruff as his appearance. The soldier had scars down both cheeks, and his dark hair was cut nearly to the scalp, showing clearly another scar that ran the length of his head. "You got no right to protection. War's coming, and wars have a way of being 'specially harsh on the countryside. Farms and hamlets being abandoned left and right, all coming here. All wanting the same thing. How many you think can fit in one city?"

"Then the children. At least let the children in," the farmer pleaded.

"Oh, that would be smart, wouldn't it? Let a bunch of plebe halfwits into the city with no one to look after them," the sergeant scoffed. "What makes you think they'd be any safer in here? Think the walls of Caelesta will protect them, do ya? This is the first place the dark one's gonna come."

"I beg you," the farmer said, his eyes filling with tears.

"Enough," the sergeant barked, placing a booted foot against the farmer's stomach and shoving him away. The farmer tumbled into the crowd and was swallowed by more just like him, another taking his place at the front of the line.

"Sergeant," came a voice from behind the guard, who immediately snapped to attention.

A Doran nearly the size of Brennan was making his way through the crowd. Brennan knew enough to tell by the medals and gold on the Doran's uniform and by the reaction from the sergeant that he was a commander of some sort. This new soldier had a way about him that bespoke competence.

"Captain, sir," the sergeant acquiesced.

The captain grabbed the sergeant roughly by the collar and pulled him slightly away from the crowd, although Brennan could still hear them clearly.

"We do not abuse the people we are meant to serve, soldier. They are scared and hungry and are under the mistaken belief that we are here to protect them. Your actions are the closest many of them will ever get to associating with the king. You want them to believe that their king is an uncaring, abusive sovereign?" the captain said, his voice calm and direct.

"Of course not, sir," the sergeant said.

"Now pick that man up, apologize, and get these people into the city," the captain ordered. As he turned to leave, he stopped briefly as his eyes passed over Chosen. He turned back, and the blood seemed to drain from his face, which moments ago had been tanned and healthy.

"Do not let him pass," the captain said, motioning toward Chosen.

"And after all that talk about service and letting the people into the city," Chosen said, his voice strange and distant. It was not a tone or accent Brennan had heard him use before. "Who *are* you, soldier?"

"I'm Captain Matthias Caelesta," the captain answered. "Of the King's Army."

"Oh my," Chosen responded, feigning surprise. "A blood relative to the king. I *am* honored."

"That I am, and a sworn protector of Leona. I know what you are, and who you serve." Matthias's hand went to the hilt of his sword.

"You know no such thing," Chosen lilted, his voice hanging eerily in the air. "*What* I am is not of your concern. I am merely passing through." Chosen closed the gap between himself and Matthias. "I am tired of talking, and you have been rude and inhospitable, not something I've come to expect from the walls of Caelesta."

Brennan expected the large Doran to seize them both at any second. He steeled himself for the fight, choosing at that moment death over prison. What occurred next left him dumbfounded.

"Of course," said the captain, his eyes lowered, his head in a reverent semi-bow. "I'm sorry for my rudeness. Please," he added, waving Chosen and Brennan through the gate.

"Please—forget it," Chosen said. To everyone around them this might have sounded enigmatic, but Brennan sensed something more meaningful in the simple statement—a feeling confirmed by the sudden blankness of the captain's face.

Chosen took Brennan by the arm, his grip ice-cold. Brennan allowed himself to be led through the gates, waiting for the guards to be out of sight before he spoke.

"What just happened?" Brennan asked.

"Not now. We need to get to the north end of the city and out of here," Chosen said, rushing them through the streets.

"That makes no sense. All that to get in here, just to leave?" Brennan stopped suddenly, causing Chosen to be yanked backward.

Chosen whipped his head around, glaring at Brennan. "You will move, now," he commanded.

Brennan felt a strange tug in the depth of his muscles. He felt compelled to move, to follow. It became for a moment the most urgent thought in his head. Panic began to consume him, sweat running down his brow and chest, chilling him to the bone. He had to follow, lest something horrible happen to him, or even the whole world. Then, from the center of his chest, he felt the warm sensation of the Tempest, and it was as if power itself was contained within him. The panic was gone as quickly as it had come over him, passing with the simple thought that it was not real. He met Chosen's gaze, seeing a twitch of fear in his eyes.

"Explain what is going on," he said, feeling the warmth spread farther throughout his body, radiating out from the center. With a violent jerk, he shook off Chosen's grip.

"You are full of surprises," Chosen said coldly, rubbing his hand and trying to regain his composure. "I don't owe you an explanation. I saved your life. How soon we forget."

"I haven't forgotten anything." Brennan felt the warmth leaving him. "But owing you my life doesn't mean following blindly."

Chosen smiled nervously. "We cannot be here. That captain wasn't as easy to fool as he pretended. He's got a hint that something is wrong, and he'll put it together soon."

"How do you know that?" Brennan asked.

"Because I do. If the Doran Army finds me with enough men, I won't be able to stop them without a great deal of killing. Is that what you want? Now hurry. There isn't time for this." Chosen grabbed Brennan's arm again and started pulling him through the street once more.

Caelesta was large, nearly two miles from the southern to the northern end. With so many Dorans on the streets, it took Chosen and Brennan half an hour before they finally reached the northern wall. Unlike the southern entrance, there was no crowd gathered.

Chosen walked straight up to one of the guards standing post at the sealed metal gates. "We wish to pass through," he barked.

The soldier looked at him in disbelief, and then at his fellow soldiers, who were chuckling behind him. "Good for you, but the gates are to remain sealed."

"Open them," Chosen said, again in the lilting voice.

The soldier seemed to struggle for a moment, but then he turned, pulled the crossbeam from the metal gates, and pushed them open. Chosen hurried Brennan into the passage. Just before the great metal gates fell together with a clash of metal, shutting them off from Caelesta, Brennan heard the alarm being raised inside the city.

15

Final Lessons

Despite the setback with Lindi, Scarlet's progress had been remarkable. Delfi—who made sure that Lindi kept her distance, allowing Scarlet to concentrate fully on magic—was quickly becoming a good friend, as the only Tounder her age who could talk to her without acting like she was a celebrity. In fact, he was really her only friend. Dakota was now more like a mentor or second father than the buddy he had been at home; Cricket seemed too overwhelmed by the newness of it all to confide in; and

Scarlet's family was caught up in trying to fit into their new life among the Tounder.

Like Dakota, Delfi also told Scarlet the truth. Not that anyone else had been lying to her, but he didn't hold back like the rest of them did. Nor was he an authority figure like Dakota, and she appreciated this above all else. It also didn't hurt that he was cute, funny, and easy to talk to.

It was Delfi who finally told her the story of how there came to be two worlds.

They had met in the tower overlooking Illuminora, and he had mentioned that only one other being had possessed the full powers of magic. "Until you and the prince, that is."

Scarlet looked at him intently, her curiosity piqued. Dakota had mentioned something about another, but he had not elaborated. "Who?" she asked.

"It was a long, long time ago," Delfi replied. "Not sure how much is true and what is just stories."

"Tell me anyway," Scarlet pleaded.

"Well, a long time ago there was a great wizard named Hulpric. And during Hulpric's time there was only one world, and it was inhabited mostly by Dorans, aside from the animals, of course." Delfi smirked. "Anyway, Hulpric was a wanderer at heart, and he traveled all over the world. What he noticed on his travels was that some Dorans had the ability to do magic, while others did not. He also noticed that the ones without magical abilities all came from the same families, and their children and their children's children all were born without any ability to do magic. Because of this, these families were treated poorly, and in some parts of the world they were enslaved. In some versions of the story, they were even hunted and killed by magical Dorans.

"Hulpric's heart went out to them, and he tried to protect them and speak for them whenever he saw these injustices, but he couldn't be everywhere at once. While he was protecting nonmagical Dorans in one part of the world, others were being mistreated in another part. Hulpric also saw what most Dorans did not—that the nonmagical Dorans had gifts of their own, powerful imaginations that helped them invent things and build.

"Anyway, one day he returned from his travels in one part of the world to find that an entire community of nonmagical Dorans had been killed because they had rebelled after being forced into slavery. Hulpric's heart was broken in two—and so, in order to protect the nonmagical Dorans, he did to the world what had been done to his heart. He broke it in two, sending all the nonmagical Dorans to one half, and leaving all magic in the other. He died of his broken heart, knowing that the two worlds could never be one again.

"But Hulpric left Satorium with a warning, a prophecy. It said that one day a Doran would develop powers like his, would try and bring the two worlds back together for his own evil gains, and would meet his match in the form of a woman born from the nonmagical world. Meant to be ironic, I guess," Delfi ended abruptly.

"That's quite a story," Scarlet said, smiling at Delfi. "Do you think it's true?"

"I don't know. I used to think it was just a legend."

"And now?" Scarlet asked.

"Well . . . here you are, right?"

Scarlet looked out at Illuminora, lost in thought. "Here I am," she said wistfully.

The day of her final lesson with Xavier came, and Scarlet entered the library, feeling nervous and apprehensive. She wasn't entirely sure why. It wasn't her first time learning something utterly bewildering and unfamiliar, and yet she was more nervous now than she had been on the first day she walked into the beautiful room.

All of the chairs and tables had been removed from the library, leaving a large empty space in the center of the room. Xavier stood alone in the center, looking graver than Scarlet had ever seen him.

"Please come in, my dear," Xavier said, his voice quite solemn.

Scarlet went to him, her nerves crying out with every step. "What's wrong?" she asked, summoning her courage. "I have been practicing very hard. If you don't think I'm ready—"

Xavier held up a hand to interrupt her. "Not at all. Not at all. You have exceeded my every expectation. It is time,

I'm afraid, that is moving a little too fast." Xavier turned and walked toward the fireplace. He motioned for Scarlet to follow, and she joined him.

"I heard about the incident with Lindi."

"Oh . . . you did," Scarlet fumbled.

"Yes, I'm afraid so. That is partly my fault. I was too preoccupied to notice her ill intentions. I purposely saved this lesson for last, and for Lindi's sake, I confess I'm glad I did."

"What lesson is this?" Scarlet asked.

"You could call it many things—but fighting would probably be the most appropriate. Attacking and defending using your abilities, which are considerable, and probably a little overwhelming at this point. This will be one of your only disadvantages," Xavier said, staring off into the fire as he did so, weariness evident in his features.

"Why does Lindi hate me?"

"Hate is a strong word, Scarlet."

Scarlet rubbed her chest. "It didn't feel like too strong a word."

"No, I guess it didn't. Lindi has her reasons, misguided though they are. Unfortunately, we don't have the time to go into what those reasons might be, as we have to begin our lesson. Our time together is running short, I'm afraid." Xavier turned away from the fire and looked gravely at Scarlet.

Scarlet started to ask why, but she stopped herself. She didn't want her time to run short. She felt safe and happy in Illuminora. At the same time, she had known from the beginning of her lessons that it had all been for a purpose.

Although it was easy to forget and look at everything she had experienced as just some wonderful dream come true, she knew that a nightmare lay somewhere ahead, and that her only choice would be to face it. Difficult as it was for her to believe, there was little doubt that she was the For Tol Don. Every story she had heard from a Tounder on the subject, all the experiences she had had, the Mortada who'd tried to kill her, and especially the aptitude with which she could learn magic, all pointed to the fact that she was Hulpric's prophesied hero.

Scarlet looked up expectantly at Xavier, her face telling him that she was ready to move on with the lesson.

"When you fight another user of magic, it is most important to keep your wits about you, Scarlet," Xavier began. "You have to think fast and react even quicker. A battle between sorcerers is a battle of imaginations. One throws some manifestation of magic at the other; the other counters with something else; and this continues until one is able to gain the upper hand. They constantly take in the world around them, searching for things to use against their opponent. There are no hard and fast rules to what curse, enchantment, or power will defeat or protect you from any given attack. There are so many factors—the power of the sorcerer, the knowledge you have amassed, your natural and learned talent, how well you conserve your energy . . . Each is vitally important.

"With time and practice you will grow stronger and more powerful, but for now, it will be important to end any battle quickly and decisively." Xavier looked at Scarlet with an intensity in his eyes she had never seen before. Despite her resolve, she felt scared and more than a bit confused.

"Maybe it would be best just to give it a try," he said, giving her his most reassuring smile.

"You mean, fight *you*?"

"I might be old, my dear, but I can assure you that I still have a trick or two up my sleeve." Xavier laughed.

"That's not what I meant," Scarlet protested.

"I know what you meant. I promise you will be perfectly safe." Xavier reached out and put two firm hands on her shoulders. "Do your best. It will be more than enough."

The two Keepers of Light walked to the center of the room and faced one another. Xavier gave a curt bow to Scarlet, who awkwardly returned the gesture. Then, after a wink and a small pause, Xavier sent a flash of light at Scarlet that began somewhat like the flash of a camera before taking the form of a hawk. Like an inverted shadow puppet, the hawk descended upon Scarlet, its beak gaping in a silent shriek.

For an instant Scarlet was frozen to her spot, watching as a hawk, born only of light yet as solid as any real bird, bared its talons and began a dive toward her. Her mind was racing. *A hawk. How do you stop a hawk?* At the last moment she fell to her knees and sent out her own animal into the room: a rabbit.

The little creature scampered forth, darting left and right, desperately searching for danger. The hawk, catching sight of this new, easier prey, banked away from Scarlet and made for the rabbit. All Scarlet could think of now was that she had to distract Xavier before he could regain control of the bird or send something else after her. As her eyes darted around the room, her mind desperately grasping for answers, one thing began to dominate her vision and mind. Books. They were everywhere. Thousands of them.

She sent out the light within her, not to one book, but to all of them. Thousands of volumes, each as bright as she could imagine. Scarlet filled the entire library with a flurry of blindingly glowing tomes, flying out from their shelves. The library was in utter chaos as the books collided and ricocheted off walls and each other. Scarlet was struggling with what to do with them when she felt the books being pulled out of her control.

The books began to spiral together into a cyclone, moving with such velocity that to Scarlet's eyes they had become one solid cone of light. The only way she could still tell that they were moving was by the horrific rush of wind that nearly lifted her off her feet. The act of illuminating the books had drained her. She felt weak and tired. The cyclone was coming nearer; in moments it would engulf her. She had to do something—now.

With all the strength she had left, she reached out for the glowing cyclone of books. Xavier was too powerful for her to take control of it completely, but if she could just manage—

She opened the books, every one of them, all at once. Like miniature sails, they caught the air, slowing before sailing out of the cyclone and into the far wall. Scarlet collapsed to her knees. She was spent. It felt as if she had been awake for days, as if she hadn't sat down in a week. Her legs quivered beneath her, feeling as if they belonged to someone else.

Xavier did not attack again. With a wave of his hand he sent the illuminated books back to their shelves and extinguished their light. He knelt down beside Scarlet, and she noticed that he too looked ragged and beat. There were dark circles under his eyes, and his skin looked sallow.

"You are remarkable," he said in a raspy voice.

"I feel like I'm going to faint. I'm so tired," Scarlet managed, her eyes beginning to close. "You could have won. I couldn't do anything to stop you right now."

"I've also been doing this for ages, my dear. You've been at it for mere weeks," Xavier said, smiling.

Scarlet slept all that night and most of the next day. When she finally woke, she didn't feel any lasting effects from her duel with Xavier. A small vindictive part of her wanted to go and find Lindi and see just how keen the Tounder girl would be to attack her now, but she knew that wouldn't be the right thing to do, and it would certainly disappoint Xavier. Instead she went to find Delfi, suddenly filled with a need to tell him all about her lesson. She thought about telling her dad first, but he wouldn't understand the way Delfi would. After all, Delfi had learned this stuff himself.

She found Delfi in the grand dining room, seated with several other young Tounder, including a pretty brunette who was hanging on his every word. Scarlet felt an instant dislike for the dark-haired Tounder before realizing that it made no sense. She'd never even met the girl. Surely she wasn't jealous. That was silly.

Scarlet sat down at the table and was greeted so warmly by everyone that she instantly felt foolish for her earlier thoughts. Within minutes she was laughing and sharing in their conversation, and it was almost like being back at the lunch table at school; for a moment she was able to forget about prophecies or wars. After a while the other Tounder got up, leaving Delfi and Scarlet alone.

Scarlet, having waited to tell him about her lesson until she could speak to him one-on-one, immediately burst out with a flurry of excitement.

"It was amazing," she exclaimed. "You wouldn't believe how powerful Xavier is!"

Delfi laughed. "Oh, I think I have a good idea."

Scarlet told him all about the books and the hawk, thinking to herself that she was not at all doing justice to how exciting it was, even though Delfi could easily tell by the tone of her voice.

"You must be exhausted," Delfi said slyly, once she had finished her story.

"Not really. I've been asleep till now," said Scarlet.

"Not from your duel with Xavier. I expect it must take a lot of energy to talk that long without breathing," Delfi teased.

Scarlet smiled good-naturedly and gave him a playful punch on the arm. They both laughed.

"What would you like to do today?" Delfi asked. "I don't have any chores, and I'm officially off probation. I have the whole day."

"Well, I thought we'd . . . " Scarlet's voice trailed off, her attention drawn by the approach of her father. The look on his face was enough to make her blood run cold.

"Scarlet," he said grimly. "We have to meet with Xavier."

"Why? What's wrong, Dad? Something's wrong. Is it Mom? Melody?" There was a frantic quality to her voice.

"It's nothing like that. Let's go," her dad said. "You can come too, I expect." He gave Delfi a weak smile. "She'll just tell you later anyway."

Scarlet and Delfi followed her dad to Xavier's study, which was on the second floor of the castle in the opposite wing from the library. What resembled a conference table was in the center of the large room, and seated around it were about a dozen older Tounder, some of whom Scarlet recognized as the council members who had stayed after the feast on her second day in Illuminora, though a few she had never seen before. Dakota was also there, sitting proudly in the corner of the room.

The group of Tounder all stood when Scarlet entered the room, and Xavier motioned her and her father toward two empty seats. Their arrival had apparently interrupted a heated discussion. Delfi remained standing near the entrance to the study, looking uncomfortable and out of place.

The group of Tounder seated around the table turned out to be the entire governing council of Illuminora, all older than the majority of the Tounder Scarlet had gotten used to seeing around the village.

"The king has sent word. The prince's army will begin its march on Caelesta any day now, and the city itself is falling from within." Xavier's voice was immediately drowned out by shocked cries and urgent whispers from the council. "Be still," he commanded. The crowd slowly quieted.

"This is not the time for panic. We knew this day would come," Xavier said sternly. He sat back in his chair, gathering himself. He looked as if he bore the weight of the world.

"What are we going to do, Xavier?" one of the Tounder called out, his cry met with a stirring from the crowd. "We have no army to meet him. His army will march unabated to the Doran king, and then all will be lost. The prince will be free."

"How quickly your hope has faded, Thaniel," Xavier answered. He did not hide his disappointment as he looked at the man. "I would have expected more from a senior member of this council." Thaniel bowed his head, no longer able to meet Xavier's gaze.

"I expect more of all of you. Fear is one thing, a loss of hope unforgivable. We have the For Tol Don. His attempts to attack her have failed, as have his attempts to find her."

"She is a child!" called out another.

"As were we all. We have the counsel of her mother and father. We have the great Lord of Wolves," Xavier boasted, not unaware of Dakota, who cringed at the mention of this title. "All is not lost. We have many trials ahead, but our history is full of great challenges that we have faced, weathered, and triumphed over."

"But Xavier, with all due respect, nothing in our history is anything like what we face in Prince Thanerbos. He has been able to achieve much more than we thought, much sooner than we thought possible." The Tounder who now spoke looked as if he might have been as old as Xavier. "I am one of few in Illuminora," he continued, "who have witnessed war. In war, it is those who control the information, whose information is sound, that win. The prince has been a step ahead of us at every turn. We barely got to young Lady Scarlet in time. He has managed in fourteen years to do what we thought would take thirty. I would never advise despair, but realism is perhaps in order."

Xavier gave the man a weak but genuine smile. "Brynn, my old friend. . . . I respect your counsel more than most, and I agree that times are dark. Very dark. I promise you all that I am not naive enough to believe that the road is easy. I assure you that I have not failed to take into account the dire urgency of our situation, or our weaknesses and strengths. I've spoken with the king, and we have a plan that I believe can succeed."

The council was silent, waiting for a miracle they dared not truly believe in, yet hoped for in spite of themselves. The next words from Xavier brought that glimmer of hope crashing to the ground.

"We will send a party to the dragon Morelpis. We will ask for his aid." With these words Xavier again lost control of the council. They erupted in a fury of cries and disgruntled wails. A few were so overwhelmed with despair that they laid their heads down and wept. Several others, overcome by anger, stood, banging clenched fists on the table and turning the anger toward each other.

"Please listen!" Xavier implored, but it was no use. He looked at Scarlet with shamed eyes. She needed strength and reassurance, not an angry, divided mob.

Scarlet, rather than feeling abandoned, felt only sympathy. With Xavier pleading to gain control, Scarlet stood, calmly facing the crowd. Compelled to do something, as much for Xavier as for the wavering hearts of the Tounder, she opened her right hand, and with her left she drew a single point of light between her finger and thumb. With a quick movement of her wrist, she tossed the light onto the table. She then held her hands in the form of two cups, closed at first and then slowly opening. As her fingers extended, so did the light, growing in size and brightness until it filled the room with a blinding radiance. The council members shielded their eyes, cowering in their seats, silent now in the presence of the light. Scarlet lowered her hands, and the light vanished.

Every eye was now fixed on Scarlet.

"Thank you, Scarlet," Xavier said, trying to sound calm, although his voice had a quiver to it.

He took a moment to compose himself. "We will send a party to Morelpis and ask for his aid," he said again.

Brynn was the only Tounder to speak, his demeanor calm and reserved. "Xavier, no creature has seen or heard from the dragon since the death of his daughter. You know the history of his vow."

"I do," Xavier answered. "And old wounds are sometimes hard to heal, but we must try."

"If you can find someone crazy enough to take such a quest. We can't possibly be hanging all of our hopes on the dragon. We don't even know if he still lives," Thaniel managed to croak out very quickly.

"*I* will go and speak to him," Xavier said.

Several of the council spoke at once.

"No, impossible."

"You can't possibly leave."

"Not now."

Xavier put up a hand to stop the cries. "We are safe here for now, but only if Prince Thanerbos's army is stopped from passing through Caelesta. I will be of little help to you if the defenses fail. Morelpis will recognize me, and he might take anyone else as an insult.

"If Morelpis agrees, the king wishes for him to block the mountain pass. That will give the king a safe haven to evacuate the city to, if need be. Give them a safe place to retreat. With Morelpis guarding the mountain, we also gain the advantage of time. Not even Prince Thanerbos's army would be able to get past Morelpis."

"Time for what?" Thaniel dared to ask.

"For Scarlet to finish her quest," Xavier said hopefully.

"These are lofty thoughts, Xavier. Lofty indeed," said Brynn.

There followed a long silence while the weight of the coming turmoil sank in fully for the crowd. Finally Xavier spoke again.

"Tomorrow Scarlet, Udd Lyall, and Mr. Hopewell will set off to complete her training."

"Is that going to be enough? Just three?" Thaniel asked.

"The prince knows that eventually she must leave the sanctuary of Illuminora to face him. The Mortada are combing the country for her, and they will expect a large group of us to protect her. If it weren't for her youth, I might even argue for just her and Udd Lyall to go."

"Where will they go?" Thaniel asked.

Xavier frowned at him, his eyes darting briefly to Dakota. "Even I will not be asking that question."

The council dispersed, and Scarlet immediately ran to Xavier, catching him before he could leave. He looked down at her with sad eyes that might have even held a touch of guilt, or at least regret.

"You aren't going to teach me more?" Scarlet pleaded. She had been putting on a show of being strong and confident in front of the council, but with only Xavier, Dakota, and her father there to hear her, she felt no need to posture now.

Xavier's expression changed to one of compassion. "I wish you could stay here with me for a lifetime, and I would gladly teach you everything I know. I care deeply for you, young lady. But I have helped you awaken the light inside you. Teaching you to wield that power as I would is not what will win the battle against Thanerbos. If that were true, then I would keep you safe under the great oak, and I would face him myself." Xavier paused, and then reached out and lightly touched her face. "It is you who will win this battle. Those you meet along your journey will help you to awaken all the magic there is time for, and then you will find the way to use that magic as Scarlet would. As the For Tol Don. Not a silly old Tounder."

"You aren't silly," Scarlet protested.

"When there is no more war to fight, you'll see that I am quite silly indeed." Xavier smiled warmly. "I have to go and get some things in order. We will speak again before you go."

Scarlet watched as Xavier left the room. Even though Dakota and her father were still in the room, she felt remarkably alone.

16

The Northern Woodlands

Brennan slept uneasily, his dreams filled with cries and screams. They'd come to the city through rolling hills and fertile farmland, and left it in the semidarkness of a long, damp tunnel. They'd passed under the moat and through the mountain pass, emerging a day later in a completely new world. The tunnel opened into a forest of majestic oaks and spruce, maples and redwoods. It was very different from the Southern Wildlands, which had been wild and untamed, filled with an overwhelming sense of danger and chaos. The Northern Woodlands exuded an air of peace, of order and comfort. Its denizens were almost all small mammals, gathering nuts and berries in the serene leafy shade and dappled sunlight.

And yet his dreams did not change. When Brennan slept, his mind was filled with images of Caelesta under siege, horrible things happening to the women and children who had hoped that the city's great walls would protect them. And always, in the center of it all, the redheaded girl . . . He woke drenched in cold sweat, striking out against some unknown force.

He had little time for waking reflection. Driven by his determination to reach the girl, Chosen insisted they wake before dawn and be on the road moments later, often not stopping to eat. Occasionally he would suddenly change direction, going east instead of west or doubling back. Often Brennan could sense the passing Mortada that Chosen had barely avoided with these maneuvers.

"They are searching hard now," Chosen offered in a rare forthcoming moment.

"Who are?" Brennan asked, not expecting any response. By now he didn't really care whether Chosen answered his questions; perhaps childishly, he found a little enjoyment in the thought that they were at least an annoyance.

"The Mortada. Like the men by the river. Apparently they have fixated on Illuminora as her hiding place." Chosen had stopped momentarily, scanning the forest for the path he'd take next.

To Brennan, the forest all looked the same. It was beautiful and peaceful, but nothing distinguished one area from another.

It occurred to Brennan that if Chosen hadn't been acting as a guide, he could easily find himself lost within these lush green woods for the rest of his life. Most of the time Brennan couldn't even tell which way they were headed.

"Isn't that where we're going—where you think she is?" Brennan asked timidly.

"That is surely where she is," Chosen snapped. "And if the idiots keep trudging around the forest in such numbers, that is where she is likely to remain for some time." His annoyance was palpable, and mixed with an anxiety that Brennan had never seen in him before. With few exceptions, Chosen had always seemed self-assured to the point of arrogance.

Brennan couldn't help but struggle over the disparity between Chosen's motives and his character. Chosen was clearly connected somehow to these Mortada. In fact, Brennan was almost sure that he was one of them. He certainly knew a lot about them, and he looked remarkably similar. And yet . . . he seemed to speak of them with such disdain. Little about Chosen fit neatly into any single formula, but it was his connection to a group that was clearly evil that worried Brennan the most.

"If you mean her no harm, why can't we just go and see her in Illuminora?" Brennan asked, feigning ignorance. One way or another, he would make Chosen admit that his intentions were not virtuous.

Chosen's head snapped around, and he gave Brennan a look of mixed anger and disbelief. "Don't test me with ignorant questions, Brennan."

"I thought it was a pretty simple, intelligent question, actually," Brennan snipped back.

"Simple, yes. Simpleminded. Nobody gets into Illuminora without being invited, and I'm not likely to receive an invitation. We'll leave it at that." Chosen selected a direction and took off at a run.

From a rise in the woods, Brennan could just make out the clearing below. At the center of it grew the largest tree he could ever have dreamed of, towering nearly fifty feet above the rest of the forest and covered in shimmering silver and golden leaves that seemed to gather into themselves all the light of the day. At the forest's edge around the clearing, Brennan could also make out the shadowy figures of Mortada, shifting about restlessly, searching either for a way into the clearing or for anyone trying to leave.

"What now?" Brennan asked.

"We wait," Chosen hissed back.

"If she leaves the tree, won't the Mortada get her?" Brennan asked, genuine concern in his voice.

"The leader of the Tounder will not be unaware of the Mortada's presence, I can assure you," Chosen said, dismissively.

"The Tounder . . . I thought they were a myth," Brennan said.

"No, they're not a myth."

They watched in silence until the sun began to set beneath the tree line. Small fires began to flicker in the forest, giving away the positions of the many groups of Mortada.

"Get some sleep," Chosen said, after the sun had completely disappeared. "I'll take the first watch. Nothing is going to happen tonight."

"And what about in the morning? What are we going to do if we can't get into Illuminora to help her?" Brennan asked, suddenly frustrated by the standstill, now that they were so close to their goal.

"The morning will take care of itself," Chosen said, taking out the root from his pocket and biting off a piece, chewing on it methodically as he continued to stare down at the clearing.

17

The Lightning Trip

Even though Scarlet woke feeling rested, it seemed as if she had just lay down when her mother shook her gently awake.

"Scarlet, sweetheart. It's time," she said softly.

Scarlet opened her eyes to find her mother sitting on the edge of her bed, tears unmistakable in her light blue eyes. Scarlet wanted to say something reassuring to her, something that would ease the worry and fear they both felt, but she couldn't think of anything satisfactory. She settled on "I love you," and threw her arms around her mother's neck.

Her mother held her tightly, rocking her gently as they both let tears fall freely. It felt good to let go. Safe, if only for a moment, in her mother's arms. So much of Scarlet's life was now unknown territory, filled with danger and uncertainty.

They met her father, Melody, and Cricket downstairs in the dining hall. When she saw her sister, Melody jumped from the table and ran to give Scarlet a hug. Her swollen eyes gave away the fact that she too had been crying.

"It's not good-bye," Scarlet said, trying to sound as reassuring as possible. "I'll be back before you know it."

"I know. That's what Cricket said. I'll be okay," Melody chirped, giving Scarlet a smile so big that she felt a lump rise in her throat.

"You are a brave girl, that's for sure," Scarlet added, giving Melody a tighter squeeze.

Everyone tried to act as normal as possible at breakfast, and for the most part they did a pretty good job. They talked about things that had nothing to do with Scarlet's coming quest, and even managed to laugh a little. Their time together ended quickly, though, and soon they were all seated in Xavier's study, going over the final preparations for departure.

Scarlet's dress was exchanged for leggings, boots, a blouse, and a traveling cloak. Looking at herself in a mirror, she had to smile. She looked like some hero from Tolkien or a King Arthur tale. Her father had changed as well. He looked wilder somehow, a thick shadow growing on his face and a desperate look in his eyes. His clothes had been exchanged for an outfit that Xavier said had been the garb of ancient Tounder warriors. It was strange to see him dressed that way, although to Scarlet, through childhood eyes, he looked dashing. His pants were made from beetle leather, and he wore boots lined in fur. His shirt, like Scarlet's entire set of clothes, was spun from spiders' silk and was certainly shinier than anything Scarlet had ever seen her father wear. According to Xavier, spiders' silk was stronger than steel, and though the clothes were light and comfortable, they could protect the wearer from knives, swords, and even, Xavier suspected, a bullet, although he admittedly had never seen one.

Charles grunted as he hefted the large pack of supplies several Tounder had just lugged into the study onto his back.

"Sorry there isn't much I can do about the weight," Xavier said. "Some things are the same whether you have magic or not—packing for a trip being one them."

Despite his conflicting emotions, Charles smiled. He was going to miss chatting with the old Tounder. "Where is Dakota?" he asked, noticing for the first time that the big dog was missing.

"He's looking for the best route out of the clearing. The woods, I'm afraid, are filled with Mortada," Xavier responded, though his face betrayed no real concern.

"Mortada!" Charles exclaimed. "We're surrounded by them?"

"Yes, but I wouldn't worry." Xavier walked over to a large chest in the corner of the study. "This is actually advantageous to us."

"How is that, exactly?" Charles said, failing to keep a sarcastic edge out of his voice.

"We're going to slip you past them, and as long as they still think you're in Illuminora, they'll remain watching over the oak while you—"

"Get a head start?"

"Exactly." Xavier smiled. "Now, I have a few more gifts for your journey." He pulled two items from the chest, each wrapped in a soft white cloth, and handed one to Scarlet and the second to Charles.

Scarlet and her father looked at each other quizzically, and then, with a shrug, Charles removed the cloth. A gilded sword, its hilt inlaid with silver in an elaborately interlaced design, glittered under the lights in the study. He pulled the blade from the scabbard, revealing metal polished to such a shine that its dazzle hurt his eyes.

"It's so beautiful!" Scarlet exclaimed.

"You realize, of course, that I have no idea how to use a sword . . ."

"When the time comes, you'll find a use for it, I'm sure. Besides, from what I understand, the premise is rather simple," Xavier said, with a little wink at Scarlet. "Sharp along the edges, pointy at the end."

Curiosity had now gotten the better of Scarlet, and she too unwrapped her package. Instead of a single item, as she had originally thought, there were several, and an odd assortment of items they were. The largest was a beautifully carved wooden staff, silken to the touch, with a small crystal shaped like an acorn wedged into a carved slot at one end. The crystal gleamed as Scarlet turned it in the light, shining a green very much like that of her eyes.

"That staff was carved from the wood of the great oak," Xavier said proudly. "A very rare and mysterious treasure. It is not often that the oak gives up her wood."

Scarlet thanked him and picked up the next item, a green satin bag about the size a child would keep marbles in, with a drawstring gathered at the top. Scarlet opened the bag and peered inside. It looked to be filled with grass seed. She looked up at Xavier, but he didn't offer any explanation. The next item was a curiously shaped stone, weightless as a piece of paper and attached to a coiled bit of leather cord. Scarlet placed it on the cloth and picked up what looked liked a black rock.

"That's flint," her father said, recognizing the familiar stone.

Finally Scarlet came to the last item, a pretty bracelet of simple interlinked white and yellow gold hoops. Scarlet placed the bracelet on her wrist, gathered up the flint, stone, and seeds, and gave them to her father to stow in his pack.

Dakota met them at the tunnel that led out of Illuminora and up to the trunk of the great oak tree. He nodded to Scarlet and her father before turning to Xavier.

"Can you maintain our current size beyond the clearing?" Dakota asked, his eyes flashing.

Xavier looked concerned. "How far beyond the clearing do you need?"

"Ideally—a mile," Dakota answered.

"I'm sorry," Xavier said. "I can possibly manage a few yards beyond, maybe a little bit more—but not much. That power is from the tree, it's not my own."

"That will have to do," Dakota said, his mind turning over rapidly. "I have a distraction in mind, but we are going to have to be moving when we break through the clearing." He looked at Scarlet and her father. "You up for that?"

"Guess we don't have much choice," Mr. Hopewell admitted. He looked to Scarlet, who managed a smile.

"Let's get a move on," Dakota said.

As they exited the castle, Scarlet caught sight of Delfi, standing sheepishly by the entrance. She waved to Dakota to give her a minute and ran over to him. Without even waiting for a word, she threw her arms around his neck.

"I going to miss you so much," she cried.

"I tried to make them let me go with you," Delfi said with deep regret in his voice. There was a touch of anger as well.

"I wish you could. It would be so much better if you could," Scarlet said, breaking her embrace with Delfi and looking up at him, tears in her eyes.

"Xavier said I was too young, and my parents were even less keen on the idea."

"But you're a year older than me!" Scarlet protested.

"I know . . . I said that. Xavier said if he had a choice in all this, you wouldn't be leaving either. Said it was the worst thing he's ever had to do, whatever that means," Delfi said.

"I'll come back, though. I promise I will," Scarlet said, her voice breaking. She hoped with all her heart that it was true, but she couldn't really know. She had absolutely no idea what was out there waiting for her.

"Take care of yourself, so you do," Delfi said, and gave her another hug.

The rest of the walk up the stone steps was solemn and quiet. No one seemed to have anything to say until it came time to move from the safety of Illuminora. The Hopewells embraced in tearful silence. Scarlet held on to her mother for a long time, feeling the weight of the coming separation and all that it meant.

When they finally parted, Mrs. Hopewell bent down to speak to Dakota. She reached out and placed a timid hand behind his ears and smoothed his rough fur. "I used to feel like my life was so in control. Now it feels so out of control, I don't know how to think about it anymore. Not to mention that I haven't even come close to understanding all that's happened."

"I can appreciate that, Mrs. Hopewell," Dakota admitted.

"I used to tell Charles that it made me feel so safe to have a big German shepherd in the house, to scare off burglars or . . . or . . ." Tears began to fall openly down Mrs. Hopewell's cheeks, and it took her a moment to regain her composure. "You keep my baby safe," she managed.

Dakota looked up at her with his piercing blue eyes. "Mrs. Hopewell, as long as I have breath, I will bring her home to you."

Breaking down completely, she threw her arms around Dakota's thick neck. Dakota stood stoically while she sobbed against him, although his eyes glistened a little more than usual. Finally she broke her embrace and went to her husband, sharing a few intimate words.

"Mr. Hopewell," Dakota announced after they had all said their good-byes. "I'll lead the charge out. Stay close to me, and I'll try to run at a human-friendly speed. The key moment is going to come when we begin to change. It's going to be a little alarming. We can't stop running though. It's very important that we keep moving."

Dakota looked out from the oak tree at the forest beyond, his eyes filled with both concern and apprehension. "At the half-mile mark, the Stidolph will attack the Mortada. It's going to be violent. You have to stay strong, Scarlet. We can't stop and help, no matter what. We have to break free. Do you understand me?"

"Yes," Scarlet said, her voice wavering.

"There'll be a time for you to fight," Dakota said, trying to sound reassuring. "Just not yet. We have a lot of work to do first."

Scarlet was scared, and her fear was clear in her eyes, which now were brimming with tears. She was leaving her mother and sister, and outside of Illuminora, where she had felt safe and wonderful, the world seemed poised to kill her, if it could. The Mortada, the evil figures who had broken into her house, who had caused her family to flee their home, were waiting outside the tree.

Then it was time. Her thoughts, her apprehension, would have to wait. Dakota took off, running a bit faster than Scarlet would have thought of as human speed. She could hear her father's footsteps pounding behind her, and although it seemed as though they had been running only a short distance, she could already feel a stitch forming in her side.

Through the haze of fear and the pain of her burning lungs, a thought occurred to Scarlet that sent a wave of panic through her. She had been thinking of the clearing in reference to when she had arrived. Then it had seemed such a short distance, but now they were no more than six inches tall. The clearing would be a great distance to someone that small. Every inch was like a foot, every foot several yards. There was no way she would be able to keep up this pace for that long.

Suddenly she felt a strange, uncomfortable sensation, and she could hear Dakota yelling at her to keep running. She felt as if every bone and muscle in her body was being stretched to its limits. The grass and weeds that moments ago had been taller than her began to shrink, first to just below her head, then to her waist. Scarlet willed her feet to continue moving forward, trying her best to focus only on Dakota bounding ahead of her.

Within a minute, the grass was being crumpled underfoot instead of waded through, and the world around her had become instantly more familiar. She had been in Illuminora so long that she had forgotten how strange it was to be shrunk. The stitch in her side began to fade, and the terrain whirled past as they dodged trees and leaped over underbrush.

Moments later the first Mortada caught sight of them, and with a call to his companions, he set off in pursuit. He was fast. Impossibly fast. Though they'd been taken by surprise, the Mortada had already closed the distance between himself and Scarlet's father to only ten feet. She dared a look over her shoulder and instantly regretted her decision. She was overcome by a feeling of hopelessness.

As the Mortada reached out to seize her father, the first of the Stidolph arrived. The massive wolf hit the Mortada like a freight train, sending the lithe figure sprawling into the woods beyond. The Stidolph was joined by several more, but, heeding Dakota's words to keep moving, Scarlet couldn't tell exactly how many. A minute later the only sign of either the Stidolph or the Mortada was the vicious growls and cries of pain and anguish that carried through the forest behind them.

Scarlet's lungs were now burning to the point of bursting, her breath coming in ragged, desperate gasps. Mercifully, Dakota suddenly stopped. With a motion of his head, he directed them all to a thicket of underbrush.

"Keep still and quiet," he whispered.

At that moment, a group of three Mortada stalked past the spot they had just vacated.

"I can smell them—we're close," one of the Mortada hissed.

"You've been saying that for the last mile," another retorted, his voice strained and irritated.

"Did you hear that?" the last Mortada asked, his voice quavering with fear and pain. "It's more of them."

"Shut your whining, they're all dead."

"You don't know that."

Scarlet put her hand to her mouth to stop from gasping. Were they talking about the Stidolph, Dakota's friends? Had they all died helping them escape?

"Let's keep moving."

"You know what he will do to us if she escapes."

"Of course I know, you imbecile. They're surrounded. She will not slip past us this time."

The Mortada moved off in the direction Scarlet, her father, and Dakota had been traveling. Dakota waited several long minutes before emerging from the brush. He lifted his muzzle and searched the air with his nose.

"They've managed to get in front of us. We're surrounded." Dakota lowered his head and began to pace methodically around in a circle.

"What do we do now?" Mr. Hopewell asked.

"I'm not sure," Dakota admitted, his voice distant, as if he was lost in thought.

Scarlet tried to calm herself, deciding to focus on the light within her. She didn't send it out or try to form it into substance, but just concentrated on it, letting it soothe and warm her. Words Xavier had spoken to her began to roll over in her mind. *You are only limited by your imagination.*

An idea struck her like a thunderbolt. She had the ability to infuse objects with light, and once having done so, she could manipulate them to her will. She could . . . move them. She thought of library books and how she had made them fly off the shelves, and then how Xavier had turned them into a cyclone. A cyclone that had moved with such speed that it appeared to be a single cone of light. Could it be possible . . .

"I have an idea," Scarlet announced.

Both her father and Dakota turned to her, looking hopeful and interested in any idea that might get them out of their predicament.

"How far do we need to go to be safe, and in what direction?" Scarlet asked.

"North—that way, probably twenty miles before we could be sure the Mortada would be off our trail," Dakota answered, tilting his head in the right direction.

"What is your idea?" her father asked.

"You'll have to trust me, Dad." Scarlet said, closing her eyes and letting the light begin to spread from within to the surface. Within seconds she had become a bright figure of light, shining like a beacon through the forest.

"Scarlet, no," Dakota shouted frantically. "You'll bring them straight to us."

There was a rustling through the woods as the Mortada began to converge on Scarlet. She did not extinguish the light, however, instead expanding it until it consumed—transformed—Dakota and her dad as well. Ten or more Mortada reached the spot, shouting curses, and beginning to conjure darkness against her.

Then, with a simple thought, Scarlet, Dakota, and her dad were gone.

Just a moment before, Charles had been standing in the forest; now he found himself on an open plain, not a tree in sight. The effect was so disconcerting that he stumbled several times before he could regain his balance. He looked around desperately for Scarlet, who was standing next to Dakota, only feet away. His own light and Dakota's had gone out completely, but Scarlet's was still fading slowly.

"This far enough?" she asked lazily, her eyes closed.

"I should think so," said Dakota, looking around and sniffing the air to get his bearings. "We're in the land of the dwarves." The big dog sounded astonished. "I've never even heard of a Tounder doing such a thing."

"Xavier said . . . your imagination. . . . I feel . . . woozy," Scarlet slurred. Then, to Charles's horror, she crumpled to the ground.

18
A Glimpse of Scarlet

Brennan had no way to explain what had just happened before his eyes.

He'd been watching from the ridge, his eyes trained on the clearing so intently that they ached. Although Chosen had pointed at the great oak, announcing that the girl had left, Brennan saw nothing at all. Then three figures seemed to sprout instantaneously out of the ground, several yards into the underbrush at the clearing's edge: a young girl, a man, and a strange-looking wolf. Could they have climbed out of a hidden tunnel? Impossible. They were already in midstride, running headlong, at the moment they first appeared.

Until today Brennan's only experience with magic had been the dark cloud Chosen had conjured against the Mortada. Neither that, nor the sudden appearance of the three running figures, could prepare him for what he saw next, though.

In the distance he could just make out the Mortada closing in on the group. He'd frozen in horror and despair—surely it was all over, before he'd had any chance to help—when suddenly the girl began to glow. Light of a startling intensity radiated from her, and spread to her companions. The Mortada were still racing toward her, with only strides to go, when the girl, the wolf, and the man lit up as brightly as the sun and then, leaving only a trail of golden light, vanished.

Brennan looked immediately to Chosen for some kind of confirmation that he had indeed just seen what he thought he'd seen, some confirmation that he wasn't losing his mind. Chosen was laughing.

"Guess there's not much doubt now," he said, still chuckling to himself.

"Much doubt of what?" Brennan asked in disbelief. "What just happened?"

Chosen stood and began to gather his things back into his bag. "What happened is, the girl just extended our trip a little."

"A *little*? She just disappeared!"

"Don't be so dramatic. She did no such thing." Chosen looked off in the distance for a moment, absorbed in his own thoughts. "I must admit, I've never seen the likes of that before. She is definitely the one."

Brennan was frustrated. What was going on? He couldn't seem to get hold of any fact before everything shifted again. "One *what*? She's definitely the one *what*?"

"It means"—Chosen's tone was dismissive—"that she is definitely the one I seek. We have a long road ahead of us. Get ready."

Within a minute Brennan had packed the few items he'd acquired on the road, a change of clothes, some food, and a bedroll, slung his pack on his back, and was jogging to catch up with Chosen. He was still mulling over what he had seen just before when he nearly ran into Chosen, who had stopped abruptly.

A large group of Mortada blocked their path. The golden-haired men didn't look happy to see them.

"We heard about what you did, Devoveo," one of the Mortada said through his teeth. "We had heard that you had become—well . . . But still, I never thought you would murder your own kind."

Chosen stared blankly at the group of Mortada, seemingly at a loss. This was alarming; Chosen hadn't seemed the least disconcerted the last time they faced a group of Mortada. In fact, his behavior was so different now that Brennan wondered whether he'd dreamed the whole episode of the Mortada in the tunnel, even though he knew he couldn't have.

"Don't act as if we're in any way beholden to our own kind, Multus," Chosen said finally, although his usual self-assurance had not returned.

"Do you know what I think I'm going to do?" the Mortada called Multus said lightly. "I'm going to have your companion kill you for me. I think that would be fitting."

Multada looked intently at Brennan and smiled wickedly. He was larger than the rest of his group, but his ashen, flaking skin, a flaw Brennan had never before seen in a Mortada, marred his striking features.

"Boy," he said, in a lyrical lilting voice that sent shivers down Brennan's spine. "Come here."

Just as when Chosen had spoken to him in Caelesta, only much more powerfully, Brennan was seized by a tremendous compulsion to obey, a fear verging on panic that if he didn't do as the Mortada asked, something terrible would happen. And then he shuddered, and a tremendous anger suffused him with heat, driving away the need to obey. He walked toward Multus, staring intently into his eyes, but allowing the Mortada to believe that Brennan was still under his control.

"I want you to kill Devoveo," Multus lilted softly, with a triumphant smirk. "I want you to strangle him."

Brennan smiled back at the Mortada, who, large as he was, was still almost a foot shorter than Brennan. With the quickness of a snake striking, his hands shot out and seized Multus by the throat. Multus's face went white with shock as he reached up and clawed at Brennan's hands, trying to wrench them away.

"What was it that you wanted me to do?" Brennan asked sarcastically.

Multus began to writhe as he struggled for breath. His fellow Mortada moved to help him, but Brennan turned, lifting Multus several inches off the ground and holding him like a shield between himself and the group. "Another step, and I'll break his neck."

The Mortada froze, but did not retreat.

The problem was, Brennan realized, he hadn't really thought this out. He'd been so wrapped up in his own anger and the need to do *something* that he had no plan beyond seizing Multus and threatening his minions to stay back. That had worked well enough . . . but he couldn't just stand there holding the Mortada up in the air forever.

"Let him down, Brennan," Chosen said coolly.

Brennan looked back to make sure he had heard correctly, receiving a curt nod. He set the Mortada down and slowly backed away, never taking his eyes off him.

Multus straightened his cloak, trying to look composed, though he was white to the lips, and clearly shaken. "Another time, perhaps," he said casually, his voice hiding his fear admirably.

"Another time," Chosen replied.

Multus and the Mortada slunk away in the direction they'd come from, and in less than a minute they were gone.

"What just happened?" Brennan asked after a moment of tense silence.

"It's too long a story for right now. You are a very brave boy, you know that? That's a very powerful and evil being you just assaulted. I have never seen fear in his face before. He is not used to anyone being able to stand up to him." Chosen bent to retrieve his pack, which he'd dropped on the forest floor. "I think he was in shock."

"You know him?"

"Yes. He's my brother."

Chosen straightened, his face expressionless, turned, and resumed his silent march through the woods.

19
Melody's Song

Melody and Cricket sat side by side, looking out from the terrace off the castle's front tower where Scarlet had once spent so much time gazing out over Illuminora. The view did not bring Melody the same peace that it had brought her big sister, however. To her, the village just looked sad. Without Scarlet, the bustling village was going to be a lonely place.

Her mom had not come back from saying good-bye at the base of the tree. Maybe Melody would feel better when she did. But now, slumping down against the wall of the terrace, she put her head in her hands and began to cry.

Cricket trotted over, lay down beside her, and flopped her large head into Melody's lap.

"They come back," Cricket murmured in a soothing tone. "Dakota and your dad and Scarlet, they all come back."

"I know," Melody said, sniffling. "But I'm going to miss them so much."

For a while, the two sat quietly on the terrace, finding comfort in each other's company. Neither noticed that they had been joined by a third person until several minutes had passed.

Melody let out a little gasp of surprise. "You scared me," she said.

"I am very sorry if I did, Melody," Xavier said, sitting down beside her on the terrace floor. It looked like it was hard for the little man to do this. He groaned a little on the way down. "I am getting to be an old fellow."

"How old?" Melody asked.

"Very," Xavier answered. Melody couldn't help but return his smile. "You are sad."

"Yes," Melody answered, trying now not to cry.

"It is quite all right, my dear. There is nothing wrong with tears. We have plenty of water to fill you back up if you need it."

Melody giggled a little. "You don't need to fill up from crying."

"Probably not. You're right. But just in case, I wanted to let you know." Xavier laid his head back against the wall and closed his eyes. "I feel like I haven't slept since before you and your family got here. I've been tossing and turning. I think, although I can't prove it, mind you, that someone . . . put frogs in my bed."

"Frogs?" Now Melody laughed outright.

"Oh yes, it is a very serious matter, frogs. They wiggle and croak. Terribly hard to sleep with frogs in your bed." The little man sounded quite serious.

"But who would put frogs in your bed?"

"I don't know. I wish I did." Xavier opened his eyes slightly and winked at her. "You know, I have heard you singing a lot since you got here. Do you like to sing?"

"Oh, yes. I love to sing."

"I thought so." Xavier sat up and turned to face Melody. "Did you know that here in Satorium there are special types of singers who sing special types of songs that are magic?"

"Really?" Melody asked.

"Yes, really. They are called healing songs, and I just bet that, the way you like to sing—well, I bet I could teach you one, and you could sing it. Would you like that?"

"Yes, I would," Melody answered right away.

"Okay, well, it goes like this:

> When e'er the road is dark and toiled,
> And travelers lose their way,
> They need not fear their plans are foiled,
> For soon there comes the day.

> When loved ones pass out of our sight,
> And sadness comes to call,
> Remember each and every night,
> Into our dreams they fall.
>
> Don't waste your time with much regret,
> The past has run its course.
> Just lift your heart and soon you'll let
> Happiness be your source,
>
> For all endeavors yet to be tried,
> From now until the grave,
> And even days when must you cry,
> Will find you always brave.

By the time Xavier had finished singing, a funny thing had happen to Melody. Although she still missed Scarlet and her father, the sadness had melted away and she felt warm and peaceful.

"That's a happy song! I mean, the song makes people feel better."

"Yes, it does. Would you like to give it a try?"

Melody nodded exuberantly, and together she and Xavier went through the song several times.

"My dear, I think that you might just be a natural bard," Xavier said, sounding excited. "You picked up the song very quickly, and when you sang it, I could feel it making things better."

"What's a bard?" Melody asked.

"Well, anyone can sing the healing songs, but only a bard can make them do magic. I might have guessed, with your sister being . . . well, it's most exciting." Xavier paused for a moment before adding, "If I were you, I would sing that song to your mother tonight at bedtime. I just bet it would make her feel a lot better."

"I will!" Melody exclaimed.

"I'll have to ask your mother tomorrow, but I would like it very much if you would learn some more songs. I would be happy to teach you."

"I would love it!"

Later that night as her mom, her eyes all puffy with tears, was tucking Melody into bed, Melody sang the song the little man had taught her. It did more than just bring a smile to her mom's face. Her eyes went back to normal, the scaredness on her face went away, and she looked much more hopeful. Maybe I *am* a bard, Melody thought, and she fell asleep happy.

20

The Hospitality of Dwarves

Scarlet couldn't have chosen a better place to take them, as it turned out. As her first piece of serious magical defense, it was a remarkably effective one. The group had to rest for a day while Scarlet regained the strength for the short walk to a nearby village, but Dakota was too amazed and grateful to chastise her for the amount of energy she'd spent performing what her father had dubbed "light walking." In truth it had been worth it; they were safe now. There had been many more Mortada than Dakota had guessed, and although he hated to admit it, he had run out of ideas when Scarlet whisked them away.

They walked only a few hours before reaching the small village, shortly after sunrise. The village was made up of huts built from straw, wood, and mud. There were no roads, or modern amenities of any kind. The people of the village were small, gruff-looking individuals—dwarves, in fact, Dakota told Scarlet. They did make her think of the dwarves she had read about in fairy tales, although they weren't quite as cheery as some of those stories made them seem.

The dwarves wore clothes made from animal hides that hung loosely about their bodies, and many of the men were covered in dirt and grime. This clan of dwarves were farmers, Dakota explained, and mostly liked to keep to themselves. They were a peaceful race, and given the choice, they'd prefer to remain far from the coming conflict.

In the center of the village was a larger building, perhaps five or six times the size of the smaller huts. Scarlet noticed as they walked inside that none of the village's buildings had doors.

As she passed a few of the dwarves, Scarlet mused that just the day before, the dwarves would have seemed like giants to her. It was only one of the many curious thoughts that came to her, and she had little time to ponder them all. But the thought of these small men—even the tallest of them was nearly a head shorter than she was—being giants struck her as funny. She was careful not to laugh or stare, though. She didn't want to be rude.

Scarlet followed Dakota into the big building, where she immediately noticed a dwarf at the far end of the large main dwelling. If she had to guess, she'd have guessed he was at least a hundred years old. He wore a long white beard that had been braided and folded over several times to keep it out of his way as he walked; otherwise, he'd surely have tripped over it. His skin was leathery from a life spent working in the sun, and his face was lined with deep-set wrinkles. Bright blue eyes sparkled out from beneath his bushy white eyebrows, and despite his coarse appearance, his smile when he saw them was charming.

"Ah, who is this who comes into my hall? I do not recognize this animal, but my eyes are very old. Come closer." The old dwarf studied Dakota closely. "This is a horrible disguise. You should keep your eyes closed," the old dwarf called out, a little too loudly, with an accent Scarlet couldn't quite pin down. "It's there in your eyes. The Lord of Wolves, I am pleased to see you again. It has been so long."

"Jud-Byr, it *has* been a long time," Dakota called back, speaking as loudly as Jud-Byr had. The old dwarf must be losing his hearing, Scarlet thought.

"Come, sit." Jud-Byr beckoned them, and then clapped his hands with a thunderous sound. "A feast, then!" he bellowed. "For old friends and long absences!"

"A feast" was perhaps an understatement. There was even more food here than there had been at the feast in Illuminora. Colorful vegetables, big slabs of meat, and giant loaves of bread were piled high on the large table. The dwarves ate heartily, laughing and singing between handfuls of food, drinking some concoction from metal goblets, the liquid sloshing to the floor in their frequent boisterous toasts. Scarlet tried her best to eat like a lady, but there were no forks or spoons to be had, and before she could even choose what she wanted, one boisterous dwarf or another would clap her on the back and pile food on her plate.

"You are too skinny, young one!" they would shout. "Skin and bones are not enough for the toils of good work."

Scarlet couldn't help but notice that the dwarves themselves could never have been called skinny. To call them fat or chubby would have been unfair, for they looked stout and muscled, but what they lacked in height, they certainly made up for in girth. Scarlet was stuffed after her first plateful, which was filled again before she could even hope to refuse.

After much time had passed in drink and song, the dwarves, who'd become so unruly they'd begun to sound uncomfortably like an angry mob, suddenly quieted, and the food was removed from the table. Several of the torches that lit the room were extinguished, giving the dining hall a more somber feel, and the dwarves as one turned their attention to Jud-Byr.

"You are waiting for a story, I assume," he jested, and the dwarves humored him with cheers and applause, although instead of clapping they drummed their fists against the table. "Okay, okay. Quiet down. I will tell you the greatest story I know."

The old dwarf settled into the ornate wooden chair and breathed deeply, as though preparing for a great ordeal, his face somber, his head lowered. Then he looked up, and a mischievous smile stretched across his face.

"This is the story of how the Lord of Wolves came to save my life," Jud-Byr began. Scarlet looked at Dakota, but he held his head down and did not meet her gaze. "He will be angry with me for telling this tale, but it is worth telling, and not having seen him for many a year, it is best.

"When I was still old, although not quite so old as I am now, I embarked on the great walking, to the village of our brothers the clan Jar-Alvis in the Northern Mountains. They were the mightiest of our clans. Miners, warriors, smiths. And it had been told to me by my father that in the Northern Mountains they had built a great dwarven city, with single halls larger than our whole village. In these halls, I had been told as a boy, they held banquets that would defy imagination. So after years of putting off my journey—the journey that is the custom of our people—I decided to visit our brothers and enjoy the spectacle of a great Jar-Alvis banquet.

"I never made it to the mountains. I underestimated my strength and my age, and when I came to the foot of the first mountain, winter had found me without any strength left. I walked deeper into the rocky forest until I collapsed, ready to face my death. I had lived a long and good life, and I knew that I would miss my clan—and they me, I hoped," he added, chortling. Many of the dwarves laughed as well, and a few teased him with jibes about not missing him at all. Scarlet, on the other hand, was too fascinated to laugh at the joke. She was desperate to hear more.

"After a day lying in the snow, freezing off bits I had forgotten I still had, I managed to drag myself into a cave, carved into the side of the rock face, and it was here I said the rites of our ancestors and prepared for death.

"Then—" He paused for effect. "I heard the breathing of a mighty beast. Then felt the warm breath against my neck. And then I heard the most terrible roar anyone has ever heard."

"Was Gunthar in the cave with you?" someone shouted, and on cue the dwarf called Gunthar let out a horrendous belch. Laughter again filled the dining hall.

"No, for in such a small space," Jud-Byr teased back, "I would have died right there. No, it was a northern bear, the mighty creature dwarf children are told about to keep them from wandering into the woods alone. His head was larger than the trunk of my body, and his teeth as long and sharp as daggers. The beast's black coat was thick and matted and smelled of rotten flesh and blood.

" 'Begone,' I yelled with all my dwindling strength, but he laughed, a treacherous horrible laugh. 'I taste old and sour, bear,' I yelled again. 'You would not like this meal.' And I beat my chest. Again he laughed. And then I heard another voice.

" 'I've always thought it rude to play with your food,' the new voice said, as calm as I was flustered. In the opening to the cave was this scraggily giant wolf.

"The bear spoke. 'After I'm done, puny wolf cub, I will have you for sport,' he said, his voice even more terrible than his laugh."

"Since when do bears talk?" someone shouted.

"You shut your trap. This is my story," Jud-Byr shouted back before continuing. " 'It is you who will die this day,' the wolf answered, stepping into the cave. 'Although it is not my wish to kill a bear as great as you, or any of the woodland creatures, needlessly.'

"With those words, which seemed to bring fury into the great bear's heart, he flung me aside with a wave of his paw and charged the wolf. Everything seemed to stand still, and then a horrible clash of teeth and fur. The great bear fell with a thud onto the floor of the cave, and there he lay motionless. I was sure that the brave wolf must have been crushed, but then there he was, climbing over the mountain of a bear, and the last thing I saw of that cave was the wolf, standing atop the bear's hide, his head tipped upward and a glorious howl escaping his throat.

"When I next awoke, I was being dragged by the wolf from the collar of my tunic, back south through the wilderness. In time I gained enough strength and warmth in my limbs to walk beside him. I learned that he was the Lord of Wolves, the same noble creature who visits our halls this night. And in time, we became great friends. But"—Jud-Byr smiled, raising his glass—"those are stories for another day."

The dwarves cheered wildly, and all raised a toast to Dakota, who nodded humbly at their praise. After several more rounds of drinks, the dwarves began to depart for their homes, and when only Scarlet, her father, Dakota, and Jud-Byr were left, the old dwarf stood and hobbled over to Dakota. He knelt down painfully.

"Thank you, dear friend, dear . . . lord. I am forever in your debt."

"No, you are not," Dakota said, nuzzling the old dwarf. It was the first time since they left home that Scarlet had seen Dakota act so tender. "It is we who need your help."

"You need only ask," Jud-Byr responded.

"We need a place to stay for a while, and . . . some knowledge."

They were seated at the end of the long table, Scarlet, her father, Dakota, and Jud-Byr, in a very different atmosphere than at the feast. Although Jud-Byr's enormous jovial spirit still prevailed, and he spoke in robust and good-humored tones, the mood was darker, more reverent.

"This is not possible," Jud-Byr said, stroking the braids of his long beard. "A human being cannot speak to the earth, know her magic."

"This one can," Dakota said, serious and determined.

"Hmmm." Jud-Byr groaned, rolling this over in his head. "You think this is the prophesied one, then? The one who will stand up to the dark one? You think she has the magic inside her?"

"I know she does," Dakota responded, with complete conviction.

Jud-Byr remained silent for a long time, taking enormous gulps from his goblet. After a while he motioned for Scarlet to come closer, slapping the empty space on the bench beside him. Scarlet reluctantly got up and sat beside the hefty old man.

"What do you think of all this, little one?" he asked, taking on a grandfatherly tone.

Scarlet wasn't sure what she thought of it all. She was scared and still a bit bewildered. She had done things, though, that she would have never imagined possible, and had exceeded even Xavier's expectations, a compliment she did not take lightly.

"This is all very strange to me still, sir," she said.

"Sir? She calls me sir? Ha!" Jud-Byr let out a bellowing laugh. "I have never been a sir before."

"I'm sorry," Scarlet said hastily.

"Don't be sorry—I like it. Sir Jud-Byr, the lord farmer dwarf . . . Ha!"

Scarlet couldn't help but smile. Jud-Byr's laughter was infectious.

"This is a lot of responsibility to put on such young shoulders," Jud-Byr said to Scarlet. "Perhaps too much." There was a slight look of reproach as his eyes shifted to Dakota and Scarlet's father.

"We agree on that," Dakota answered.

"Do you want me to teach you, child?" Jud-Byr asked.

"Very much." Scarlet knew this was the truth.

"Okay—I will try. Because I owe Udd Lyall a great debt. And . . . because you call me sir. It is the cutest thing ever I see. Plus, Udd Lyall knows my weakness." Jud-Byr chuckled.

"What's that?" Scarlet braved.

"Redheads. My first wife was a redhead. Never could say no to her, neither. We begin tomorrow."

Morning came extremely early for Scarlet, and although the sun had barely risen, it was painfully bright to her tired eyes. She wondered with a hint of amusement if there had been something funny in the drinks they had consumed at the feast. She dressed and tied back her hair, not sure exactly what she needed to ready herself for; the dwarves were farmers, after all, and Scarlet had a feeling that nature magic might just involve a bit of dirt and labor. As she only had one outfit, it wasn't difficult to choose what to wear.

She trudged out of the hut she had shared with her father and Dakota and into the orange light of dawn. Many of the dwarves were already up and about, tending to their gardens and fields. They waved cheerfully at Scarlet as she passed the large hut where they'd had the feast. Jud-Byr was waiting outside the hut, leaning against one of the porch posts and smoking a giant pipe that would have looked large held by a man three times Jud-Byr's size.

"Do you like it?" Jud-Byr said with pride, gesturing with his huge pipe. "I won this in a game of cards off a giant from the Northern Mountains."

"I don't know much about pipes," Scarlet admitted. "It's quite . . . big, isn't it?"

"Ha, that it is." Jud-Byr tapped the ash from the pipe and set it down beside a chair on the porch. He then walked out to meet Scarlet, offering her his elbow. Scarlet put her arm through his, and they began to walk toward a garden. "Udd Lyall tells me that you are a Keeper of Light, like the little ones."

"Yes . . . I guess . . . I mean, I can do light magic, if that's what you mean." Scarlet was unsure of herself, not wanting to sound boastful or disrespectful to Xavier, who was the true Keeper of Light. "Xavier taught me a little."

"A little, yes, well, I hear tell more than a little." Jud-Byr chortled. "Could you show me a little? Don't make yourself tired, though—something small."

Scarlet thought for a moment and then picked up a pebble from the ground. With minimal effort she filled the pebble with light and let it float, bobbing in midair before sending it shooting off across the sky.

"Ha. To my knowledge, little one, you are the first non-Tounder to ever master the light. Ha." Jud-Byr stroked his beard. "There may be hope. Maybe. I expect that nature's magic is not as hard to learn as light. After all, many more can do it than just one group. Light belongs only to the Tounder, dark to the Mortada, but the earth is known to many. How do you speak to the light?"

"Speak to it?" Scarlet said, puzzled.

"Yes, girl. When you talk to the light, what do you say?"

"I don't *say* anything," Scarlet admitted.

"Hmmmm. Then how do you get it to come to you? Is it the sun—does the sun speak to you? A talisman, perhaps?" Jud-Byr seemed both confused and curious.

"I don't think it works that way—with the light, I mean. I kinda feel it inside, and then I send it out."

"Ha. The light comes from inside *you*. No wonder it is so difficult." With a broad, dramatic gesture, Jud-Byr put his hands up in the air and then let them fall to his sides. "Well, nature's magic is different. You have to learn to speak to nature. To ask it to do as you wish. You must develop a relationship with it."

Scarlet thought for a moment about trying to explain what Xavier and Dakota had told her about the For Tol Don and all magic coming from inside her, but thought better of it. She could figure that part out later. "You mean . . . actually talk to it?"

"Yes, talk to it," Jud-Byr responded, a little incredulous.

"Okay, how do I do that?"

"You have to learn its language. Let me show you," Jud-Byr said, walking over to a scraggly tree that was little more than a bush. He bent slowly down, looking very much like an old man as he gingerly placed his knees in the dirt. Leaning close to the tree, he began to whisper, his voice too soft for Scarlet to distinguish the words. He turned his palms upward, still whispering to the tree, and slowly, by mere slivers of inches, the tree began to grow. The dry ground cracked as the tree's roots thickened, its growth beginning to accelerate. Suddenly it rose several feet above Scarlet and Jud-Byr, green foliage budding from its once spindly limbs.

When the tree had finally settled, Jud-Byr turned to Scarlet.

"Do you see? I asked the tree to grow—to sprout new leaves and roots—and it did. It did this for me because it sees me as a friend, as a guardian, and so it trusts me." Jud-Byr smiled at Scarlet, as if he had said the simplest, most basic thing in the world. *First you put one leg in your pants, then the other.*

"What language does nature speak?" Scarlet asked, and then flushed. She knew the question was naive.

"It doesn't matter what words you choose." Jud-Byr seemed frustrated. "You don't understand. It's not what you say—it's how you say it."

Scarlet felt confused. She knew that Jud-Byr was getting frustrated with her. For some reason—perhaps it was just the difference in teaching styles—when Xavier had begun her training, even though she still felt disbelief, it had been easy. It had made sense. Here with Jud-Byr, she understood neither what he was explaining nor what he wanted her to do.

"Come here, girl," he said, taking her hand and leading her over to a half-dead bush. "You see this bush?"

"Yes, of course."

"It is old for a bush. It is dying. Ready to return to the earth. But you could ask it to stay a little longer, if you needed to. . . . If you wanted to." Jud-Byr motioned to the bush and gave Scarlet a nudge.

Feeling incredibly silly, she obeyed, kneeling in front of the bush. She cleared her throat. "Um . . . Mr. Bush . . . if you could please . . . um . . . grow?"

Jud-Byr shook his head. "Mister Bush. What are you saying, child? Mister Bush. It is not Mister Bush."

"I'm sorry. It's just that I've never talked to a bush before. I don't know what to say."

"Just sit quiet and think about it. It may come to you," Jud-Byr said. "I'll leave you here for a little while."

As good as his word, he walked off, leaving Scarlet kneeing by the bush alone. She sat quietly for a long time, unsure of what to say or do. After a while she reached out and felt the bush's twigs and leaves. They were hard and brittle.

"I bet you could do with a bit of water," she said absently. One of the leaves came off in her hand. "Oh, I'm sorry." Scarlet looked at the limb where the leaf had come off. A small bud was forming.

Did I do that? As if in answer, several more buds formed on empty branches.

"Are you dying? Like Jud-Byr said?" Scarlet of course received no answer, but she did feel like she might be on the right track. There was a feeling she was getting from the bush—a connection. "Could you grow a little bit," she asked timidly, "before you fade away?"

Very slowly, almost imperceptibly at first, the bush began

to rise a little higher into the air, its limbs spreading a little wider.

Scarlet squealed with delight.

"Thank you," she said to the bush, no longer feeling quite so silly.

For a while she sat quietly, reverently, watching the bush grow. Then finally, unable to contain herself anymore, she ran off to find Jud-Byr.

21
Magic Seeds

Scarlet spent the remainder of the day attempting to talk to any and every plant she saw, sometimes with great success, although often with none. Regardless of the outcome, she found the whole idea of communicating with nature so fascinating that she continued, undaunted by her numerous failures. Not until later on in the evening did she finally catch up with Jud-Byr. He was standing with her father and several dwarves, staring at a barren field that was by far the largest in the village.

Scarlet approached the group apprehensively. She could hear a heated discussion about the state of the field. Something was clearly wrong. The dwarves were obviously deeply concerned.

Noticing Scarlet, Jud-Byr beckoned her closer. "This is a good lesson for you, child. Come here."

He waited until she'd come close before continuing. "You see this field?"

"Yes," she answered.

"This field has produced most of all the food and medicine we depend on for our livelihood. But now it is barren. Even the earth is affected by the evil rising in the south. Now you may ask me why I don't ask the crops to grow."

"I guess . . . yes, why don't you?"

"Because you can't speak to what isn't there. You create your light from within you, you said, but it is not so with nature. I cannot create the crops—I can only ask them to grow or move or spread. I can only ask the insects and the birds to carry seeds to fertile soil. I cannot create the seeds or the birds. Do you understand?"

"Yes, I do. I've been trying what you told me. They listened," Scarlet said excitedly. "Well—sometimes they did."

"I glad to hear that, child. You'll have to show me later. Right now I must figure out what to do about this problem. I will talk to you later."

Scarlet nodded and was turning to walk away when something caught her eye; a figure was hobbling toward the village in the distance. From the way he was walking, he appeared to be hurt.

"Who is that?" Scarlet asked, getting the adults' attention.

They all looked up at once, and seeing the figure, Scarlet's father took off at a run toward it. "Bring blankets," he shouted.

Scarlet started to run after her father, but Jud-Byr held her back with a firm hand. Several dwarves ran after her father with blankets and water. Scarlet watched as he reached the figure, catching him as he collapsed. Her father lifted the figure in his arms and began carrying him back to the village.

"We need a bed!" he shouted as he passed Scarlet.

Scarlet gasped. It was Delfi. He looked horrible, as if he had been beaten, and was very thin. Delfi tried to whisper something to Scarlet as her father carried him past, but she could not make out what he was saying. Despite Jud-Byr's attempts to hold her back, she rushed past him and followed her father into the hut.

Scarlet's father laid Delfi on a straw bed and began to look him over.

"Can you tell me what happened?" he asked softly.

Delfi blinked, as if he was dizzy, and opened his mouth to speak, but the words were so quiet that Scarlet's father had to lean his ear against Delfi's lips to understand him. He listened for a long time before rising again and telling Delfi to rest; then he walked over to Jud-Byr and pulled him aside. Although they too spoke in quiet tones, Scarlet could make out what they were saying.

"He said he light-walked, like Scarlet did," her father whispered. "He saw her do it, and wanted to find us to help."

"What is this light-walk?" Jud-Byr asked, his eyes fixed on the wounded Tounder.

"I'm not sure I completely understand it myself. Scarlet turned us into light, and then suddenly we were gone—transported here, just a short walk from your village."

"Fascinating. Truly. I've never heard of such magic. Troubling, though. Quite troubling," Jud-Byr's voice was grim.

"Why?"

"Well . . . I would guess the reason I never heard of this magic before is because it would take too much of oneself to use it. Your daughter is obviously special. This boy Tounder might have spent so much of his life's energy, there will be no coming back." Jud-Byr shook his head solemnly. "Why is he so scratched up?"

"He said he crawled here from the place where he landed. He also said that he hit the ground hard. His wings look ripped," Scarlet's father admitted.

"Only the other Tounder would be able to help him with his wings. They are part of the Tounder's gift from the great oak," Dakota said, joining the conversation.

"There is no way to get him to the Tounder, if the Mortada are searching the forest for you all." Jud-Byr stroked his beard worriedly. "That is the least of his worries, though. Our fields are barren. We have no medicine to help any of his wounds, or any ingredients to make a tonic to bring up his strength."

"Oh, the poor boy," Mr. Hopewell said. He rubbed his face in frustration. "I knew they were close, he and Scarlet. I meant to say something to Xavier, but . . ."

"He will rest tonight. Maybe tomorrow we can think of something."

Scarlet sat by Delfi's side, tears running down her face. She felt responsible. He had tried to find her, and if it weren't for her stunt with the light, he would still be in Illuminora, safe and sound. Now Jud-Byr said he was going to die. She couldn't let that happen. She just couldn't. Her mind raced with ideas of how she could help. The only thing she kept coming back to, however, was traveling back to Illuminora and getting Xavier. There was one major problem with that idea. After she had light-walked the last time, she had passed out. If she passed out in the forest outside the great oak, she would be helpless, easy prey for the Mortada. Besides, who was to say that Xavier could even do anything? No one had ever traveled the way she had before, and maybe even Xavier couldn't do it without ending up like Delfi.

Night fell, and everyone but Scarlet went to sleep. There was nothing to be done, and since Scarlet had insisted on staying with Delfi, they left her to watch over him. In the silence she kept running it over and over in her mind, trying to focus on some plan to help Delfi that didn't involve light-walking. The idea came to her slowly, like something seen through a fog. Then it became clear. She got up and tiptoed to where her father slept. She slid his bag from underneath his bed, careful not to wake him. Reaching inside, she slipped the green satin bag Xavier had given her from the pack. Walking past the sleeping dwarves, she made her way out of the hut and to the barren field.

She couldn't be sure that this was the right thing to do, but it felt right. She walked to the middle of the field, took a handful of the seeds from the bag, and tossed them out into the field. She repeated this process until only a handful remained, which she decided to save. Kneeling down in the field, Scarlet began to talk to the seeds, speaking as she sometimes did to her little sister after a bad dream.

In reassuring tones, Scarlet encouraged the seeds to grow, pleaded with them for help. She told them about her friend, and the farmer dwarves who stood to suffer with a barren crop. Several hours passed in this way, Scarlet speaking to the seeds and then waiting. Nothing happened. She received no answer in the form of budding plants or fruits or vegetables. Her heart sank. She had failed Delfi, after he had risked everything just to come to her.

With a heavy heart and tear-filled eyes, Scarlet went back to the hut and sat back down at Delfi's side. She gathered his hand in hers, laid her head on his chest, and quickly drifted off to sleep.

Scarlet woke with a start. Someone had screamed. Then she heard it again. Not screaming, but shouting. There were many shouts. She quickly made her way outside toward all the noise. Jud-Byr, Dakota, her father, and a large group of dwarves were all standing in front of the barren field, blocking

Scarlet's view of it. She rushed to the group and gasped when she caught sight of the field. It was filled with all manner of plants, some familiar, some incredibly strange.

"How did this happen?" one of the dwarves exclaimed.

Jud-Byr turned to Scarlet. "Perhaps our young guest might have an explanation. You *are* the For Tol Don. You have created this from inside you, like the light magic." He smiled warmly at her.

"No," Scarlet said timidly. "Before I left, Xavier gave me a bag. . . . It seemed like the right thing to do."

"Indeed," Jud-Byr said, with a deep laugh.

"Are there the right ingredients to help Delfi here? Can you save him?" Scarlet asked, desperately.

"I think you are the one who saved him," Dakota said. "But yes, the right plants are here." He gave her a wink as the dwarves set off at Jud-Byr's command to collect the needed ingredients.

Jud-Byr had administered the draught that gave Delfi back a good deal of his strength. He still wasn't a hundred percent, and Dzakota had insisted that he remain in bed resting for another several days, but it was now certain that he would recover.

"I can't believe you came after us," Scarlet said.

"I've been stuck in Illuminora all my life," Delfi said groggily. "Besides, I couldn't let you go off on this adventure alone."

"But I'm not alone, silly," Scarlet teased.

"Well, you were the only one who knows light magic. What if you had questions or needed to practice?" Delfi said. He looked a little embarrassed.

Scarlet was going to tease *him* about needing the practice, but decided it would hurt his feelings. "What did Jud-Byr say about your wings?" she asked.

Scarlet could see a flash of anguish in Delfi's eyes, though he quickly recovered, pasting on a warm smile. "They're going to fall off," he admitted. "Too damaged. Besides, not much they could do outside Illuminora anyway."

"Oh, Delfi, I'm so sorry," Scarlet exclaimed, tears running down her cheeks.

"Don't cry," Delfi pleaded. "I'll be okay. Besides, I'm going with you, and it would have been odd to have a giant Tounder walking around drawing attention, wouldn't it? Now I can fit in."

"Because I don't stick out traveling around with a giant German shepherd?" Scarlet elbowed him.

"Well, you got a point there," Delfi said, joining in her laughter.

It took Delfi several days before he was fully up and able to stroll with Scarlet through the fields and meadows. Occasionally Scarlet would show Delfi how she was learning to talk to nature, a skill she was rapidly becoming more proficient in, and try to teach him how she did it. Delfi, however, proved to be completely incapable of this sort of magic, and after a while Scarlet stopped trying.

They would also engage each other in silly duels, vying to conjure up the most ridiculous animal out of light and then setting the glowing creatures scampering about the meadow.

Scarlet found Delfi's presence a great comfort, and it did wonders to ease her sadness at having left her mother and sister. It was also nice just to have someone her age around, someone she could share her feelings with without feeling childish, as she always did around Dakota and her father. Although she was sure they didn't mean to make her feel that way, and probably didn't even realize that they did, it was difficult, considering she was supposed to be some great savior, to act childish around them. She worried that they might be disappointed somehow.

Dakota and Scarlet's father, with the help of Jud-Byr, were planning the next phase of their adventure, and Scarlet was happy for the moment to stay out of the decision making. She didn't know anything about Satorium anyway, and she didn't feel that any insight she might possess would be particularly helpful.

She had practiced light-walking a few times, for very short distances, and found that if she didn't travel far, only a few hundred feet at most, she could do so without much ill effect. Delfi, after his near-death experience, watched apprehensively as she practiced; he'd apparently lost all interest in trying it again.

They had been guests in the dwarven village a whole week when at last Dakota and Scarlet's father called Scarlet and Delfi into the hut to announce that they would be setting off the following morning. Although the feeling wasn't quite as strong as it had been when they left Illuminora, Scarlet felt a twinge of sadness at the thought of leaving another happy and comfortable place. The dwarves, like the Tounder, had been gracious and kind, and Scarlet had enjoyed her time in their village very much.

The next stop on their journey was to the Western Mountains, where they were going to seek help from the spirits of the phoenixes. Scarlet felt a wave of excitement that helped to push away the twinge of sadness. Phoenixes, Scarlet knew from reading, were magical birds that died in a burst of flames and were reborn from their own ashes. That they were real, and that she was going to see them . . . well, it was almost unbelievable. If she was to be honest with herself, however, it wasn't really any more unbelievable than most things that had happened to her over the past few months.

The next morning they said their good-byes. To the old dwarf's obvious surprise, Scarlet gave Jud-Byr a long, tight hug.

"You take good care of yourself, young lady," Jud-Byr said in his most grandfatherly tone, giving her a pat on the head. He turned to Delfi. "You—you owe me a life debt," he announced seriously.

Delfi lowered his head, nervous and a little scared of what Jud-Byr was about to ask of him. The dwarf had saved his life, but he didn't want to leave Scarlet.

"You will pay this debt by watching over the little lady. You guard her with your life."

Delfi smiled. "You can count on it." He extended his hand—this time with much more assurance than the first time he and Scarlet met—and Jud-Byr shook it firmly.

There was little left to say after that. Dakota and Jud-Byr exchanged a few private words, and then the four companions set off to the west. Scarlet looked back over her shoulder once at the dwarven village growing smaller in the distance, feeling a little pang. Taking leave of that place of merriment and order felt almost like leaving her own childhood behind.

She gave herself a little mental shake and turned forward again, calm and resolute.

Her quest, she knew, had just begun.

22
A Forced Good-bye

They tore through the meadows at a full sprint. Chosen ran as if he were being chased by death itself, and Brennan was struggling to keep up, despite his youth and longer legs. Something bad was happening. Brennan could feel it as much as he could see it on Chosen's twisted face. Time itself was against them.

There were other signs that something was amiss. A series of darkly luminous clouds had appeared on the horizon, unlike any Brennan had ever seen before. They had a purplish glow and moved quickly in circular patterns, almost as if they were searching for something . . . or someone. As ominous as the clouds were, and as uneasy as they made Brennan feel, it was in their direction that Chosen ran. Brennan had no choice but to follow.

Chosen offered no explanation for what was happening, or for the sudden need for such haste, and Brennan was so caught up in the rush that he didn't ask.

They'd been at it all day, and with each mile the clouds grew closer, the sense of foreboding stronger.

At a small rise in the land, Chosen halted suddenly. Brennan came up alongside him, drawing in great gulps of air. Chosen was scouring the countryside, desperately searching for something.

"She is close. But where?" he said to the air.

Without a word, they took off again.

Dakota seemed uneasy. They had been traveling nearly two whole days, keeping a steady pace, and although Scarlet was enjoying the time with her father and Delfi, she couldn't help noticing the change in Dakota's manner. Something about the storm clouds behind them seemed to bother him greatly, for he kept stealing glances back at them, and stared fixedly that way whenever they stopped to rest.

The clouds did look odd, tinted a luminous purple and moving in a strange swirling pattern. They almost seemed to be following the four travelers, although Scarlet was sure that was just her imagination. In any case, Dakota's attitude worried Scarlet more than the clouds themselves.

By the time they stopped for lunch on the third day, the clouds were so close that Scarlet's father had begun searching the relatively flat landscape for a place to take shelter. "Do you think we'll be able to reach a patch of woods or the base of the mountains before those clouds get over the top of us?" he asked Dakota.

Dakota didn't answer; he seemed to be concentrating intently on something. Scarlet's father turned to her instead. "You guys stay here and finish eating. I'm going to scout ahead and see if I can find some kind of shelter. That storm looks bad."

Scarlet and Delfi nodded, busy eagerly filling their empty stomachs, laughing between bites.

"There they are!" Brennan shouted. He could just see the tiny figures of Scarlet, Delfi, and Dakota far ahead under the lowering darkness, which had descended like a curtain to just above their heads.

Chosen looked desperately around, searching the air for an answer; they were too far away to reach the cloud in time. He turned to Brennan.

"I'm going to send you after her," he shouted. "We don't have time. Just find her and keep her safe until I find you."

Brennan tried to speak, but suddenly felt himself being hurled through the air. For a moment he could still see Chosen shrinking in the distance, his hands held together in a sort of prayer. Then the black mist wrapped around Brennan, cutting off his vision and hurtling him toward the massive vortex ahead. Then he felt something pull at him, slightly at first, and with tremendous force. The world seemed to spin. He was no longer aware of what was up or down, where sky and earth began. He was only aware of the sensation of falling in all directions.

Charles had left his pack with the group and set off at a jog toward the west, hoping to come across something that could shield the group from the storm. The terrain was flat in all directions, though, and after jogging for ten minutes, he realized that there was nothing anywhere near that would help.

A stray thought struck him as he stopped and turned to walk back to the group. In fourteen years, he had never taken Scarlet camping. It seemed like such a fatherly thing to do, and now, in this strange and dangerous place, they were doing exactly that.

He was musing wryly that he'd have much preferred a nice quiet campsite somewhere in a national park when an ear-splitting *crack* echoed through the plains.

It sounded as if the earth itself had opened up. Charles felt his spine turn to ice as an overwhelming fear swept through him. And then a sound even more terrifying filled the air—the sound of Scarlet screaming.

Charles took off at a full sprint toward the group, toward Scarlet. With each step he took, the sky grew darker. Across the plains he could see that the purple vapor had descended to the earth just behind Scarlet, Delfi, and Dakota, framing them as they ran desperately toward him, away from the clouds bearing down on them.

"Run!" Charles shouted, his own legs feeling rubbery as they pounded the earth. The cloud was gaining on Scarlet. At any moment it would swallow her up, and though Charles had no idea what that would mean, his fear had pushed aside all rational thought.

Dakota, who had hung back to stay between Scarlet, Delfi, and the cloud, was the first to be engulfed. One second he was galloping along, barking encouragement to the two young ones, and the next he'd been lifted off his feet and sucked into the black shroud. Charles watched in horror as Delfi was sucked away next, leaving only his precious daughter, a fraction of a second from vanishing into the vortex. Charles was only steps away. He reached out just as she was lifted off her feet, clutching the first thing his hand touched, his fingers locked grimly around on the strap of Scarlet's pack.

For a brief moment, everything seemed frozen. Charles gripped the strap desperately, looking into the terrified eyes of Scarlet, who was suspended in the air above him, only held down by her own grip on the pack. He knew that he was screaming, but he could not hear himself. Everything seemed to have gone absolutely silent.

Then, without warning, the sound of ripping fabric tore the silence apart.

The strap of the pack had come off in Charles's hand; its stitching had not held. Charles fell to the ground, still clutching the now useless strap. Scarlet had disappeared. He reached out to her, and felt the oddest sensation as it entered the blackness, as if his arm were no longer connected to his body. Struggling to his feet again, he made to charge into the cloud after her, but it was gone.

Before him stretched only a clear blue sky, and the amber grasses of an endless plain.

23

Welcome Home

Scarlet landed hard in overgrown grass; her head thumped against the earth, sending a burst of sparks up behind her closed eyelids, and a dull ache throbbed in her brain. It took a moment to reorient herself, and when she did, she sat up gingerly, feeling numerous muscle twinges and bruises that were sure to bother her for several days. Her first clear thought was that she had landed somewhere familiar, a place she knew quite well, and yet she didn't—*did* she? This place had a wild and deserted look that didn't fit her memories.

Scarlet suddenly remembered her father, Dakota, and Delfi. She got to her feet and began to search frantically for them. Dear lord, she hoped that she wasn't here alone. Relief came quickly as she caught sight of Delfi getting to his feet several yards away, and then Dakota emerging from the woods not far from them. But where was her dad? She looked down at her pack, her oaken staff tied to the top. One of the straps was torn off. An image flashed into her mind with dreadful clarity: her father's arm, momentarily reaching out for her and then vanishing as she was swept away. An enormous wave of grief rolled over her, pulling her under. What had happened to him?

Delfi reached her just in time to catch her as she collapsed in tears. He didn't need to ask her what was wrong, just held her while she cried. Dakota came up beside them, allowing Scarlet her moment of sorrow, while he took stock of their surroundings. He thought he knew where they were, but what had happened? There was something very wrong here.

Soon Scarlet's tears began to subside, and she managed to look up at Dakota. "Is he dead?"

"No," Dakota answered, almost too quickly. "The fog just faded before it got him, that's all. He's fine."

New tears began to fall down Scarlet's cheeks, but she was able to keep control of herself.

"Where are we?" Delfi asked, still keeping a firm arm around her shoulders.

Dakota looked around, his eyes glowing fiercely. "I'm lost for an explanation, but—"

He stopped abruptly, as if reluctant to continue. Scarlet had hardly registered his words, anyway. She'd shrugged off Delfi and was walking away, toward the nearest building—there had to be a building under that mound of vines—as if drawn by a magnet.

Yes, there was a way in—that must be the front door through that gap in the tangled vegetation, she thought as she got closer. Or—not a door. Just an opening. The door was gone, she saw now. She kept moving forward like a sleepwalker, though she could hear Delfi protesting behind her.

"Wait, Scarlet! It might not be safe. You don't know what's in there."

She went on, walking across the door itself, which was lying flat in the opening, the wood almost disintegrated, some shelf fungus sprouting from one side of it. She was in a hallway, with stairs in front of her. She stopped short, looking at the carved ball at the end of the banister. Could it—

She stepped forward and looked through an open doorway to the side. A room covered thickly in dust and cobwebs, pale tendrils of vines creeping over the floor. A television, its screen shattered. For a moment she saw a ghostly image in front of the TV: a gangly half-grown German shepherd, ears pricked, watching the weather forecast with calm concentration. Then she felt a nose touch her hand, and came back to the present.

With Dakota stalking protectively by her side, she crossed to the warped, decayed mantel and reached for a framed picture. She brushed away the thick layer of dust on the glass with her hand. Looking back out at her was a young girl, flushed with happiness, holding a puppy with big paws and startling blue eyes.

The house was absolutely still, not a breath of movement in the air. Scarlet sat on the bottom step of the stairs, her head in her hands. Delfi sat beside her, and Dakota lay at their feet. She couldn't remember putting the picture down, or walking out of the room.

"I don't feel as if I'm that girl anymore," she said, sniffling. "Everything's so different. This can't be home. I don't even know where home is."

Delfi just patted her hand; he obviously had no idea what to say. Looking at his anxious face, Scarlet realized she needed to pull herself together. They couldn't just sit around while she felt sorry for herself. She had a couple of worlds to save, she thought ruefully.

"Come on. We'd better get going," she said, standing up and turning to offer Delfi a hand. Suddenly a soft breeze filled the hall, blowing down the stairs from above. It felt good, and Scarlet tipped her head back to feel it on her face. Then it grew stronger, and a blizzard of paper filled the air. Pages were floating down the stairwell, spinning in circles, filling the hall.

Reaching out, she caught one of the dancing sheets of paper. There were a few lines of writing on it—her own handwriting, notes from a dream:

... I'd come to a magical village, sparkling with light, beneath a great oak tree. At the foot of this tree would be my family and friends, greeting me as if they'd been waiting for me for years. It would be the grandest homecoming . . .

"Well," she said, not sure whether to laugh or cry, "this isn't exactly the homecoming of my dreams."

Outside, they looked around. Only a few other houses in the neighborhood were still standing, and even those looked as though they wouldn't hold up to the roots and vines much longer. There were no cars on the broken pavement of the road, no people anywhere to be seen. No lights shone anywhere, though dusk was coming on.

"It's as if we've been gone for ages. How is that possible?" Scarlet asked. "It's only been a few months."

"I wish I had the answers, but I don't," Dakota confessed. "Something is very wrong. Something Xavier didn't see."

Darkness was coming quickly upon them as the sun sank beyond the western horizon. Sounds began to disturb the stillness. Although the familiar croaks of frogs and the rhythmic ebb and flow of crickets were clearly evident, they could also hear strange, wild cries, the calls of animals that were surely out of place in the once-suburban landscape.

"We need to get away from here," Dakota said, looking apprehensive and a touch wild himself. "Whoever is responsible for this, we don't want to be found exactly where they sent us. We need to find some sort of shelter to rest and make a plan."

Scarlet thought for a moment. "What about my school?" she asked. "It was a tornado shelter and everything. It should be safe, shouldn't it? I mean, it's not too far."

"You mean we have to go to school?" Delfi kidded, trying his best to lighten the mood. Scarlet could see that he didn't want her to get upset again.

"I think it sounds like an excellent idea. That school's as good a chance as any to find shelter," Dakota said firmly. "Stay close to each other and keep your eyes on a swivel." In response, Delfi looked at Scarlet and rolled his eyes in dramatic circles.

They set off quickly to the main road and toward the school. It was only a mile up the road, and they reached it in under half an hour. Made of brick and steel, the school did appear to be intact. Scarlet's hunch had proven accurate. Although the school was covered in vines and overgrown plant life, the simple, single-story structure was doing its best to hold out against the unchecked overgrowth around it. This made getting inside the building, however, a little bit difficult; every door they tried proved to be either locked or completely blocked by plant life. Vines and thick foliage covered the windows as well.

It took several minutes before Scarlet remembered magic. Something about being back in her world, wild and strange though it was, had pushed the idea from her mind. She was staring at the front door to the school, which was slightly ajar and blocked by the thick intertwining roots of a willow tree that was growing through the pavement. A smile lit up her face.

She leaned forward and whispered to the roots, which responded immediately, retreating from the doorway and revealing a clear path to the inside of the school. Scarlet was amazed at how quickly it happened. She wondered whether the plants in her world, unused to magic, did not have the same resistance to it that the plants in Satorium did. She made a mental note to ask Dakota about it once they had gotten inside the school and had a chance to discuss what was happening. To be honest, whether or not the plants back home reacted more quickly to magic was the least of the many questions that needed answering.

Although it didn't really matter what room they chose to rest in, Scarlet found herself leading Delfi and Dakota to Ms. Thandiwe's classroom. The halls were completely dark, the windows covered and the electric lights not working. Scarlet and Delfi sent a few spheres of light out ahead of them to light the way. In certain parts of the hall tree roots had broken through the floor, although in the absence of light, no other plant life had flourished inside the building.

Once inside Ms. Thandiwe's classroom, the three companions collapsed onto the floor. There were still many desks and chairs in the room, but for the moment the floor looked much more comfortable.

"What happened?" Delfi asked, not really expecting an answer but feeling the need to voice what he knew everyone was thinking.

"I can only guess," Dakota answered. "But I think Xavier must have underestimated the prince's strength. He has done something to this world."

"He's here?" Scarlet cried in alarm.

"No, no. Of that I am sure. If he had escaped, we would certainly have known. But that doesn't mean he hasn't found a way to act upon this world from his tower prison. It's as if he's sped up time, and I'm nearly positive he must have sent some of his minions over to begin preparing for his eventual escape. We were oblivious over there, and all the while this world has been under siege." Dakota looked as angry as he was uneasy.

"So we aren't safe here," said Delfi.

"Certainly not," Dakota answered. "Why else would he have sent us back here?"

"Can you send us back to Illuminora?" Scarlet asked, hope in her voice.

Dakota remained silent for a long, uncomfortable moment. "Without Xavier's direct help, I have no way of sending us back. Even with his help, it took fourteen years to break the barrier, and a considerable amount of planning to hold it open long enough to get us back."

Dakota's words fell on them like a heavy curtain cutting short a promising show. There was a finality in his simple statement that drained away the last vestiges of hope, leaving only a foreboding sense of doom. How could Scarlet learn magic if they couldn't go back? Would any of them ever see their friends and families again?

"We should rest for now," Dakota said. "Perhaps in the morning things will look different."

There was no argument from Scarlet or Delfi. They found places on the musty carpet and prepared for what was sure to be a sleepless night.

"I should ask the roots to close the doorway again, just in case. That way nobody else can get in," Scarlet said.

Dakota nodded. "Be quick, and be careful."

Scarlet returned to the school's main entrance and whispered to the willow. The branches quivered at the sound of her voice, and in less than a minute the entrance was again sealed. On her way back to the classroom, Scarlet noticed something she hadn't before: a flyer hastily taped on every classroom door. She took one down and looked at it. A few lines of what looked like verse followed a short note:

Dear Students,

This letter is to tell you where to find us. It's in a riddle in the hope that the monsters won't understand and be able to find us. I have no idea how intelligent they are. The school is no longer safe. Leave as soon as you can, and follow the clues in the riddle. Be careful, and good luck.

—Ms. Thandiwe

A presidential donation, given forth, the citizens to enlight.
The 3rd's great love, kept safe behind vaulted doors.
A mighty building, we hide in plain sight.
Where the 2nd and 4th are our neighbors.

Scarlet wasted no time. She went immediately to the library; the thought of finding Ms. Thandiwe, an adult who she trusted and could help explain what had happened, was too much to pass up. The library was dark and wild. Many plants had invaded through the numerous windows. Scarlet sent several spheres of light into the cavernous room and began looking for books on US government. The riddle had mentioned a president, so books about the government seemed like a good place to start. She got history books, assuming that since the riddle mentioned the third, it would be about older presidents.

Scarlet gathered together a stack of books and was about to leave when she stopped to pick up a book about Washington, DC, as well. She then hurried back to Ms. Thandiwe's classroom, where Dakota was about to leave to find her.

"Where have you been?" he asked, deep concern in his voice.

"I found this," Scarlet answered, showing the flyer to Dakota, who read it quickly. Delfi came over and read it as well.

"What does it mean?" Delfi asked.

"Ms. Thandiwe was one of my teachers in school. She's obviously found a safe place, but she didn't want to give it away to whatever has come over. It's a riddle." Scarlet sat down on the floor and began flipping through her books. Delfi picked one of them up as well, although he had no idea what he was looking at.

"First we have to go to school on my first visit to your world, and now we have homework," Delfi jibbed.

Scarlet smiled but ignored his joking.

"The third president was Thomas Jefferson," Scarlet read, although she had been pretty sure of that before reading it. "Now we have to figure out what he donated."

Delfi had found Thomas Jefferson in his book as well. "It says he wrote the American Declaration of Independence," Delfi offered.

"We saw the Declaration of Independence once when we went to DC. It's in the . . . National Archives Museum, I think." She turned to the map in the book about DC. "Here it is, she said pointing to the Archives on the map. "DC isn't that far away, either. It used to be only a thirty-minute trip by car. Without traffic, that is."

"What's a car?" Delfi asked.

"It's a . . . a . . . machine . . . that can move people around faster," Scarlet explained.

"What else is in the Archives?" Dakota asked. "What are the neighbors being the second and fourth?"

Scarlet turned in the book about DC to the section about the National Archives Museum. She didn't see anything that she thought might have anything to do with second or fourth. There was also the section in the riddle about Thomas Jefferson's great love. Surely he loved the United States, but was the Declaration of Independence enough of a connection to explain that part of the riddle?

Scarlet looked up at Delfi. "Who does it say in your book that Thomas Jefferson was married to?"

"It says Martha, but she died before he became president. Wow!" Delfi exclaimed.

"What?" Scarlet asked.

"Only two of their children survived to grow up, and they had five. That is so sad." The Tounder lived remarkably long lives, and to hear that a couple's children could almost all die was deeply disturbing to Delfi, who'd had never heard of a Tounder child passing away.

Scarlet and Delfi continued reading for a while before the answer presented itself to them. Scarlet found the answer first in a minor sentence in one of the books, but from there the riddle began to unfold quickly. Thomas Jefferson was a great lover of books and had donated his extensive library to the people of the United States of America. A little investigation revealed that his books were held in the Thomas Jefferson Building in the Library of Congress, whose other buildings were the Adams and Madison Buildings, named after the second and fourth presidents of the United States.

The only question now was how they would get there.

"The problem is, we have no idea what's out there," said Dakota.

"But that's why we should go and find Ms. Thandiwe. She can tell us more about what's happened here," said Scarlet.

Dakota was pacing the room, obviously conflicted about what to do. They seemed safe for the time being, talking shelter in the brick school building, which was surrounded by protective trees and vines. Nevertheless, the danger of the prince's rise to power was not gone just because they found themselves in Scarlet's home world, and they could do nothing to stop him while they were hiding out in a school. They needed a new plan to develop Scarlet's magical abilities. They couldn't afford to hide.

Eventually Dakota stopped pacing, having made his decision. "We'll need to try and make it to this library in one day, if we can. I have no idea how dangerous it is out there or what other shelter we might be able to find along the way."

"We can do it," Scarlet said, feeling a stir of hope and excitement.

"Tomorrow morning then," Dakota announced. "first thing."

24
New Friends

Brennan woke in a tangle of brush, surrounded by trees. It was dark, and he had no idea how long he had been unconscious. Cautiously he pulled himself up and tried to gain some familiarity with his surroundings. The area was not like any forest he had ever seen; just a short distance away, he could see a series of strange dilapidated buildings that had been overrun by plants, almost as if the forest had swallowed a village.

He tested his legs and feet. Apart from being a little sore, and having a good-size lump on the back of his head, he found no apparent injuries. The first thing he needed to do was find the girl, and after that . . . well, he wasn't sure. He had no idea what had happened to him, where he was, or when Chosen would find him, if he ever did at all. Searching the area for any signs of the girl or her companions, he was able to find signs of disturbance in the brush, leading to a clearing behind a stone pit about the size of the other buildings. Beyond the clearing, though, he had no idea where they had gone.

Brennan tried to put himself in their shoes. A young girl, a boy, and a wolf. What would be the first thing they'd want to do after waking up in this awful place? With night falling, they'd definitely want to seek shelter. Brennan looked around at the buildings in the area. None of them appeared to be suitable to take refuge in; hiding in any of them looked more dangerous than staying in the open. Deciding that they would not have gone back into the trees, either, Brennan headed out toward the road, which to his amazement proved to be made entirely of one long piece of black stone.

He had been traveling about ten minutes when he heard sounds that made his blood run cold; in the distance, hopefully a long way behind him, came the unmistakable roars of tiranthropes. It was a sound he would never forget as long as he lived. Having no desire for another run-in with one of those creatures, let alone what sounded like several, Brennan quickened his pace, now searching with a degree of panic for somewhere to take shelter.

If there was one thing Brennan's time with Chosen had done for him, it had turned him into a proficient long-distance runner. He quickly covered the distance on the open road, coming to a large building made of red stone and covered with roots and plants. Unlike the taller buildings he had seen, this one was single story and looked to be fairly intact.

Brennan circled the building several times, finding all obvious entrances completely blocked by thick roots and foliage. There was no way for the girl and her companions to have gotten inside—at least, not that he could see. He wished Chosen had told him something about where he was being sent. He wished Chosen had told him anything useful.

A light flickered in the corner of Brennan's eye, catching his attention. He turned to look at it, but it was already gone. For a moment he thought it had been his imagination, and he was about to ignore it when it happened again. It came from the cracks in the foliage entwining one of the windows. It then reappeared several windows down, moving in the direction of the largest entrance to the school, the one covered by the entwined thick roots of a tree.

Brennan hid himself behind a bush where he could still view the building. The sun was just beginning to peek out over the roofline. Suddenly the roots from the front door began to writhe, recoiling back toward the tree to leave the door exposed. Brennan steeled himself for a fight; he had no idea what might emerge from the building. His only hope was that it was the girl.

The first figure to emerge was the strange wolf, followed by the girl and boy. Brennan let out a sigh of relief. Luck, it seemed, had turned in his direction. Then came the growl, and this time it was definitely not far off in the distance. It was close. Too close.

Only the wolf had time to react as the tiranthrope came bounding around the far corner of the building, on top of the group before the girl and boy could respond. Having little option, the wolf threw himself at the tiranthrope, the two crashing in midair as they leaped toward each other. The sounds of the two animals attacking one another was ferocious, almost blocking out the screams from the girl.

If the wolf wasn't able to beat the tiranthrope, the girl would be killed in seconds as it turned to its next victim. Brennan couldn't let that happen. He didn't feel the warm tingling in his muscles that signaled the onset of the Tempest and had enabled him to beat the tiranthrope before. Maybe though, if he and the wolf attacked together—

Brennan darted from his hiding place behind the bush, running silently, straight at the tumbling tangle that was the fighting tiranthrope and wolf. There was a yelp from the wolf, just as Brennan reached them. The tiranthrope tossed the wolf aside and turned to the girl, taking no notice of Brennan, who threw his shoulder into its midsection, sending them both to the ground. Brennan landed hard on top of the huge snarling creature, sprang up before the tiranthrope could get hold of him, and stepped back, ready to defend himself against the next attack.

The girl had gone to the wolf. She was crying, but the wolf was rising to its feet. The boy was still behind Brennan.

The tiranthrope got up slowly and let out a horrific roar. "You are going to die for that," it cried.

"I don't think so," Brennan said coldly, his voice sounding much more brave than he felt. He could feel the boy coming around from behind him. "Stay back, boy!"

"My name is Delfi," the boy said, anger in his voice. "Those are my friends it attacked."

Without another word, the boy sent a beam of solid light directly into the tiranthrope's face. The reaction was immediate, strange, and disturbing. The tiranthrope began to flail and clutch at its eyes, screaming in pain as it backed away from Brennan and Delfi. Brennan turned to glance at Delfi, unsure of what had just happened.

"Scarlet!" Delfi cried, "it can't take the light. There's something about the light!"

Scarlet didn't need any further explanation. Furious that her beloved Dakota had been injured, and tired of being afraid, she rose to her feet, summoned the light within, and sent a beam of light, more powerful than she had ever produced before, streaming into the tiranthrope. Knocked off its feet, the creature slammed into a brick wall several feet away and slumped to the ground, where it lay motionless.

Brennan looked from Scarlet to Delfi, who appeared somewhat shell-shocked—much as Brennan imagined he must have looked the first time he encountered a tiranthrope. The wolf was staring at him with suspicious glowing blue eyes. Brennan walked cautiously over to the tiranthrope and prodded it with his foot. It didn't move.

"We should go back inside," Brennan said, turning back to the group.

"*We* aren't doing anything until you explain who *you* are," Dakota snarled.

"Dakota, he saved our lives," Scarlet pleaded.

"I don't care," Dakota snapped. "We can't afford to be trusting."

Brennan looked around, concerned that there might be more tiranthropes. How was he going to explain what he didn't really understand himself? Brennan decided a quick version of what had happened to him would have to suffice.

"I was in a slave prison," he started, "and this strange man came and rescued me. He said that he needed me to protect a girl he was searching for, and we traveled across the whole of Satorium to find her . . . to find you," Brennan said, nodding toward Scarlet. "Look . . . we don't have time for this."

"We are going to have to make time," Dakota snarled.

"Except, when we got to you . . . well, the man I was with, he said time was running out. There was a black cloud descending on you, and he said he was going to send me to you, and I was to protect you until he found us."

"How exactly did he send you to us?" Dakota asked suspiciously.

"I don't know exactly. He did some kind of magic, and the next thing I knew, I was flying through the black cloud. I woke up in some trees here—wherever *here* is."

Scarlet supposed that Dakota had good reason to be suspicious, but it was hard for her to feel the same way. After all, the young man had risked his life to save them from the monstrous cat thing. She took a moment to look over the man, trying her best to get an impression of him. He was by far the largest man Scarlet had ever met, like she imagined a football player or a basketball player might be, only even taller. He wasn't skinny like a basketball player, though. He was very broad, and his arms were thick and very muscular. He had kind marble-like eyes, shoulder-length blond hair, and his face, although weathered by the sun and strained from hardship, was young and slightly wild.

"What's your name?" Scarlet asked.

"Brennan. I'm the last of my people, the Conquered—the Satorians."

At these words, Dakota's ears perked up. He walked closer to Brennan, his nose in the air, as if trying to sniff out the truth of Brennan's statement.

"You are the last Satorian?" Dakota said, a hint of intrigue in his tone.

"As far as I know, my mother and I were the last. She was killed when the slavers found us," Brennan said.

"That's awful!" Scarlet cried.

Something about the mention of Satorians had seemed to put Dakota at ease. At least his voice showed a little compassion the next time he spoke to Brennan.

"What do you know about the man you were traveling with?" Dakota asked.

Brennan lowered his head and was silent for a moment before he answered. "I don't think he's a good man," Brennan confessed. "We fought several groups of . . . of Mortada, he said they were, on our travels, but I think—in fact, I'm sure—that he was one of them." Dakota's hackles rose. "Listen, though, I'm not with him. He just saved me from the jail, and I had nowhere else to go. I didn't have many options."

"You are here under his bidding," Dakota snarled.

"I swore that I would protect the girl. I have no home or place to go and no purpose anymore. I spent my whole life running with my mother, and now she's gone. I decided that if a young girl was in danger . . . well, then that was as good a purpose as any. I swore to myself that I *would* protect her, even from him if necessary. In that way, I would give what my mother did . . . It would be like honoring her."

Scarlet could not take her eyes off Brennan's face, contorted with a grief he was trying gallantly to hide. His eyes glistened with tears that he was not allowing to fall. A long, uncomfortable silence followed.

"I believe you," Dakota said finally, releasing the tension. "And I am very sorry for your loss," he added solemnly.

"I think we should go inside your fortress," Brennan said, pointing at the school. "I heard more of the tiranthropes on my way here."

"No," Dakota said firmly. "We need answers, and Scarlet still has a job to do. We have to get to a place that might give us both answers and safety. We think it's about a day's walk, and we haven't any time to lose. If you truly mean to protect her," he added with a hint of reluctance, "then you can come with us."

Brennan didn't argue. He simply nodded and said that he was ready to go whenever they were.

"My name—" Dakota paused for a moment, as if unsure of which name to give. He had not had to introduce himself in so long, and had spent so much time ashamed of the honor his original name bestowed, that he was at a loss. Then he decided, and it brought him a great deal of peace to be proud of the name he gave. "My name is Dakota. This is Delfi of the Tounder, and this is Scarlet. If you mean what you said, truly, then for now I will just tell you that she is the most important person in all of Satorium—and in this world, for that matter. Her life is worth all of ours."

"I'm not—" Scarlet began, but Dakota interrupted her with a stern look.

"On my honor," Brennan said, his voice stern and unwavering. "I pledge my life to her safety."

Dakota bowed his head slightly at Brennan's vow, and without another word they set off toward Washington, DC.

25

Monsters in the Capitol

It was strange for Scarlet to see what had once been so familiar be so foreign to her. It was as if the entire world had been abandoned. Forsaken houses, all in the same wild state, overrun with trees and vines, were everywhere. Cars sat unattended in driveways and streets. They saw no sign of anyone, friend or foe. All of northern Virginia had become a ghost town, and it looked as if it had been that way for many, many years.

They walked along the interstate because it seemed the quickest and simplest way to get into DC. Scarlet wished she knew how to drive. Most of the cars they saw along the interstate still had keys in them, and taking them would have shortened their trip considerably. She thought about asking Brennan to try, but he was so disoriented by everything around him that she was sure that even trying to explain to him how to drive a car would be impossible.

It was dusk before they could see the first hints of the Washington skyline. The Washington Monument still stood tall against the fading gray sky. Night brought new sounds to the stillness of the day, as strange creatures awoke with the coming night. The unmistakable growls of the tiranthropes were present, but so were other sounds that were just as alarming, perhaps more so because they were unknown.

"The creatures the prince has let loose on this world are obviously either drawn to the darkness or can only survive within it," Dakota said, looking out across the abandoned capital. "We're not safe out in the dark."

"Well, between Scarlet and me, we could take care of some of that," Delfi said bravely.

"No, I don't want us to draw attention to ourselves if we don't have to. There's no way to know how many are out there."

"How far is it to this library?" Brennan asked.

Scarlet looked at the map she had taken from one of the books. She traced the roads between where they were and the Library of Congress. "If we head to the Washington Monument—sorry, that tall tower there—then we can just walk straight to the Capitol Building. The library is behind it."

Delfi looked over Scarlet's shoulder at the map. "It doesn't look too far," he said. "As running through the open in the dark with monstrous creatures lurking everywhere goes, that is."

Dakota did not look amused. The sounds were growing louder. "Let's get a move on."

They began to run toward the Washington Monument. Although they reached it without any problem, the sense that danger was coming ever nearer increased with every step. The distance up the Mall to the Capitol in the distance seemed much longer than it should have. The sun had disappeared completely, leaving a vast starry night above and a silvery glow across the lawn below. The moon was full and bright, and with no artificial light to mask the grandeur of the night sky, the scene over the city was one Scarlet could have only hoped to view in a planetarium. If it hadn't been for the deep apprehension and genuine fear of death, Scarlet would have been mesmerized by the beauty of it all.

"We're going to just have to make a run for it," Brennan said, after waiting for them to catch their breath. It was not a plan that instilled a high degree of confidence, but no one had a better one to offer.

"Brennan, you stay at the back, and I'll take the front." Dakota peered intently over the open ground. "Delfi, Scarlet, you two stay between us. If we get attacked, Brennan and I will try to hold whatever it is off you while you two make for the library. If you get attacked again, defend yourselves, but be careful not to use up all your energy. You'll still need to get to safety even if you're able to get rid of whatever it is.

Then head for the nearest building, whichever one of these it ends up being," he added, motioning to the Smithsonian museums that flanked the Mall.

The group nodded their understanding and, Dakota in the lead, took off across the lawns. Legs burning, lungs cramping, they reached the middle of the Mall without incident, and even Dakota was beginning to feel like they would make it to the library without an altercation. The feeling would not last.

Dakota stopped suddenly, his sharp canine eyes the first to see them; only as Scarlet, Delfi, and Brennan came to a halt did they too see what blocked their path. Five Mortada stood in a line between them and the Capitol. It was as if they had appeared out of nowhere. One second Dakota had been staring at a clear path to the large white structure in the distance, and the next, the Mortada had materialized there.

Dakota bristled and growled. He could face a few Mortada, but five was more than he could possibly handle, and Scarlet was not yet ready to face magic as dark as theirs. They would sucker her into expending every last bit of energy she had, until there was nothing left but death. His only glimmer of hope was the remote stories he had heard of the Satorians; maybe, just maybe, Brennan could pick up where Dakota's strength failed. Even though he knew that if he hadn't changed, he never would have been able to get to Scarlet, Dakota silently cursed the weakness of his new form.

All Dakota's thoughts, plans, and regrets would prove pointless, though. The Mortada let out a maniacal laugh, raised their arms as one, and then, bringing them down, turned the clear sky into a dense dark haze. An impenetrable black fog descended upon the group, and before any of them could act, Scarlet, Delfi, and Dakota fell silently to the ground.

Brennan struggled to see through the nearly opaque mist. He felt the now-familiar pull on his senses, his muscles and skin—an intense desire to obey, to lie down and go to sleep. He resisted the best he could, and soon the feeling passed, replaced by the rage and indignation he always felt after a Mortada tried to compel him against his will. He could just make out the outlines of Scarlet, Delfi, and Dakota lying on the ground in front of him, although he didn't know whether they were alive or dead. They had not been able to resist the powerful magic cast by all five of the Mortada.

The Mortada had been warned of Brennan, and as a result they kept their distance. Although immensely powerful, without magic they were no more or less than any other man. Brennan, on the other hand, was not an average man, and against him, without magic, they would have little more power than children in a fight. Instead they had debilitated those who could use magic; now they only need wait for the tiranthropes to come and finish the job. Brennan could already hear the terrible cries of the beasts in the distance, closer with each passing moment.

Brennan struggled to figure out what to do, his mind racing; once the tiranthropes arrived, all hope was gone. One of the creatures was really more than Brennan could handle;

any more than that was not to be contemplated. By the sound of it, many more than one were headed his way. There was only one thing to do. He would have to carry Scarlet, Delfi, and Dakota to safety.

This wouldn't be easy. Dakota, small as he might be for a Stidolph, still had to weigh close to two hundred pounds. Scarlet was small enough, but Delfi was a healthy young man and surely weighed over a hundred pounds. Each second wasted decreased their chances of survival exponentially. He had no time to agonize over what he'd have to do; he'd just have to get on with it.

Lifting Dakota by the legs, he slung the great dog over his shoulders and around his neck. He gathered Delfi and Scarlet up in his muscular arms, cradling them like babies, one on each side, and trudged forward. He could feel the extra weight on his legs instantly, and for a moment he considered turning back. He would never reach the library in time.

To make matters worse, the fog was more than just vapor; it had a density that fought against Brennan's every step. It was like walking underwater, each footfall a tremendous ordeal. His muscles burned, screaming at him to stop, to put down the weight, but he continued to move, one carefully placed step at a time. Behind him the tiranthropes drew nearer and nearer.

By the time he'd made it almost to the paved road in front of the Capitol, his legs were in agony. He wobbled slightly, almost dropping Scarlet and Delfi. If he could just get out of the fog, then maybe they would wake up and help. The tiranthropes had entered the Mall. They were close—very close. The fog seemed to extend all the way to the building.

Another minute passed. Brennan's mind was numb except for one thought . . . *Keep moving.* One step. Another. He reached the steps, steps that might as well have been a mountain, and began to climb. Suddenly a sharp, slashing pain sliced across his back, and he fell to his knees, doing his best to set Delfi and Scarlet down as easily as he could. He had been so focused on the stairs, he had not heard the tiranthrope behind him. Hefting Dakota off his shoulders, he whirled to face the monster behind him. The fog had grown so thick it was hard to make out anything.

A flash, and Brennan slumped down again, a searing pain throbbing across his chest. He couldn't see where the tiranthrope had gone, it moved so quickly. It seemed to have none of Brennan's difficulty in the haze. Stumbling to his feet, Brennan searched the darkness for his opponent. The tiranthrope attacked again, this time from behind, slashing the back of Brennan's right leg, which buckled underneath him.

He was going to die, and after that, so would Scarlet and her friends.

Warmth began to rise in the pit of Brennan's stomach, and he welcomed it like a friend he hadn't seen in a very long time. The Tempest started to radiate outward, first to his bones, then his muscles, and finally to the very tips of his fingers and toes. His sight sharpened, and shapes began to appear through the darkness. The pain in his chest, back, and leg disappeared. Brennan got to his feet once again. He could hear the tiranthrope approaching.

Brennan spun on the tiranthrope as it attacked, grabbing its wrists as the daggerlike claws slashed out at him. Pivoting on his heel, he flung the beast, all four hundred pounds of it, far into the distance. Not waiting to hear it hit the ground, he hefted Dakota back onto his shoulders and scooped Scarlet and Delfi back up in his arms. With the Tempest raging through him, they seemed almost weightless, and Brennan took off at a full run, into the entrance of the Capitol, through the building, and out the other side. Seeing the Library of Congress just a short distance away, he made a break for it.

As he bounded up the steps to the library, he emerged from the fog; it did not rise as far as the main entrance. The large doors to the entrance had been barred from the inside. Brennan set down Delfi, Scarlet, and Dakota, who had begun to stir. With one mighty heave, he ripped the door off its hinges and kicked aside the desks and shelves that blocked his way inside. Grabbing Delfi and Scarlet, one in each hand, he heaved them inside, then did the same for Dakota.

They had made it, but Brennan did not feel safe just yet. He grabbed the door he had ripped away and took it inside with him. Then he lugged a desk out of the rubble and wedged it into the empty space left by the door. Grabbing the door, he drove it several inches into the marble floor and then braced it against the desk. He stepped back, feeling that it would take a great deal of effort for anything to come through there now.

Scarlet, Delfi, and Dakota had awoken, and as Brennan turned to face them, he was met with looks of bewildered gratitude. They'd been unconscious, so they had no idea how he had done it, but Brennan had gotten them all to safety.

Scarlet was about to speak when another voice broke the silence, taking her completely by surprise.

"Miss Hopewell!" Ms. Thandiwe said, standing at the top of a set of stairs that led to the second landing of the library. "It can't be!"

26
Explanations

"You must be Scarlet's granddaughter," Ms. Thandiwe said after she had led them to the main reading room. The main reading room had been an awe-inspiring sight when Scarlet visited with her family just a year before. The room had been bathed in soft golden light, its towering columns encircled in rose-colored stone and topped with statues. A magnificent domed ceiling soared over arches, reading tables, and beautiful sculptures. She had never been inside before, only having seen it from the visitors' gallery. Standing in the room, she thought the space, now lit by numerous candles, was even more brilliant.

Scarlet turned to Ms. Thandiwe and smiled at her. "No, ma'am. I *am* Scarlet Hopewell."

"That's impossible. Scarlet would be nearly sixty-four by now," Ms. Thandiwe said incredulously.

"You mean it's been fifty years since I left?" Scarlet asked, quickly doing the math in her head. Even the question itself seemed incomprehensible.

Ms. Thandiwe took a long moment to study Scarlet and then Delfi, Brennan, and especially Dakota. "Yes, it has been fifty years since I had Scarlet Hopewell in my class," she said finally. "Fifty years since *they* came, and the world went crazy. What do you mean, 'since you left'?"

It took a long time for Scarlet to explain what had happened to her, from the night the Mortada had broken into her home all the way up until she made it to the library. At times she felt so foolish telling the story that she was afraid to continue, but for her part, Ms. Thandiwe seemed to listen with rapt attention, her face never showing any sign of judgment or disbelief. At one point Dakota interjected to help explain some things, and Ms. Thandiwe's eyes widened when he first spoke, but even then she managed to recover quickly. When Scarlet got to the part about being taken from her father, she broke into tears. Ms. Thandiwe gathered Scarlet into her arms and held her until she had finally let out the grief she'd been bottling inside.

In many ways Ms. Thandiwe was just the same as Scarlet remembered her—the same kind, caring eyes, the same long hair tied neatly in a bun, the same gaudy pink glasses hanging from a chain of beads around her neck. Her voice still had that youthful drawling South African accent, but it was impossible to ignore the obvious difference: Ms. Thandiwe was old. Her caring eyes were framed by deep-set wrinkles, and her hair was now cotton white. Her frame was still quite thin and bony, and although wrinkled, her skin was still clear and unblemished.

When Scarlet finished her story, Ms. Thandiwe took a moment to process all that she had heard before announcing, "Well, if you had told me this fifty years ago, I would have thought your imagination had run away with you. But this is no stranger than what we have been through ourselves."

"We?" Dakota asked.

"Yes, me and the children. I had them hide downstairs when I heard the commotion."

"Children?" Dakota said quizzically. "Where are all the adults?"

A sad and distant look came over Ms. Thandiwe. "The tiger men attacked five years ago. I was too old to fight, so I stayed inside with the children of the few adults still left. Their parents were all—they were all killed. Afterward the tigers just left—they didn't care about us. It's been quiet ever since, and I've done my best to take care of the children. There is a group of men—they were teenagers back then—who managed to survive, and still wander around trying to hunt and fight the tiger men and the other monsters. They bring us supplies every couple months. I hope and pray for their safety. They are very brave, but young. What they do is dangerous."

"The beasts haven't attacked you since then?" Delfi said, surprise in his voice.

"No. It was strange that they attacked that time. Something about the library—they don't like it, and they've always avoided coming close. I sometimes wonder whether, if the adults had just stayed inside, instead of going to fight them, they would still . . ." Ms. Thandiwe's voice faded away as tears fell down her face. She made no effort to hide them or wipe them away, and somehow this only made her look more dignified.

"Can you tell me, please, ma'am," Dakota said reverently, "what has happened over the last fifty years? It's of great importance."

Ms. Thandiwe dried her eyes with a lace handkerchief that she drew from her sleeve. "It was about fifty years ago. The sky went dark all over the world. The weathermen had no idea what was going on. They couldn't explain it. Then the trees and plants began growing wild, and the tiger men came."

"Tiranthropes," Delfi interjected.

"Yes, the . . . tiranthropes, you call them? They began killing all the men in the military and police. There was a horrible war all over the world. So much death. The plants destroyed our power plants and our factories. Without electricity, the military couldn't communicate, and they were eventually defeated. Without them to help keep the monsters in check—well, it was awful. So many people died. That was about thirty years ago. Ever since, we who survived have lived in hiding." Ms. Thandiwe looked as if reliving the events had taken a lot out of her.

"What made you choose this library?" Dakota asked.

"I don't know exactly. I have always loved the library and books. Here in the capital, the buildings are made of stone and steel and haven't been taken over by vegetation. Most everything else was destroyed. Also—well, never mind, it doesn't make sense," Ms. Thandiwe said with embarrassment.

"Please. It may not make sense to you, but you'd be surprised what is important," Dakota said reassuringly.

"Well . . . I was drawn here. I can't explain it," Ms. Thandiwe admitted. "Does that help you or make any sense?"

"It might. Perhaps we should get the children now, and introduce ourselves," Dakota said.

The children turned out to be twenty boys and girls of varying ages, some as young as six, a few as old as fourteen. Having been born and raised in this new version of the world, they were not at all taken aback by Dakota talking, or the mention of magic. A few seemed apprehensive about Brennan, who towered over them, but his calm, easygoing manner soon brought them around. The entire group of them looked skinny, but otherwise well cared for, and at seeing Ms. Thandiwe a few of the younger ones rushed over to her and clung to her side.

"Thandy," one of the youngest said, tugging on Ms. Thandiwe's skirt. "Have they brought us more food?"

Scarlet smiled at the little girl's accent. Doing quick math in her head, Scarlet realized that Ms. Thandiwe would have raised the little girl since shortly after she was born.

"No, sweetheart," Ms. Thandiwe said to the little girl. "They have come to stay with us." She turned to Scarlet. "They call me Thandy. Many have tried to call me Mommy, but I did not think that was right. They all had mothers. Brave and wonderful women. Ms. Thandiwe is just too formal, though, don't you think?"

They all ate in the reading room, which seemed to serve as the general living area for Ms. Thandiwe and the children. The meal consisted mainly of canned goods, although Ms. Thandiwe made a point of placing everything out as best she could so that they ate in some semblance of order, like a real family. After dinner Scarlet was treated to something she had dearly missed since leaving her home: Ms. Thandiwe read to all the children, her lilting voice filling the chamber. For a moment, Scarlet as well as the children felt carried away from the painful memories and danger that lurked outside the walls.

Later that night, Brennan and Dakota pored over a floor map of the Library of Congress, paying special attention to the building they were in, the Thomas Jefferson Building, and the tunnels that led to the Adams and Madison Buildings, as well as the Capitol. It was a lot of ground to defend. There were so many possible entrances that it seemed almost impossible to secure them all.

"What about what the old woman said about the tiranthropes staying away from the library? Do you think there's something to that?" Brennan asked.

"I don't know, and there's no way we can be sure," Dakota confessed. "It might be that there was just nothing they really cared about inside before. After all, once the adults left, it was only Ms. Thandiwe and a group of children—hardly a threat. Besides, we are going to have to leave soon. Scarlet has to complete her magical education if we are ever to have a chance at beating Prince Thanerbos. I don't like the thought of leaving them here, with things the way they are."

Although Dakota was initially reluctant to tell Brennan about their plans, his actions to save them in the Capitol Mall had earned Brennan the right to know. Dakota was still guarded, considering Brennan's involvement with a Mortada, but until something proved him to be other than an ally, Brennan had gained Dakota's reluctant trust.

An idea had suddenly occurred to Brennan. "Back at the school, the door was covered by roots and then right before you came out, they moved aside. Was that your magic?"

"No, it was Scarlet's. Why?" Dakota asked.

"Maybe she could do it in reverse. Put up roots to block the doors to the buildings and tunnels," Brennan suggested.

"I'm afraid that might take a great deal of energy. I'm not sure she'd be up to it," Dakota said, feeling particularly overprotective.

They studied the map in silence for several minutes before Dakota spoke again.

"Perhaps if we combine a little magic with some heavy lifting, we might be able to get it done. Have Scarlet close a few of the key entrances and work on barricading the rest," Dakota suggested.

"I could certainly gather up some of the older boys and Delfi. If we worked at it, I bet we could make a fair bit of progress," Brennan offered.

The next morning Brennan talked to Ms. Thandiwe and informed her of his intentions. He'd expected her to object that the tiranthropes naturally stayed away from the library, but she was in fact keen to improve the security of her chosen refuge.

Brennan, Delfi, and three of Ms. Thandiwe's boys—a small, thin boy of fourteen named John Farrington, who had thick curly hair and thicker glasses, and two pudgy boys of thirteen, each with the same narrow eyes, who remained so quiet that Brennan never learned their names, only that they were brothers but not twins—worked the entire day emptying shelves and desks and using them to barricade the library's entrances. It was hard, slow work. Brennan was pleased with how eager the boys were to pitch in. Their small size and undernourishment meant that they couldn't lift much at a time, and worked slowly. When evening finally came and

Brennan called the work done for the day, they had managed to block up seven entrances. Scarlet, he found out when they met up again, had managed to seal up the tunnel to the Madison Building.

At dinner Scarlet looked exhausted, and Brennan began to understand what Dakota meant about conserving her energy. At the current pace, Brennan figured, it would take a week to cover all the entrances.

As it turned out, they would have only one more day.

27
Jefferson's Last Stand

The following day began the same as the first, with Brennan and the boys working on entrances. The only difference was that Dakota insisted Scarlet rest, and not try to close up another tunnel until she had fully recovered. In the evening they all met in the reading room for another canned meal. Despite the less than inspiring food, good spirits seemed to prevail—at least, until the first roar pierced the inner sanctum of the library. More disconcertingly, it was not a faint, far-off call, but the loud, clear yowl of a tiranthrope announcing his presence just outside the walls.

Brennan, Scarlet, Delfi, and Dakota all rushed to the third floor to look out the windows. What they saw sent their stomachs tumbling to the floor. Tiranthropes, Mortada, and creatures neither Brennan nor Scarlet had ever seen before thronged around the library.

"Incruetati," Dakota said, answering Brennan and Scarlet's unspoken question. "I haven't heard of them being seen in Satorium in ages."

Whatever behavior they might have displayed before, the evil beings outside did not appear to be the slightest reluctant to cross onto the library grounds now. The new creatures, which looked like crosses between bats and men, had taken posts above the rest, perched on unlit streetlights and the roofs of the adjacent buildings.

"We can't possibly fight all of them," Delfi announced with a slight tremble in his throat, although his face wore a determined expression.

"No, we can't," Dakota admitted, "but we're going to have to." He turned and put his head through the railing, calling down to Ms. Thandiwe. "Take all the food you can carry and get yourself and all the children into one of the vaults downstairs."

Even though Ms. Thandiwe would have liked to protest and stand by Scarlet's side, she could not argue with the fact that twenty children needed her. She began to gather up the children, giving each as much food as he or she could carry and ushering them down the steps toward the vaults below the building.

"I don't understand," Scarlet began in a rush. "Ms. Thandiwe said that the beasts stayed away from the library."

Dakota looked at Scarlet and Delfi. "Maybe it's the Mortada. Maybe they weren't here before. I don't know, but I want you to listen to me. You need to stay safe. I want you to stay inside."

"No," Scarlet protested. "You can't go out there alone."

"He won't," Brennan said quickly.

"I thought this was my destiny," Scarlet pleaded. "To fight against the prince and his army," Scarlet pleaded.

"Yes, but first you have to be ready for the prince." Dakota didn't mince words. "It does the world no good if you die first."

"But I can't lose you too, Dakota. I can't!" Scarlet threw her arms around him, hot tears falling down her face.

"You have to be strong, Scarlet. Stick with Delfi. Take care of each other. Find a way to continue if I don't come back—do you understand?" Dakota said, his voice trembling slightly.

"I don't know what to do without you," Scarlet said, burying her face in Dakota's thick fur.

"You will, sweetheart, you will." Perhaps it had something to do with the time he had spent as a puppy, snuggled beside her as she slept, perhaps it was just some deep-seated sentimentality he hadn't known he possessed, but in that moment Dakota knew that he loved Scarlet. He loved her as deeply as any dog had ever loved his master, and that, he knew, was saying quite a lot.

Scarlet finally let go, and Dakota trotted off. Brennan extended his hand to Scarlet, who took it in both of hers. "I hope I see you again."

"Me too," Scarlet called out as Brennan ran off after Dakota.

Brennan and Dakota left through one of the entrances that had yet to be sealed. The sky above them was pitch-black, not a star in the sky. The moon hung eerily alone, full and bright, giving a pale silvery light to the scene in front of the library. Framed by the looming Capitol, which seemed to drink in the moonlight, was the army of Mortada, tiranthropes, and incruetati. Brennan and Dakota stood on the steps before the army, looking insignificant in the face of such overwhelming odds. The tiranthropes snarled at the odd pair of warriors, itching to attack, but for the moment stayed in place.

"Legend has it that your people have an inner power that gives you supernatural strength," Dakota said offhandedly to Brennan, his eyes fixed on the army. "Any chance that legend is true?"

Brennan smiled. "It's true. Problem is, I've got no control over when it comes and goes."

"Well, at least that's something," Dakota quipped in a rare moment of frivolity—brought on, no doubt, by the fact that he was surely facing his death.

One of the Mortada stepped forward from the ranks. "Udd Lyall, is that you?" Multus, the Mortada with the strangely flaking skin who Brennan had attacked in the woods, called in a lilting almost whimsical voice. "We had heard rumors

, that you had . . . well, changed." The Mortada laughed. "Lord of Wolves indeed."

Dakota held his head high and said, "I am Dakota." Thoughts of his father passed through his mind at that moment. The love and pride his father had shown him. The hope that one day, he, Udd Lyall, would succeed him as the leader of the Stidolph, and how after his father's death, Dakota had shied away from such responsibility. Well, no more would he carry that shame. "I *am* the Lord of Wolves," he added defiantly.

Multus laughed again. "You are revered in Satorium—although I must point out that we are not in Satorium." Several of the other Mortada joined in the joke, laughing in a creepy, unnatural chorus. "All the same, our lord would wish that we uphold at least the ancient courtesies. If you leave the field and step aside, you may go in peace. We will not seek you out. You may live out your remaining days as a dog, doing whatever you please."

"I know this Mortada," Brennan whispered to Dakota. "He was the one Chosen was afraid of. Didn't seem too eager to deal with me, though."

"I know him as well," Dakota whispered cryptically. Then he spoke boldly to the Mortada. "I will not stand aside. You will not have the girl, this night or any other."

"I thought you might say that. *Hoped* is more like it," Multus sang out, though his voice had lost a great deal of its whimsical quality.

Multus swept his arm toward the pair, and the tiranthropes sprang forward, quickly closing the distance. Brennan and

Dakota ran out to meet them, and blood and fur flew as the fighting began. Dakota leaped and spun, snapping out at the tiranthropes and dodging most of the blows that came his way. Brennan, locked in a wrestling match with two of the tiranthropes, quickly failed under the weight and strength of them.

Scarlet watched the scene unfold with growing horror from the third floor of the library. It wouldn't be long before both Dakota and Brennan were killed. The sound of voices and footsteps below brought Scarlet's attention away from the window. Ms. Thandiwe and the children had come back up into the main lobby.

Scarlet rushed to the railing. "What's happened? Why aren't you in the vault?"

Ms. Thandiwe looked ashen. "They are coming through the tunnel from the Capitol. They'll be here any minute."

Scarlet had to do something—she just didn't know what. She and her family hadn't gone through all of this, hadn't learned all this, to have it end here. Her first and most pressing thought was to do something to save Dakota and Brennan, and it took a tremendous effort for her to put that aside. Dakota had been clear. She needed to stay safe.

Scarlet ran to the reading room, where Ms. Thandiwe had gathered the children. Wide with fear and shock, their eyes pleaded with Scarlet. Not knowing what else to do, she lay on the floor, her cheek against the cold stone, and began to whisper to the earth. She prayed to it for understanding, for it to grant what seemed impossible. She remembered Jud-Byr's warning about his magic: he could not create what wasn't there. He could not speak to nothing.

But Scarlet was the For Tol Don. She had not wanted to fully accept that, but if it were true, as all her friends believed, then her magic—all magic—could come from within her. The legend was that she, unlike the dwarves, had the power to create what wasn't there. She remembered Dakota's explanation from what now seemed like ages ago.

Scarlet closed her eyes and rose to her knees, searching within herself for the power that must be there. She had to believe. She had to conjure forth something that would save them all.

For a terrifyingly long moment, nothing happened. Then the ground began to shake, the walls trembled, and hideous wails filled the air. And suddenly Scarlet knew what was happening, though she wasn't sure how she knew. It was almost as if she could see it. Enormous roots were erupting through the floor of the tunnel, crushing the Mortada coming through the tunnel, killing or injuring many and cutting the rest off from the building. Across every entrance to the Thomas Jefferson Building, every door and window, roots were bursting violently from the ground, completely encasing the building in a thick woven armor of living wood. When Scarlet finally stood, dizzy and nearly fainting, the Thomas Jefferson Building had become an impenetrable fortress of wood and stone.

Delfi ran to Scarlet's side, catching her as her knees buckled. "Help me to the window," Scarlet pleaded, her voice weak and distant.

Delfi did not argue. He motioned to one of the eldest boys, and they helped her up the steps and to the window that looked out to the front of the building. Scarlet waved her hand, and the roots rearranged themselves, opening a small gap to allow them to see the battle below.

The Tempest had come to Brennan, and given him the strength to keep himself and Dakota alive. They were both weakened by grave wounds, however, and now the Mortada had joined the fight, casting their dark spells as the incruetati began circling over Brennan and Dakota's heads.

"They won't last much longer," Delfi cried. "I should go. I should go and help them."

Scarlet put a hand on his shoulder. "No. You'll die."

She felt so weak, so drained. But she had to do something. Charging out of the building wouldn't help—the Mortada would be on her before she got a foot out the door. And Delfi had been just as susceptible to their dark magic as she was; he wouldn't last any longer. She suddenly realized what she had to do. Dakota would be furious; it went against his wishes directly. It risked everything. However, For Tol Don or not, she was not a person who could let her friends die. She just couldn't.

Scarlet allowed herself to fall to her knees. Delfi went to help her up, but she bade him back with an upraised hand. Closing her eyes, she drew deep within herself . . . deeper than she had ever gone before. She searched not just for her inner light but for the very origin of that light. She allowed it to build, adding her rage, her fear, her love, her sorrow. It was a living thing, wild and untamed, unlike the restrained and controlled magic Xavier had taught her to master. When at last she could hold it in no more, she raised her hands to the sky and let it out, falling to the ground as darkness overtook her.

And now a sphere of light exploded out from her, so bright and powerful that it penetrated everything in its wake in concentric rings as it spread. It passed out of the Thomas Jefferson Building and into the night, illuminating all of DC in a light brighter than the sunniest of days. The tiranthropes, Mortada, and incruetati cowered in the intolerable glare. Some attempted to flee. All were swallowed up in its brilliance.

When the light faded, they had all vanished.

28
The Sorrowful Return

For a week Charles had been wandering over the plains, hoping against hope for a miracle—for any sign of his daughter, any hint at how to get to her. Finally, starving and dehydrated, he decided with a heavy heart that his best chance at finding Scarlet was to return to Xavier. If anyone would know what to do, it would be the wise Keeper of Light.

The hike back to Illuminora was excruciating. His mind could not turn off the grief. It hollowed him out, made every step an agony. He made no attempt to disguise his presence as he trudged through the forest. If any Mortada had been left in the area, they would have captured or killed him as easily as an orphaned cub. Looking back, he would never understand how he made it back to the great oak at all.

After all the time Charles had spent underneath the oak tree, it amazed him how small the opening in the trunk now seemed to be; it seemed a lifetime ago now that he had come here for the first time with his family. With Scarlet. He fell down at the base of the tree, crying out for Xavier.

Moments later, the dancing lights of the Tounder surrounded him, and he began to shrink. Once he'd reached the right size, the Tounder gathered him up and whisked him quickly away to the castle in Illuminora. They carried him to the room he had shared with Allie and sent for Xavier at once.

Charles was near delirium by the time Xavier arrived with Allie, Melody, and Cricket. Seeing the state he was in, Xavier asked Cricket if she could take Melody downstairs for a while. Although Melody nearly pitched a fit at being taken away from her father, she eventually followed Cricket out, leaving Xavier and Allie to tend to Charles.

"Charles," Allie sobbed. "What's happened? Where's Scarlet?" She was doing her best to hold off hysterics, but they weren't far away.

Xavier was checking Charles over, whispering chants, and occasionally bathing him in light. He examined Charles's right hand especially carefully, then called for a Tounder waiting outside the door to bring water. "He has a fever and is severely dehydrated," Xavier said to Allie. "His hand has been exposed to a powerful bit of dark magic."

After the Tounder returned, Allie raised the glass of Tounder water to her husband's lips while Xavier performed a series of light incantations over his hand. Finally, Charles lapsed into an uneasy sleep.

Xavier took Allie to the side, away from the bed. "He's going to be fine. In a couple of hours he'll be able to speak to us. I won't lie to you—something has gone very wrong."

"Is Scarlet . . . is she . . . oh God!" Allie wailed.

"No, no. Scarlet is alive. We are connected now, through the magic we share as student and teacher. I would know if she wasn't. I promise you."

Xavier's promise seemed to give Allie a small degree of peace. It didn't help explain where her daughter was and why her husband had returned without her, though. She went back to the bedside and sat down in a chair, taking her husband's hand as she wept.

Charles woke several hours later with a start, calling out for Scarlet. It took him a minute to realize where he was, and before he could say anything, Xavier had appeared beside Mrs. Hopewell.

"Where's Scarlet?" Mrs. Hopewell asked, unable to wait a second longer.

Tears pooled in Mr. Hopewell's eyes as he looked from his wife to Xavier, his face contorted with sorrow and guilt. "I should never have left her," he cried. "I walked ahead to find us some shelter from the storm, and it came for them—for her. I had her—the strap tore off."

"What storm?" Xavier asked a rising panic in his voice.

"Black. Endless black clouds that sucked them away. I waited for days. There was no sign of them. They just disappeared."

"Black clouds. Like a fog. It took them away," Xavier repeated. Charles nodded. "I'm sorry," Xavier said suddenly. "I must go. I'll be back soon, or if you feel up to it, meet me later in the library." And with that he vanished, moving more quickly than Charles had ever seen him move.

Allie leaned down and wrapped her arms around her husband, holding him tightly as they both wept.

An hour later, although he still felt weak and emotionally drained, Charles forced himself to get out of bed and go find Xavier. He was in desperate need of answers, and he couldn't wait any longer to get them. Wherever Scarlet was, she was alive; Charles had gathered that much from Allie. What mattered now, more than anything else in the world, was finding his little girl and keeping her safe. The weight of guilt that bore down on him as he made his way to the library was crippling. Regret over letting Scarlet go on the quest, letting himself be sucked into the idea . . . He couldn't help but feel that he had failed her as a father. He hadn't protected her.

Xavier was sitting in his high-backed chair when Charles found him, desperately searching through the enchanted leather-bound book. The patience he'd developed with old age, the ability to let the passages he wanted come to him, had failed him, it seemed. Not until Charles had come all the way into the library and was standing before him did Xavier notice his presence.

"You look much better." Xavier's voice was full of weariness. He looked as if he had aged considerably in the past few hours. "You'll need more rest, though."

"Where is Scarlet?" Charles demanded. "Where is my little girl?"

Xavier sighed. "She is back in your world, with Dakota and Delfi."

"How is that possible? I thought . . . I don't know what I thought. What is going on?" Mr. Hopewell's voice was full of desperation. Unable to stand still any longer, he began to pace feverishly in front of Xavier.

"I have made a horrible miscalculation," Xavier admitted, his eyes deeply apologetic. "Prince Thanerbos has played me for the old fool that I am. The attack on Leona, the Mortada he stationed around Illuminora, it was all a ruse. A misdirection."

"What do you mean, a misdirection?" Charles demanded.

"To distract me from what he has done to your world, Mr. Hopewell. He is still imprisoned—I've had word from the king confirming as much—but his powers are far stronger than I had guessed. He has sent an army to your world. He has torn the very fabric of time. Only months have passed here in Satorium, but fifty years have passed in your world. While we were training for the coming battle, preparing for his eventual escape from prison, he has destroyed that world." For a moment, Xavier looked completely vanquished. He bowed his head, as if to accept his defeat. But the moment passed. When Xavier looked up, his face was set in a determined smile—more to reassure Charles, he thought, than a reflection of his true feeling.

"How do you know all this?" Charles asked.

"Some of the pieces fell into place when I reread old texts of the prophecy. Others I have received from the Doran king. Lastly"—Xavier shrugged—"well, I guessed."

"You guessed?" Charles was incredulous.

"We have some catching up to do," Xavier announced briskly, avoiding Charles's question. He stood and began to make his way out of the library.

"Catching up?" Charles followed Xavier as the old Tounder strode out of the library.

"We will leave in the morning. He may have won the first round, but the war is not his. We will defeat him." Xavier briskly led the way through the castle's mazelike passages, stopping every so often to issue orders to a castle Tounder.

Ten minutes later, Charles found himself in the conference room with Xavier and the rest of the Tounder council. This time there was no grumbling or heated debate; all, even Thaniel, sat in silence, waiting with bated breath to hear what Xavier had to say.

"It has come to my attention that Prince Thanerbos has succeeded in mounting an attack on the human world. While we have been preparing here over the course of the past months, a fifty-year battle has been waged in the land beyond—a battle that has been lost. Minions of the dark prince have overrun the world of Mr. Hopewell and his family. Those humans that remain do so in hiding, or in small pockets of resistance." Xavier took a moment to let his words sink in.

The members of the council all looked somberly at Charles, and a few offered their condolences.

Brynn placed a comforting hand on his shoulder. "We may be divided by magic, but we are all creatures of the earth. We will do whatever we can to help your world."

"That we will," Xavier chimed in. "I see only one way to do that now. The two worlds must be no more."

There was a series of gasps from the council. Thaniel huffed so loudly that he had to look away in embarrassment when Xavier's flashing eyes locked on him. The council member managed to gather enough courage, however, to add incredulously, "You mean to undo what the great Hulpric brought to pass eons ago?"

"Times change, Thaniel," Xavier said sternly. "What was right then is not always right now. The few that remain in Mr. Hopewell's world are defenseless against the plight they face each and every day. They have fought for fifty years against hopeless odds, and it is time that we come to their aid."

"I agree," Brynn interjected. "I must ask, however, what this means for our plans against Prince Thanerbos."

"It only strengthens them, old friend. And in our current circumstance, the two goals are one. Lady Scarlet, the For Tol Don, is trapped in that world. Without access to Satorium, she cannot hope to complete her preparations. Prince Thanerbos now controls the ability to cross over. Our only hope is to take that control away from him by making it obsolete.

"Before this new development, I had plans to ask Morelpis for his help in repelling the prince's army from invading Caelesta. I will still make this trip, and I hope that Mr. Hopewell will agree to accompany me."

Charles was taken aback. "You want me to go and see the dragon?"

"Yes. He was once a father, like you, and I believe that your story and your anguish over Scarlet will appeal to him in ways that I cannot. Morelpis is the only creature living now who was alive in Hulpric's time. If anyone can help us merge the two worlds and reach Scarlet, it will be he."

"What of Hulpric's book?" Brynn asked. "Does it say nothing of this?"

"I'm afraid that if Hulpric wished us to know how to join the two worlds, he made the information difficult to find. Perhaps he did not want the venture taken too lightly."

"Perhaps he didn't want the venture taken at all," Thaniel snapped.

"There is no choice left to us," Xavier responded. "He separated the two worlds to protect those without magic. His goal is now being threatened by the very means he used to achieve it. The separation only serves to keep the human world in eternal danger now. I will speak to Morelpis. I—*we*—will not let our worlds fall to Prince Thanerbos."

In the early morning light, Charles knelt beside Melody's bed, running his fingers through her thick blond hair. She was safe here with the Tounder and her mother. With all the things that he didn't understand, with all the things that overwhelmed his emotions and his senses, for some reason this one known fact brought him a small measure of peace.

It had been such a short time to spend with his wife and youngest daughter that when morning came, Charles had felt as if it were no time at all. For the second time in a week, he was saying good-bye with no real knowledge of when he would see his family again. Everything seemed so wildly out of control. He wished that he could freeze time and catch his breath, try to wrap his mind around it all.

He debated now whether he should wake Melody; her sleep seemed so serene. He did not want her to wake and find him gone, though, and so he lightly rubbed her shoulder until she stirred.

"Daddy," she whispered, rubbing the sleep from her eyes.

"Hi, baby. Daddy's got to go." A lump rose in his throat.

Tears came instantly to Melody's eyes, but she did not sob. She reached out her small arms, and Charles picked her up, holding her tight to his chest. "I love you, Daddy."

"I love you too, baby."

He held her for a long time before setting her back on the bed. "I want you to listen to me," he said firmly. "I'm going to bring your sister back, okay? I'm going to bring her back."

Melody nodded, a few tears running down her cheek.

"You be good for Mommy and take care of Cricket, okay?" Charles added. "I'll be home soon." Home. A strange concept. Illuminora had now become their home.

He picked up Melody again, and she began to sing. As Charles held her, listening to her soft voice, he felt a peace deep in his heart he had not known since losing Scarlet. When she had finished, he laid her down and tucked her back into bed.

"That was beautiful," he said, leaning down and kissing her cheek.

"It's a healing song, Daddy," Melody said, letting out a big yawn, her eyelids heavy.

"That it certainly is."

Cricket was sitting at the foot of the bed, looking solemnly at him with her big brown eyes. "You take care of her, you hear," he said to her.

"I will," she replied simply.

Charles and Allie's good-byes were longer. Charles held Allie as she sobbed, her head buried in his chest. Letting her go was one of the most difficult things he had ever done.

"I don't care how cranky that dragon ends up being," she said sternly at last, brushing away her tears with determination and setting her hand lovingly on Charles's chest. "You get him to agree. You get him to help us get to Scarlet."

"I will, darling."

"Maybe you shouldn't mention that you're a firefighter, though," Allie said, managing a smile. "Him being a dragon and all."

"I was hoping that might work to my advantage. Put some fear into him." Charles smiled back at her, and they both chuckled nervously and embraced one last time.

Xavier was waiting in the entrance hall, wearing a heavy pack and carrying a staff much like the one he'd given Scarlet. He and Charles had both put on new spider's-silk traveling clothes.

"Are you ready, Charles?" Xavier looked as determined as Charles had ever seen him, the aged, wizened professor giving way to the ancient warrior.

Charles took one last deep breath of the peaceful air of Illuminora, and looked around one more time. He would find Scarlet. He would find her and bring her home.

"Let's go meet a dragon," he said. And perhaps for the first time since he'd arrived in the land of Satorium, such words did not sound at all strange coming from his lips.

29
Hulpric's Book

Scarlet opened her eyes to soft candlelight. She wiped the sleep from her eyes, and waited for them to adjust to the dim light before looking around. She was in a small room that had been used for private study and reading in the days when the Thomas Jefferson Building was just a library, Ms. Thandiwe had told her. She felt hungry, and a little woozy. In a stiff wooden chair nearby, Delfi was propped up, sleeping with his head in his hands. His chestnut hair was a mess, standing up at weird angles all over his head, and even though he was asleep at that moment, he had the look of someone who had not slept in days.

"You're going to get a horrible crick in your neck," she said, waking Delfi, whose head slipped from his hands as he woke with a jolt.

"You're awake!" Delfi exclaimed. "You—you woke up! Just a second—wait just a second."

Delfi got up and opened the glass door to the tiny room. Scarlet could hear him yelling so loudly that everyone in the library must have heard him.

"How long have I been asleep?" Scarlet asked. She raised herself into a sitting position, her muscles feeling a bit stiff from lack of use.

"Two weeks," Delfi answered, the smile on his face so broad it seemed it might wrap around the side of his head.

"Two weeks!"

"Dakota was afraid you might not wake up at all," Delfi said, frowning. The memory was a painful one.

"Dakota's alive?" Scarlet exclaimed. "And Brennan?"

"You saved them both. It was amazing. Never seen anything quite so powerful, not even from Xavier. Dakota said it was foolish to risk your life, but I expect he's gonna be proud all the same." Delfi's smile returned as quickly as it had vanished.

Just then Brennan, Dakota, and Ms. Thandiwe rushed into the room. They were all jammed in like sardines. Dakota wedged his way to where she lay.

"You silly girl," he barked. "You risked the fate of the

entire world just to save us? Do you have any idea what could have happened to you?"

Scarlet just smiled back. Despite the sternness in his voice, she could see the tenderness in his deep blue eyes. Besides, it was best just to let him get the fear and frustration off his chest. After all, he'd been waiting two weeks.

Dakota softened a little. "What you did was . . . very brave. Thinking about it now, I probably should have locked you in a closet. I don't know why I expected anything different from you. You wouldn't . . . well, you wouldn't be you if you hadn't."

Brennan leaned down toward Scarlet. "Thank you." His face and arms still bore the marks of the horrific battle he had fought. Looking at his wounds, Scarlet guessed that he'd carry some of those scars for the rest of his life.

After another night's rest, Scarlet felt well enough to leave her makeshift hospital room and venture out into the rest of the library. Delfi had been busy. Some of the trees Scarlet had called forth to block the tunnels were fruit-bearing. Delfi had added spheres of light to the darkened spaces, and the enchanted trees had responded with a steady supply of apples, pears, and figs. He'd also exposed fresh earth by breaking up some of the tunnel floors, and there was talk of finding seeds and growing vegetables.

Scarlet gathered her father's pack, removed the green satin bag containing the seeds she'd saved when she sowed the dwarves' field, and went to find Delfi. She found him in the Madison tunnel, looking over a pear tree and making sure his sphere of light gave it enough energy to bear fruit.

"Pretty brilliant," she said, sneaking up behind him.

Delfi jumped, spun around, and then laughed when he saw Scarlet. "Yep, you are."

"Me, I didn't even have a clue what kind of trees I was calling up. Giving them light and harvesting the fruit—now *that's* brilliant."

"Hungry is more like it." Delfi grinned.

Scarlet picked one of the pears and bit into it. It was perfectly ripe and extremely juicy. "Oh, these are for you," she said, handing Delfi the bag.

"What are they?" he asked, answering his own question as he looked into the bag. "What kind of seeds are they?"

"I don't know. Xavier gave them to me, and I gave most to the dwarves. They sprouted into all sorts of stuff in their field. Some of it's what they used to save you."

"I can't believe you thought to save some. This is going to be amazing." Delfi bent down and dropped a few into the freshly cultivated soil.

"So what happened after?"

Delfi laughed. "After you sent out the lightie wonder ball, you mean?"

"Lightie wonder ball?"

"It's what the little ones call it. I think it sounds pretty menacing, so I like to use it. It's become its official title." Delfi smirked. "As I was saying, after you conjured up the lightie wonder ball, it radiated into the army outside. They were all repelled—or anyway, just somehow disappeared. Funny thing was, Brennan and Dakota made their way back to the library, but there was no one to ask the trees to stand aside. They had to go to a back entrance and hack their way through. Took them the whole night."

"Oh no," Scarlet exclaimed. "No wonder he's mad at me."

"He's not mad." Delfi raised his eyebrows. "He was so worried about you. It was killing him not to be able to get to you."

He took her hand. "Come on, I want to show you something."

"Oh, Delfi," Scarlet cried, suddenly realizing what had been bothering her. "Your wings!" They were completely gone.

"What, those?" Delfi craned his neck to try and look at his back. "Don't worry about it. It's a relief to have them finally gone, all tattered and hanging down like they were. A bit uncomfortable. Besides, I've got something to show you." He tugged on her arm, nearly hopping up and down in his eagerness.

Scarlet followed, giggling, as Delfi led her up to the second floor and walked her around to the window where she had watched Brennan and Dakota fighting. The small opening in the roots was still there outside the window.

"I should probably close that," Scarlet remarked.

"Not necessarily. Take a look." Delfi pointed.

Scarlet peered through the hole in the vines and gasped. Like a colossal bell jar set down over the library, filled with a golden radiance, the dome of light she'd created shone steadily, cheerfully.

"Mortada and tiranthropes have been trying to get past it for days, sending out dark magic spells or charging it. They haven't gotten anywhere. The incruetati have tried from the air as well. Same thing."

"I don't understand. How could I possibly . . . I would still have to be concentrating to maintain something that big. I wouldn't have the energy."

"I figure it's like when the craftsmen in Illuminora make those toys. They make them out of light, and they are permanent. They don't have to think about them anymore—they just are what they are. You've done the same thing, only with an enormous burst of light energy. Never heard of anything like it—but after all, you *are* the For Tol Don."

Scarlet smiled, and then sighed. "Yeah, I guess I am."

After lunch—at which, thanks to Delfi's horticultural activities and to Brennan, who'd found tables and cleared a space for a proper dining room, they ate fresh food, seated like a family—the children were allowed to play outside, sheltered by Scarlet's dome of light, for the first time in their lives. She asked the trees and vines to draw away from the doors, and with timid steps at first, then running full tilt, the children poured out of the building and onto the grassy lawns surrounding the library, shouting with joy.

To the immense surprise of everyone who knew him, Dakota let some of the younger children climb onto his back, where they held tight, some wide-eyed as he carefully walked around the lawn, some of the braver ones giggling madly as he galumphed about like a big puppy. It was a golden moment of peace and merriment. Scarlet lay on the grass, watching them. When had she last felt so content, so carefree? Surely this had been one of the best days of her life, she thought as the children filed back into the library, tired but contented. If only the rest of her family had been there with her, she could have asked for nothing more.

She'd grown up so much since that fateful day when her father brought home the skinny puppy with the big paws and the deep blue eyes. Sometimes she felt like an entirely different person, like the heroine of the legend, even, but others she still felt like an awkward schoolgirl. It was hard to imagine that once life had been so simple.

She thought about the stories she used to write. Now she knew that it was Satorium in those stories, Satorium she had been dreaming of. It must all have been part of the prophecy; somehow Satorium—Xavier, perhaps—had been calling to her through the barrier. She had never told him about her dreams or her writing, and she now wished that she had. It wasn't only that he might know what they should do next; she just wished that he were here, so she could ask some of the million questions they hadn't had time for before.

She stood up to head back inside too, but then stopped, her head tipped back as she looked up at the Library of Congress. In the enchanted light the building seemed almost translucent, glowing from within. It was as beautiful as it had ever been, yet utterly changed. In this fortress of enchanted living wood and earthly stone, the two worlds seemed joined as one.

That evening Dakota, Brennan, Delfi, and Scarlet met in what had once been a conference room to discuss their next move. They had a secure base from which to plan now, and the children and Ms. Thandiwe were safe. Now they had to find a way to complete Scarlet's education, and to anticipate Xavier's and Prince Thanerbos's next moves so they could either help or thwart them.

"Is there a way Scarlet could learn any of what she needs to know here, in this world?" Delfi asked.

Looking at Delfi standing with the rest of her friends, his face so grave, Scarlet thought that he had also grown up a lot in the short time she'd known him. She felt a deep gratitude that he had risked so much to be with her.

"I don't know. I've never heard of any magic on this side. I wouldn't even know where to begin. In Satorium it was always clear who to ask for help, and where to go." Dakota's forehead wrinkled as he thought. "Can you think of any legends or stories in this world that could really be true?"

"Sure, loads," Scarlet answered. "Greek mythology, the Nordic sagas, the legends around Christmas, fairy tales—even some great works of literature are about imaginary worlds, and magic. Tolkien, C. S. Lewis, even Shakespeare," she said, thinking about Ms. Thandiwe.

"That may be worth researching," Delfi added. "We *are* in a library, after all."

"Or we could find a way to get back to Satorium," Dakota said, looking doubtful. "I just don't know how we could do that without—"

But he never finished the thought. Just then a small boy, maybe eight years old, burst into the conference room. "Scarlet, Scarlet, you have to come quick!"

"What's wrong, young one?" Dakota barked.

"It's in the rare books part of the library. We were playing, and—you just have to come look!"

The group got up and followed the boy to the rare books room, where Thomas Jefferson's personal books, among other treasures, were kept. The boy pointed up at one of the bookshelves, nearly hopping up and down in his excitement. "I've played in here loads of times, and that's never been like that before."

High up on the shelf, a book was glowing softly.

A little gingerly, Brennan reached to get the leather-bound volume down, handing it over to Scarlet at once. It looked familiar, somehow. Opening it reverently, she watched in amazement as the letters and the lines of the woodcut pictures rose off the page like a flock of tiny black birds, spiraling in the air and then settling back down on the page to create new images and stories. At one of the new pictures, Scarlet's breath caught in her throat. There were words below the image. She began to read.

In the land of Satorium, in the Northern Woodlands, beneath a great oak tree, lies the village of Illuminora, the home of the Tounder, the Keepers of Light . . .

Again the letters rose in a swirling cloud, and again they settled on the page like blackbirds on a field.

And from humanity will rise a great sorceress, and the people will call her the For Tol Don. She will stand against the dark one, for only she can match his power. And though she may doubt herself, though she may struggle through fear and disbelief, she will find the magic within . . .

The adventure continues in the second book of the Scarlet Hopewell series...

Scarlet
and the Dragon's Burden

Three young men sat huddled around a campfire that sputtered and sizzled under a steady rain. They were cold and hungry, but filled with a hope that they had not felt for a long time. If the stories they'd been hearing were true, they might just have a chance against the monstrous plague that had ravaged their world, robbing them of their families, of their dreams, of any hope of peace, leaving only dread. Two of the three, born after the world had already succumbed to the destructive force from Satorium, had never known what it was to feel safe.

The story that most concerned the three young men had traveled by word of mouth around the wild, war-torn earth.

It told of a cunning dog, a fairy, a giant, and a young sorceress who traveled by starlight and possessed powers that might help her vanquish the dark creatures. Sixty years ago, had they heard such a story, most would have dismissed it as the plot of a children's novel or a fantasy movie. But those carefree days were gone. There were no longer any theaters to take the kids to, no Barnes & Nobles in which to browse while sipping coffee on a busy weekend. The world was now a savage, cruel place.

"How much farther to the city?" one of the young men, Brian, asked, raising a tin cup full of hot soup that was little more than flavored water to his lips.

The eldest of the group, whose name was Gerald, looked out toward the eastern horizon. "Another day, I figure," he said, although he had no idea if this were true. In fact, he'd been saying the same thing for days now. His companions never complained. It was as good an answer as any, and better than admitting that he didn't know.

"How much do you think is true?" The youngest and smallest of the three men directed his question to Gerald, as he always did.

"I don't know, Mike. I guess I'd have to hope all of it." Gerald offered his most reassuring smile. In addition to being the reluctant leader, and a surrogate big brother to the other two, he was also the most skeptical. In his mind, the stories must contain some grain of truth if they'd reached all the way to Tennessee, but he wasn't ready to believe them wholesale. In his life thus far, if something was too good to be true—well, actually, if it was good at all—it was not. He had agreed to travel to Washington, DC, not because he expected to find answers there but because it was better than cowering in some cellar or cave, waiting to die.

"I think they are," Mike said wistfully. "I mean, they gotta be, right? Everywhere we go, no matter who we talk to, it's always the same. That's gotta count for something."

Gerald dragged his pack in front of him and began taking inventory by firelight. "The stories are not all the same, though. And if we're being honest with ourselves, they've gotten more outrageous the closer we've come to DC." Instantly he regretted that he'd spoken his feelings out loud. Mike and Brian didn't need his doubts weighing them down. Let them believe if they wanted to. Heck, he wished he could.

"Well, the safe haven hasn't changed. The Sanctuary. That part has always been the same, no matter where we go," Brian said, his voice confident. "No one person we've talked to has ever described anything different. A great sphere around the Library of Congress that keeps the darkness out____"

"Where safe haven is to be had for any human seeking refuge," Gerald cut him off. He was tired and out of sorts, and he didn't feel like going over it all again. "You're right, Brian. That part's always been the same."

"Who wants first watch?" Mike asked, trying to change the subject. He also hoped that if he brought it up, Brian and Gerald would offer it to him. It was so much easier to stay up late and then sleep without interruption until morning.

"I'll take it," Gerald answered quickly. "I don't have a good feeling about tonight. I'll take a long watch, let you two get some extra sleep."

Neither Mike nor Brian argued, partly because they'd learned it was useless to argue with Gerald once he'd made up his mind and partly because extra sleep was a rare luxury. They rolled out their sleeping bags, placing them as close to the fire as possible. As they crawled inside, ready to take advantage of Gerald's generosity, a sound carried across the night and straight up their spines.

"How close?" Mike whimpered.

"Too close," Gerald whispered back.

Quickly and quietly they began stuffing their things back into their packs. Gerald stomped out the fire, cursing himself for having lit it in the first place. It had been such a cold night. . . . Still, he should have known better. They had come all this way, and now they were done for; there was no use pretending any different.

The roar of the tiranthropes came again, already much closer. The three young men began to move away from the campsite as quietly as they could. With any luck, the creatures would spend a while sniffing around the campsite and lose interest. The area was thick with trees, and Gerald was pretty sure that a river lay not too far to the east. If they could get across it, maybe they could lose the tiranthropes. Surely the beasts couldn't follow scent across a river.

A tiranthrope let out a bloodcurdling roar. The creature must have reached their campsite. The river was their only hope, Gerald decided. Abandoning any pretense of stealth, he motioned to his companions and they took off in a full sprint toward the east. The ground was uneven and thick with underbrush, slowing them but also offering some cover from the keen eyes of the tiranthropes that would be bearing down on them any minute. The three men plunged headlong through the forest, dodging trees and jumping logs, their ears straining for the unmistakable sound of heavy footsteps on their heels.

The forest thinned, and they broke into a clearing. At its center stone steps led to a flat marble edifice, surrounded by uniform white headstones. In the distance was the river, and beyond, a towering white obelisk.

"It's a graveyard." Mike's voice quivered uncontrollably.

"This is the soldiers' graveyard." Gerald pointed toward the Washington Monument. "That's DC. We were camped right across the river from it. It's right there."

Brian grabbed Gerald's shoulder and pulled at him. "We gotta go," he said frantically. "They're coming."

Gerald shook his head clear, his momentary sense of wonder replaced by a primal fear. He could hear the tiranthropes approaching, their heavily muscled legs pounding the earth as they tore through the underbrush. The three men dropped their packs and ran as hard as they could for the river. Never had anything seemed so blissfully close and yet so painfully far away.

The tiranthropes broke through the trees as the three men reached the middle of Arlington National Cemetery. The average man can run maybe twelve miles an hour, the average tiranthrope, closer to fifty. With nothing but open ground ahead, the three men stood no chance. At the Tomb of the Unknown Soldier, Gerald stopped running. He had made his decision. He would not be run down like a deer; he'd fight like a man. He'd fight as his father had, when Gerald was newborn and the world not yet fallen. His companions stopped as well, ready to stand beside him, but Gerald waved them on, pushing them away.

"Maybe I can buy you some time," he said, sounding braver than he felt. "Find the Sanctuary. Find safety."

Brian and Mike remained frozen by indecision, trapped between their desire to survive and their instinct to stand by their friend. And then it was too late; the tiranthropes had bounded up the steps, stopping mere feet from the three young men.

"Should we play with them a little?" one of the creatures growled, deep and menacing.

There were three of the giant feline figures, lithe despite their massive size, each standing near eight feet tall, covered head to foot in a tiger's fur, their faces more cat than man.

One, set apart from the others by his snow-white coat, stepped slightly forward and sniffed at the air. "I don't think you'd play with them long before they all dropped dead. You can smell the fear on them thicker than their blood." His laugh sounded more like a roar.

"Better not, then," the first answered. "I like my meat fresh. I hate it when their hearts give out before the first bite."

The tiranthropes moved in, and then stopped abruptly. The white tiranthrope's nose again searched the air. This time his eyes, focused on something behind Gerald and his friends, narrowed in alarm, not in amusement. Gerald turned his head to look: behind him, a man was walking up the steps. As the newcomer neared, the tiranthropes stepped back.

"Times must be getting desperate, for you to be hunting this close to the Capitol," the new figure said.

At once the three young men knew who he was: this was the giant of the stories they'd heard.

In reality, Brennan was significantly smaller than the tiranthropes who seemed so afraid of him. True, next to Gerald, Brian, and Mike he was a very large young man, nearly seven feet tall, thickly muscled and broad-shouldered. But it wasn't his size that identified him. The young men, now spectators in an exchange they didn't understand, could see why he'd been described as a giant. It was the way that he carried himself.

"There are three of us, Satoriun," the white tiranthrope said. His attempt to sound confident came out more like pleading. "You are outnumbered."

"Am I?" Brennan said, his voice calm and even.

From the left side of the monument, a German shepherd padded into the invisible circle around the tiranthropes and men. He too was quite large.

Gerald looked from the giant to the dog to the tiranthropes, utterly bewildered. Not half an hour ago, he hadn't been sure whether he believed any of the stories, and not five minutes ago he had been sure that he was about to die. His mind struggled to process what was happening and what, if anything, he and his friends should do. It certainly didn't seem smart to remain between the giant and the tiranthropes.

The next development in the odd standoff served only to further baffle Gerald. There was a flash of light, and two teenagers appeared, seemingly out of thin air, on the right side of the monument: an elfish boy and a beautiful girl with long red hair.

"Seems you got the odds a bit wrong," Brennan said as he stepped through Gerald, Brian, and Mike, pushing them behind him.

Slowly the three young men began to back down the steps. Although a part of Gerald wanted to see what would happen next, it was not a large enough part to overrule his desire to escape.

"We won't let them leave," the white tiranthrope growled. "That is our prey."

"You don't have a choice," Brennan responded, standing like a stone sentry between the young men and the tiranthropes.

The white tiranthrope's eyes blazed with anger, and he charged Brennan, his fellow beasts close at his heels.

Gerald watched in horror, his head craned over his shoulder even as he turned to run. There was a blinding flash of light, and the world went white. Gerald tumbled down the last few steps, reaching out for Brian and Mike, who'd been knocked over as he fell. There was snarling, and then a thwack as a body hit the marble above. Gerald tried to blink away the blindness, but his eyes were agonizingly slow to readjust. Then he heard footsteps coming down the stairs toward him.

"Get back, get back!" Gerald screamed, lashing blindly out at the air. His inability to see made his fear so overpowering that tears began to flow down his face, and his body shook.

"It's okay," said a feminine voice. "You're safe now."

It was the sweetest voice he had ever heard.

Brandon is the author of the Scarlet Hopewell series of books for young adults. When not writing, he works as a firefighter and paramedic in the state of Virginia, where he lives with his wife and daughters.

Made in the USA
Middletown, DE
03 June 2015